THE EXECUTIVE'S DECISION

THE KELLER FAMILY SERIES ~ BOOK ONE

BERNADETTE MARIE

5 PRINCE PUBLISHING

The Executive's Decision

ISBN Digital 9781465932723

ISBN Print 9781939217974

4th edition

5 Prince Publishing, LLC

PO Box 865, Arvada CO 80001

books@5princebooks.com

Published by 5 Prince Publishing

Original Publication 2011

For Stan
As always I can write about true love because I live it.

ACKNOWLEDGMENTS

The journey to bring THE EXECUTIVE'S DECISION to light was not undertaken alone. As always, I have had so many supporters. I must thank my husband, who weathers my mood swings as I feel what my characters are feeling so that I can get their emotions onto the page. He has never faltered in his belief in me. My children, the five most wonderful little men any one woman could have been blessed with, are my biggest fans and I love them dearly. A big thanks to my sister, who jumps in to edit, critique, and enjoy all my books no matter which state they are currently in. I was blessed with supportive and loving parents who have always smiled and nodded as I've rambled on and on about real or imaginary people. An ENORMOUS thank you goes out to my editor Susan. Without you I surely would have fallen flat many times. Your spirit lifts me up. Your knowledge makes me better. Your friendship is invaluable. Judy, thank you for coming along with me on this journey. Knowing those I work with makes it so much better. June, I look forward to many journeys with you. Connie, thank you for always being there at the head of the line to read my books. You are the very best kind of fan to have. Theresa, having you be part of this was special. You are my sister from another mother, and I love you as I love my own sister. And last but certainly not least, to all my readers who make me want to get up every morning and write something. Knowing you look forward to my next books lets me know I'm doing the right thing with my life.

ALSO BY BERNADETTE MARIE

Date for Hire

THE EXECUTIVE'S DECISION

CHAPTER 1

*T*hunder rippled through the gray clouds that loomed overhead. Regan Keller raised her eyes to the sky.

Please, please don't rain, she sent up the silent prayer as she felt the first drop hit her forehead.

The nervous flutter in her stomach quickened as she looked down at her watch. Surely her day couldn't get any worse. But the sky opened up, and those around her crowded together in the bus stop shelter. Her hair, tied in a tail at the base of her neck, dripped rain down her back as she hunched in her coat. How could she have forgotten her umbrella? Had her car been running, she'd have the one tucked safely away in the glove compartment because spring in Tennessee often meant sudden storms. She should carry one in her bag, but she had suffered a lapse in memory, having opted for the sunny beaches of Hawaii for the past two years.

As the bus arrived, those under the shelter huddled onto it ahead of her, claiming every seat. Soaking wet, Regan wedged herself between two people and held onto the handrail above her head. She looked out the window at the commuters driving themselves to work in the pouring rain. That should have been her.

A bitter-faced old woman sat below her, her oversized bag occupying the next seat. Regan bent to ask her to move it, but the woman glared up at her and gave a grunt that sounded like a dog's bark. Regan flinched and tried to look away. But she was compelled to keep an eye on the woman.

The man to the other side of the vacant seat snickered. Regan looked down at him in his long black overcoat and perfect hair. Hemmed in between the old lady's bag and an overweight man in a jogging suit, he was as pinned in his seat as she was to the people around her. She would have given him a piece of her mind for laughing at her had the bus not jolted to a sudden stop, lurching forward then back and tossing Regan onto the man's lap.

"I would have offered you my seat," he said with a bright grin as the bus lurched again.

Regan heard the gasp she'd let out, but no words followed. She struggled to free herself, but the crowd moved in tightly around them as the bus bounced down the street. The pace of her heart ticked harder, and she could feel sweat bead on her brow.

She hadn't been this close to a man in over a year, and the panic of having him actually hold her on his lap was making her more than uncomfortable.

"I need to stand up," she said.

"You might as well sit." He wrapped his arms around her and looked up at the people who crowded around them. "It doesn't look like you'll be standing again anytime soon."

Regan took a few deep and cleansing breaths of stale air. She forced down the panic that was filling her body and tried to push it away. The man didn't know his arms around her in the crammed bus was causing an anxiety attack.

Michael Hamilton, the reason she was back in Nashville and on her way to a new job, thought she was dead. He wasn't there to hurt her, and there should be no danger in sitting on the lap of a nice-looking man. Taking another breath of thick air, she thought she should find it within her to enjoy the experience and focus on something else.

So she turned her focus on the man who's arms encircled her. He didn't have an accent native to Tennessee like hers. Perhaps the rain had caught him off guard as well. Perhaps she should start a conversation based on that—his accent. But still there were no words.

If she didn't relax, she'd have a heart attack, and the nice gentleman, who wasn't from Nashville, would probably be blamed for her death on the bus on his way to work.

Accepting her current predicament, she decided this would be a prime opportunity to let go of bitter feelings for the opposite gender. This man offered her protection, even if it was just from a crowed bus. Though after what she'd been through in the past year, she wasn't sure she could let go of the worry and fear that accompanied being so close to a man. The very thought of another man touching her made her palms sweat and her stomach clench.

The man smiled at her, and a dimple formed in his cheek. "This is your first time on this bus, isn't it?" He pushed back a wet wisp of hair from her forehead, and she flinched away. "It's always crowded, but I know I would have seen you."

"My car wouldn't start this morning." She pressed her hand to her jittery stomach and willed it to settle. "I start a new job today. Car trouble couldn't have come at a worse time."

"New job? Congratulations. So what is this new job?" he asked and she knew he was making small talk to ease her obvious nerves.

Easing her eyes to meet his, the fluttering in her stomach intensified. God, he was handsome, and wouldn't it be nice to enjoy the ride? But she wasn't. "Executive assistant." The words shook as she spoke.

"Pretty important."

"You think it's just some glorified secretary, don't you?" She clenched her teeth and her fists. Why wouldn't she be angry? The last man she'd worked for had interpreted the title of executive assistant as a license to run her life and to ruin it.

"No. I was serious. It's a very important position." His eyes carried his sincerity. "So where is this new job?"

"Benson, Benson and Hart," she blurted out the name of the firm and then wished she hadn't. She didn't know this man, or any of the people around her. Why would she go and tell someone where she was going?

"Real estate development."

"Yes." Her breath was becoming harder to push through her lungs. "I should get off your lap."

"You'd ruin my day." He laughed easily, so she tried to relax. "So whose executive assistant will you be?"

"Zachary Benson's." She looked around for a space to stand.

"CEO? He must have been very impressed with you."

The stranger on the bus knew who the man was she was going to work with. She was in over her head, she thought.

"I've never met him. His current assistant is having a baby and leaving the company for awhile. He was out of town when she interviewed me." She thought about Mary Ellen, his current assistant. The interview had had a motherly quality to it. She wasn't sure whether it was because Mary Ellen was pregnant or that worried for her boss and was looking for the right person to coddle him. "I think she takes good care of him. It'll be a hard pair of shoes to fill." And if that hadn't had her stomach tied in knots, here she was having a conversation about it with a man she didn't know while sitting on his lap. Had she completely forgotten the last man she'd gotten this close to tried to kill her? No, she hadn't forgotten, and that's why she was nearly sick to her stomach sitting on the man's lap.

"I'm sure he'll be pleased with her choice."

"Thank you." She wanted to wiggle away from the hard muscles she could feel in his chest, from his arms that held her tight against him, and from the legs of a man who obviously kept in shape. She couldn't, so she kept talking as if it were protecting her. "I hope he likes me. I can't imagine him not wanting to meet me first."

"Maybe he's ugly."

Finally a laugh rolled from her throat. "That's not what Mary Ellen said." She tucked in her lips. "She says he's a hottie."

"Hottie?" His voice lit with humor. "Well, you'll enjoy your job then."

"Strictly business here. I don't get involved with the boss," she said sternly. Not anymore. This was, after all, her chance to take back her life after making such a mistake.

The bus stopped, and the old woman stood and grabbed her bag.

"Move!" She shoved her way through the people who climbed on and made her way out the door. Before Regan could stand and claim a seat, the crowd around her pushed her closer against the stranger, whose arms remained wrapped tightly around her as others dropped down beside them.

"Your stop is the next one," he offered, and she nodded. "So what's your name?"

"Regan."

"You're native to Tennessee, aren't you? Your accent gives you away."

"I was born in Memphis. I spent most of my life in Nashville though. I did a stint in Los Angeles and then lived in Maui for the last two years. I missed home though." The more she tried to suppress her nerves, the more she talked, spilling personal information as if she couldn't stop herself from doing so.

"Los Angeles? Tried your hand at Hollywood?"

"No." She shook her head. "I worked for a prominent lawyer

who had some big-name clients. But I wasn't seeking fame and fortune."

"Well, Ms. Executive Assistant, I'm glad you came home or this would have been a very boring ride this morning." The bus stopped, and most of the people began to move to the door. "This is your stop."

She finally stood and turned to exit with the crowd without looking back.

The man caught her hand and held it. Her very core shook, and her first instinct was to rip her hand away. But she needed to move on and not be so damn afraid of every man that gave her attention.

"Would you have lunch with me?" he asked.

"What?" She looked back at people climbing on. If she didn't exit the bus now, she'd miss her stop. "Oh, I don't think so."

"Meet me at the hot dog stand at noon just on the north corner of your building," he said with a wink and a nod.

She couldn't think to speak. She nodded as she hurried off the bus.

The rain had subsided for the moment. Regan was still wet from the burst of rain that had soaked her before climbing on the bus. The smell of the man's cologne lingered on her coat. She closed her eyes and breathed in the scent of him.

She stopped as she neared the door and turned to see the bus drive away. He was watching her from the window, and he waved. It occurred to her she didn't even know his name.

She looked down at her hands. They were shaking.

Get over it. She told herself. *Move on. Not everyone wanted to hurt her. Not every man was evil with ulterior motives. No, some are just nice men who want to take you to lunch.*

Well, it wasn't like he'd asked her to stay at a hotel. He'd offered to buy her a hot dog. Really, it was harmless. And he'd assume she was too busy with her new job if she just didn't show up.

But she wanted to.

Well, there was no better time to move on with her life, and no better way to get to know the man on whose lap you'd ridden to work than over a hot dog.

A tingle of hope shot through her. She needed to start taking back her life. No more mistakes. No more regrets. It was her life now, and she was going to enjoy it.

CHAPTER 2

*M*ary Ellen Rothchild, the very pregnant assistant to Zachary Benson, was waiting for Regan as she exited the elevator. "There you are. I was worried." She held her hand out.

Regan took her hand, giving it a firm, professional shake. "Car trouble. I had to ride the bus."

Mary Ellen crinkled her nose and let out a grunt. "I hate the bus."

"So do I," she confessed as Mary Ellen led her through the office toward the break room. "But this morning wasn't too bad. It was wet and crowded, and there was this really mean old lady." She laughed, and Mary Ellen glanced at her. "When the bus jerked, I fell and landed right in some guy's lap."

"How did that go?" She raised her eyebrows playfully.

"I have a lunch date with him at noon on the corner." Well there, she'd committed to it. And suddenly her stomach gurgled and she knew it wasn't as much from hunger as it was from excitement for the chance to have a normal moment with a man. A stranger.

Mary Ellen showed her to her locker, where she could hang

her coat and secure her purse. She introduced her to a few people and headed to her new office. Her new corner of the world. Her new beginning.

"This is your office," Mary Ellen said as they entered a small office away from the cubicles in the main area. "Mr. Benson's office is right through here." Mary Ellen walked into the other, larger office behind hers. "This way he can still have you near, but be shut off from the rest of the floor. His private conference room is right through there." She pointed to the adjoining room. Both had full walls of windows that looked out over the river that ran through downtown Nashville.

Mary Ellen walked her into Zachary's office. "He likes coffee in his own pot." She filled the pot with water and poured it into the coffeemaker on the counter. "He likes it strong. So four scoops and set it to strong brew." She stuck out her tongue as if she could taste it. "Later in the day check on it. The man cannot remember to turn it off." She started the machine.

Mary Ellen dusted off her hands and looked around the office. "His bathroom is private. This is important. He often showers here and sleeps on the Murphy bed." She pointed to a set of doors in the wall. "That is a secret only you and I know, but you have to know it so you don't startle him or yourself. He never brings anyone up with him, so no worries there," she added with a wink. "He does have a private entry from the parking garage, so you always, always, always want to knock before entering. Again not to startle him or you."

A man who would be forgetful of his coffee and slept and showered in his office could not have much of a social life. Perhaps Mary Ellen was his only source of companionship. He would be in short supply of that from Regan. Mary Ellen did say he was a hottie, but she just couldn't picture it.

"From the sounds of it, having him scare you has been a problem in the past?"

"When he first took over this office, I'll admit I walked in a few times and screamed out loud. Even last week I thought I'd go into labor, he'd startled me so badly." She snorted a laugh and rubbed her oversized stomach. "I've never caught him in an awkward situation, but to think you're alone and to find him sitting on the couch is a bit of a shock."

"I can imagine." The image of a balding, middle-aged man sprawled out on the couch with his feet up on the coffee table filled her head.

Mary Ellen walked toward his imposing cherry wood desk situated in the corner of the room. "He likes to catch up on the news and stocks when he gets in. He'll want twenty minutes to get settled, and then you can come in with any messages or business for him to attend to."

Regan nodded, absorbing her new instructions.

They walked out of his office and settled into their office. Regan pulled a chair up next to Mary Ellen, who flipped on the computer screen and began going over everything Regan would need to know to assist Zachary Benson, one of the most sought-after real estate developers in the nation.

"I really hope I don't screw anything up." Regan felt the knot in her stomach tighten again, and she feared her nerves were going to get the best of her. Lord knows she'd screwed up the last job she'd had. Suddenly every place the last man she'd worked for had hit her throbbed with the memory of the bruises and broken bones.

"You'll screw up plenty," Mary Ellen said, and Regan shifted uncomfortably in her chair. Mary Ellen smiled and laid a gentle hand on her arm. "But that's how you learn."

"Great." She wasn't reassured.

"He's a softy. He only fires people once in a while."

"And if he's a softy, what makes him fire people?" Regan's attempt to hide the fear in her voice didn't completely work.

"If you lose him a contract, he'll fire you on the spot," she said matter-of-factly. "I don't think you'll have to worry about it."

Mary Ellen set forth to help Regan understand contracts and bids. Though Regan had been around many of the forms before, she worried that she was once again placing herself in the position of caretaker of a very powerful man. Why would she think that she was doing the right thing when all she could do was concentrate on the physical pains she'd recovered from? Why hadn't she taken the job her brother had told her about at the hospital? She'd be filing papers, not making sure some CEO's coffeemaker was turned off, and his papers were on his desk in order.

When the phone rang, Mary Ellen handed her the wireless headset and pushed a button.

Regan's eyes widened. She put on the headset and heard the line go live. Her body stiffened. She swallowed hard. "Good morning, Mr. Benson's office," she said, having heard Mary Ellen offer the greeting moments earlier.

"Good morning. May I speak to Mary Ellen Rothchild?" the man on the other end asked.

"Of course, let me connect you." Regan fumbled for the hold button and let out a sigh. "It's for you."

Mary Ellen's eyebrows pinched together as she took the phone. "This is Mary Ellen... yes... are you... Okay, I understand. In ten. That's fine." Her voice grew agitated as she replaced the receiver with a shake of her head. "Well, looks like you get to run the desk yourself for a few minutes. I have an urgent meeting in the lobby. I'll be back in just a few minutes. If anything comes up and you don't know the answer, just write it down and take a message. In a week you're on your own anyway." She adjusted out of the chair and rubbed her side. "This is a good time to try and fly solo."

Mary Ellen retrieved a legal pad and a pen from the desk drawer and then headed toward the elevator.

Regan tried to settle into her new space, more than a little annoyed that she'd been training to be Zachary Benson's assistant and he hadn't even shown up yet. How could someone run an empire if they didn't even show up for work? Obviously, he was the kind of man Michael Hamilton had been. The kind that pushes his employees to perform and then takes the credit for their success.

She took a moment to browse over Zachary Benson's schedule in the computer and become familiar with the kinds of appointments she'd probably have to make excuses for when he didn't show up.

There were plenty of meetings, both in Nashville and as far away as Los Angeles. She assumed she'd be present at most of them. Mary Ellen had made sure she had a very flexible schedule and could attend early and late meetings. She also needed to be available for business trips that lasted a week and that came up at the last moment. Sadly, this was something her life would allow. Her only commitments were to her family. She had dinner with them once a month, and it too was something she could reschedule if necessary.

For today, he had a meeting off site at two and a conference call at six. She assumed, looking at the other days in his schedule, this was a laid-back day.

Mary Ellen returned a half hour later and tossed her legal pad onto the desk. "Any crisis?"

"A Jason Agston from Steeple Concrete called and said the order was delayed and there was nothing more he could do about it. He'd appreciate if Zach could call him personally and get everything straightened out. A Ms. Simone Pierpont called and said, '*That would be fine.*'" She waved a hand in the air with her French accent flowing, and Mary Ellen smiled. "And his mother called and tried to get me to spill my life story when I said he wasn't in."

"She's a talker. She's gets lonely during the day when her husband plays golf or is swimming. She knows someone here will always answer the phone."

"Will that impact my schedule much?" Did the job include taking care of his mother too?

"Only if you marry him."

That certainly wasn't going to happen.

She looked at her watch, which now read ten fifteen. "So where is he?"

"That was him in the lobby. He's taken on a lunch meeting. He'll be in this afternoon."

"He's not coming up to meet me?" Regan snapped, though she hadn't meant it to sound as angry as it did. Didn't he care whose hands he was going to be in?

Mary Ellen shrugged. "I'd say he's a pain in the ass, but really he's not. I'm not sure what he's doing today. He's usually up to his eyeballs in contracts by this time of the morning. Well, at least he'll be your concern soon."

Mary Ellen sank into her chair, and her eyes misted. She turned away, but Regan had noticed.

"I have a feeling you'll miss him."

"Nah," Mary Ellen said, rubbing her stomach again and adjusting herself in her seat. "It's only been ten years. I can just walk away." She winced. "Really, though, I interviewed forty people out of one hundred applicants. You were the one I knew would take the best care of Zach."

Regan wasn't sure what to say to that. She'd hoped her vast knowledge of contracts had been why they'd hired her, not because she was most qualified to take care of Zachary Benson's personal needs, especially when he didn't have the decency to meet her. The thought left her uncomfortable with the prospect of the job at hand. Once she'd had a job for the same reason, and it hadn't ended in the best way. She didn't want to go through that again.

CHAPTER 3

*I*t was past noon when Mary Ellen announced she needed to eat because her head was spinning. Regan hadn't wanted to stop her from showing her everything just so she could meet a total stranger for a hot dog. Now she wondered if he'd even be there.

She grabbed her purse and joined the crowd in the elevator. There were four different conversations going on at the same time. She loved the banter. She'd missed corporate America.

When she walked through the lobby, sunlight streamed across the marble floor. The sun was shining for her experimental moment of moving on.

Just beyond the door, she stopped and took out the compact from her purse and gave herself a quick glance. A quick gloss over her lips, and she had to look better than she had that morning. She walked around the side of the building to find the hot dog cart.

A variety of people in suits and skirts mingled with a few tourists in shorts in the small court between the buildings. Would she recognize him?

A laugh escaped her throat. She knew exactly what he looked

like. His sandy hair and green eyes had burned his image into her mind. A shudder ran through her when she thought of his arms wrapped around her, protecting her—enticing her.

"I hope you weren't waiting long."

Regan's heart hitched, and she spun around to find him standing behind her with a bouquet of daisies.

"I just got here." She tried to catch her breath with him standing right before her. He was even more handsome in the full light of day than under the dingy glow of the bus lights. "I forgot to ask …"

"These are for you." He handed her the bouquet and interrupted her thought on asking his name.

"Thank you." She took the flowers from him, careful not to let their fingers meet. She was already feeling the surge of anxiety threaten her triumphant moment.

"So how is that new boss of yours?" he asked as they walked to the hot dog cart. "Working you too hard?"

"He hasn't even shown up." She blew out a breath of irritation then rubbed her fingers over her forehead to ward off the mark she knew was forming from her scowl. "You'd think that since I'll be in charge of his every move by the end of the week, he'd want to meet me."

"I'm sure he has good reason." They approached the cart. "The usual, Frank. What will you have? Sky's the limit." He smiled a brilliant white smile.

He was taller than she'd realized. "Well then, I'll take the Polish sausage with sauerkraut and mustard, a bag of chips, and all caution thrown to the wind today, a Coke."

"Caution thrown to the wind?"

"I don't eat chips, drink soda, or eat hot dogs. But when a charming man asks…" When his smile widened, she stopped. It was okay to flirt with a man again, wasn't it? Fresh start, she reminded herself.

"This way." He led her around the building to a courtyard that overlooked the river. An enormous fountain sat in the middle of the yard with stone tables all around. "There's a nice spot over here."

He started toward a blanket that had been set down under a shady tree.

She let out a long breath. "Your usual spot?"

"I suppose you could say that." He laid down his lunch. Then he took hers and set it on the blanket as she maneuvered a seat in her skirt.

"So this is where you bring all your lady friends?" She could hear the jealousy bubble in her voice and she hated it. She didn't want to care about this man and his life. She was being pleasant and having lunch with him because he'd asked.

"Well, I haven't had one of those in a long time. Usually my assistant comes with me, but..." He stopped at that and bit into his hot dog. "I must say, I'm glad you took the bus today."

"Me too. Otherwise I would have had to pay for lunch." They shared a laugh, though his sounded more relaxed and natural than hers. Her eyes skimmed over him again. He was someone she could definitely find herself wanting to get to know better, if she'd only allow herself to do so. It was nice to have normal, female feelings toward the opposite sex again, but it scared her to the core.

"So will you be riding home with me as well?" he asked, biting down on a chip he'd taken from her bag.

"No, sorry. I have someone picking me up. He would have brought me to work, but I would have been late."

"Had you known your boss wasn't even going to show up..."

"I would have missed out on lunch." She bit into her Polish sausage.

"Good thing you didn't know, then." He reached over with a napkin and wiped her upper lip, leaving a smudge of mustard on the napkin. The intimacy of it made her avert her eyes. He leaned back on his arms. "I suppose you're going to get that car of yours fixed."

"Of course." She kept her eyes low.

"Too bad. I'll be stuck with that old lady and her giant bag." When she lifted her eyes to him, his danced with humor. "I guess I could stop running home in the evenings and just drive."

If her brother couldn't get her car running it wouldn't be so bad. "You run home?"

"I've been known to. It frees my mind after a chaotic day."

His phone rang and he pulled it from his pocket. Regan quietly sat and finished her lunch as he answered the call.

"I'll be there." He shook his head. "I said I would." He sipped his soda while he continued to nod his head. "You did? How did she sound? I'm sure she'll do a great job." He glanced toward Regan, who desperately tried to give him his privacy. "Okay, I'll talk to you tonight."

Regan tucked her trash into her chip bag and finished off her soda. She noticed him glance at his watch and she realized her very nice lunch date was over.

"I suppose I should head back to my office." He stood and helped her to her feet. "Thank you, Regan, for a very nice lunch."

"Thank you." She picked up the blanket and folded it neatly as he carried their trash to the can. "Thank you again for the flowers. It was very nice of you." She handed him the blanket and pulled the bouquet to her chest.

"I'm sure I'll see you again." He turned and walked away with the blanket tucked beneath his arm.

Regan stood still for a moment and watched him. It seemed as though he was leaving in a hurry. She wondered who had been on the other end of his phone call that would be waiting for him tonight, and guilt weighted her innocent lunch in her belly.

Tears began to burn her eyes as she wondered if she'd been betrayed again. Was there a wife innocently calling her husband and there he sat with a woman he'd only met? No, he was a nice, honest man, she told herself. Nothing had happened. It was lunch. The flowers were generous, and she'd set them on her desk as a gift for her first day at a new job.

Regan started toward the building that housed the offices of Benson, Benson and Hart. Perhaps her new acquaintance simply had a meeting to rush off to and everything was okay.

Then again, he'd interrupted her before she get his name and she'd forgotten to ask again.

CHAPTER 4

When Regan returned to the office after lunch, Mary Ellen's fingers were flying at the keyboard. "How was your lunch?" she asked without diverting her eyes from the letter at her side.

"It was very nice." She placed her hand on her stomach, feeling the discomfort that had surfaced. It wasn't so much the food as the phone call and her date's speedy departure.

"Just nice?" Finally, she looked up. "I thought maybe there would be dinner plans?"

"No." She shook her head fiercely. "No dinner plans."

"Let me finish this up." Mary Ellen sent the document to the printer. She stood with her hands on her back and let out a long, uncomfortable sigh. "He brought you daisies?" she asked, but her manner was more of concern than delight.

"Yes." Regan smiled, looking down at the bouquet in her arms. But when she looked back up, Mary Ellen's jaw had set and there was a pulse throbbing in her neck.

"Nice." She shook her head and pulled the letters from the printer. The daisies had set her off, and Regan hoped it was a hormonal reaction.

Mary Ellen showed her the papers. "Changes in the conference call." She noted the letter. "I just have to put these on his desk."

"Let me. You should sit. You don't look very comfortable." Regan took the letter from her and headed back to the office.

The door was open, and Regan strolled in and laid the letter on the desk. She turned quickly to leave, still not comfortable in the space.

A man was sitting on the leather couch, his feet propped up, and an enormous grin on his face. She screamed, recognized him, and muffled the sound with her hands. He was stalking her. The last time a man appeared out of nowhere, he'd beaten her nearly to death. Now here was this stranger who had never introduced himself, and she was paralyzed.

"God, what in the world?" Mary Ellen ran through the door as quickly as she could. "You're not supposed to sneak up on us like that. That's the rule. That's your rule." Then she reached for her stomach, and that brought him to his feet.

"Mary Ellen, I'm sorry. Sit down." He took her by the arm and helped her to the couch.

"Well, I guess you've met the elusive Mr. Benson," she said, wincing as she rubbed her stomach.

Zachary looked up at Regan and smiled. "Yes, we've met."

"You!" It was all she seemed to be able to blurt out. "You!"

"I knew I recognized those daisies." Mary Ellen struggled to get comfortable on the couch. "I assume this is your handsome mystery date?" She nodded in his direction.

He laughed. "Please, handsome? She said you thought I was a hottie."

"You told him that?" Mary Ellen looked at Regan.

Regan stood with her mouth open. Her professional demeanor had taken a nosedive. "Well yes, but I didn't know…"

"Really, you think I'm a hottie?" He looked back at Mary Ellen, who rubbed the side of her stomach.

"Get over yourself." She laughed as she jabbed him in the ribs with her elbow.

Regan watched the banter. She'd seen it before, been part of it even. It was like the relationship she had with her brothers and her sister.

The two of them continued. She knew they weren't related, but they had obviously been together long enough that there was a line between professionalism and friendliness, and it could be crossed at any time.

When silence fell between them, they both looked at her. Regan was still stunned into paralysis. The handsome stranger from the bus sat before her. He was her boss. He was a multi-millionaire. He was a liar.

She turned to leave the office, but he stood and reached for her arm. "Regan, please don't be angry."

His hand held hers, but his fingers didn't hurt her. He wanted her attention, but he wasn't causing her pain. She relaxed, but only slightly. "Angry? Do I look angry?"

"Yes, you do." There was that handsome smile on his lips, and it infuriated her.

"I think I need to get my things and go." She tried to move from him, but he blocked her way.

"It was just a misunderstanding." His eyes were soft, and so was his voice.

She wanted to believe that he was a good man, but she couldn't trust her judgment. She had leave. It was best to forget the job and the new beginning and just leave.

"Misunderstanding? You lied to me."

"I didn't lie." He took a step back, a big concession for a man with such power. "I just didn't tell you who I was when you confided in me who you were." He let out a breath. "Okay, when I say it that way, it does sound pretty lousy."

"Why were you riding a bus? Saving money?"

"How about the environment? One less car…" he offered.

"Great. I feel so much better." She walked past him and out of the office.

She had already put on her coat and pulled the few items from her locker when Zachary Benson found her. The talking in the break room died down to a murmur the moment he walked through the door.

"Could we talk before you walk out?" He kept his voice low and leaned against the locker next to hers.

"I don't think so."

"Regan, I'm sorry. I should have told you who I was on the bus. Mary Ellen picked you just for me, and I need you." Regan held up a finger to stop him, but he continued. "Professionally, that is."

She didn't speak right away. Instead she stared into the empty locker, willing her unease to subside. She wanted to trust him. "If I choose to stay—and I'm not saying I will—but if I do, I do it for Mary Ellen." And for myself. She couldn't be scared for the rest of her life. This was her chance to move on.

"That's fair."

"I'll talk to you, but it's strictly business."

"From now on."

"No more lunches under trees, no more daisies, and no more sitting on your lap on the bus, or…"

"Regan, you're ruining my day." A smile broke on his lips. This time it unraveled her nerves, making her hands shake and her heart flutter. She took a deep breath.

The silence of the other employees made the room uncomfortable. She looked around at her new colleagues, who had all averted their eyes from what had to be the latest source of juicy office gossip. She contemplated her position and looked back at Zachary. He was a powerful man who was willing to say he was sorry. That wasn't something she'd run into in the past. Maybe Zachary Benson was different.

It was worth her new beginning to give him the benefit of the doubt. If she was wrong, she'd just walk away.

"C'mon, you have a meeting in an hour." She closed the locker and walked out of the break room with him a few strides behind her.

Mary Ellen was standing at the door to Zach's office, her skin pale and her breathing labored. Regan took one look at her and raced toward her.

"My water just broke. I need to get to the hospital." She bit her lip and wrapped her arms around her stomach.

CHAPTER 5

*R*egan had watched Zach go as pale as Mary Ellen. Men were no good in a crisis. She supposed that was why he relied on an assistant so heavily.

"Okay. Let's go." Regan took her arm.

Zach moved in on the other side of Mary Ellen. Crouching, he laced her arm around his neck. "My car is in the garage. We'll take my elevator down."

He stood and carried her into the office without looking back at Regan.

She realized she would soon see the secret workings of the River Front Building.

The elevator was concealed behind what she'd thought was a closet door in the corner of his office. They crowded inside; the elevator car was only big enough for the three of them.

She shifted her glance to Zach. "You have a car? Here?"

"Yeah."

"And you were on the bus this morning why?"

"Am I not allowed public transportation?"

"You—"

Mary Ellen screamed through a contraction, cutting off her verbal bashing.

"Your conference call," Mary Ellen blurted out.

Regan shook her head. "I'll go back up when he gets you in the car, and I'll reschedule it."

"Like hell," Zach said as the elevator slowed to a stop. "You're going with us."

"I need to run your office."

"I can't do this alone," he argued as they helped Mary Ellen to the Lexus parked in the parking space marked with his name.

"I'll catch a cab once I'm done, and I'll meet you at the hospital." Regan held tighter to Mary Ellen as he dug in his pocket for his key fob and pushed buttons.

"Just get in. I'll call someone else to fill in."

Mary Ellen let out a yelp and they both diverted their attention to her. "Sorry for the interruption," she scolded as she gripped her stomach again.

Regan climbed into the backseat, and Zach helped Mary Ellen into the passenger seat, easing her down carefully. When Regan looked at Zach and realized he was as pale as Mary Ellen, she had to bite back the temptation to offer to drive. Men—what would they do if they had to bear children?

The hospital was only ten minutes away from the office, but it could have been an hour, as nervous as Zach was maneuvering through the early afternoon traffic. He had his cell phone in his hand calling another executive to cover his meeting.

Mary Ellen handed her phone to Regan as they swerved through traffic.

"Call my husband. He's on the speed dial under two. "She winced with another contraction as Regan followed her instructions and called her husband.

"He'll meet us there. He said he's fifteen minutes out." Regan closed the phone and handed it back to Mary Ellen.

"God, I hope he makes it."

"First babies can take hours."

Zach's eyes met hers in the mirror. "How do you know?"

"Inside source." Her voice cracked, and she averted her eyes out the window. She tried to focus on the world that passed beyond the car and not on the year she was trying to move on from.

Zach pulled into the unloading zone near the emergency exit. He helped Mary Ellen from the car, and Regan climbed out from the backseat. She retrieved a wheel chair from the entrance and pushed it to the car. Zach held tight to Mary Ellen and helped to ease her into the chair.

Regan spun her around and headed toward the door. "Go park the car. We'll be on the second floor."

"How do you know where you'll be?" he called back to her.

"Inside source," she said again and disappeared through the door to the hospital, hoping her slip of words would disappear in the chaos of the moment.

The process was far more streamlined than Regan remembered. When they hit the second floor, nurses jumped from their stations to get Mary Ellen into the right place and start monitoring her. Mary Ellen threw her purse at Regan, who pulled out her identification and the envelope she'd labeled DELIVERY. A laugh caught her. She wondered if she'd ever be that prepared for anything outside of work. Then she thought of the morning and her lack of an umbrella. No, Regan Keller would never be that organized in her personal life.

Most of Mary Ellen's information was on file, and she relayed necessary details to Regan, who filled in the blanks. By the time the forms were complete, a monitor had been strapped to Mary Ellen's stomach, and Zach walked through the door with Mary Ellen's husband right behind him.

Regan and Zach found themselves pushed to the corner of the room as people came and went. It would never cease to amaze Regan how many people it took to deliver just one baby.

"Are you all family?" The nurse asked as the room grew more crowded.

"No." Regan answered for Zach and herself.

"You'll need to wait outside. The visitor waiting area is just down the hall." She pointed them in the direction.

Regan headed toward the door as quickly as she could. She'd become much too uncomfortable with the situation once Mary Ellen was in capable hands. The delivery room was not where she wanted to be.

"Are you all right?" Zach asked as they left the room.

"Yeah, I'm fine."

"You look a little shaken up now that it's all over."

Of course she was shaken. She was standing in a hospital with a very powerful man, and around them were birth, sickness, and death. "I'm okay. I just don't like hospitals much."

"Let's get some coffee."

She'd rather have gone back to the office, but that would be cowardly, so she followed him.

Zach fed quarters into the machine in the waiting room and checked his phone's messages as they waited for the instant coffee to be dispensed into a cup. "I'll bet you've never had a first day on a job like this one." He closed his phone and placed it back in his pocket.

"No, this would definitely be one of the most exciting." She took the paper cup he handed her and sipped the strong coffee as they sat at a small round table by the window.

"So your last job was in Hawaii?" He sat back in his chair, draping his arm over its back.

She despised small talk, but she'd let him attempt to get her to warm back up to him. Whether she chose to warm up was another matter. "Yes."

"I love Hawaii. What would make you want to leave?"

Regan forced the lump down her throat. "The job ended," she said and sipped again at the coffee, but it was as bitter as her attitude toward the subject of her last job. She pushed it to the center of the table.

"When was that?"

"Eight months ago." She looked around the room at the other waiting families and wished for a way out of the conversation and the room.

"What has Regan Keller been doing since then?" He sipping his own coffee.

She dropped her hands to the table and looked across at him. Damn, she'd hoped the handsome man on the bus was going to be a steppingstone for her. She'd hoped she'd be able to open herself up again. But finding that same man was her boss brought back the fear and anxiety all over again. She wiped her damp palms on her skirt under the table.

"Mr. Benson, do I still have my job?"

"Of course you do." He drew his eyebrows together. "And it's Zach."

"Fine. Zach. Then is it necessary to interview again?"

He pushed his coffee to the center of the table and leaned in. His superior posture softened and, again, so did her attitude toward him. "I didn't mean to pry, Regan. Things didn't start as they should have. I apologize."

"I wish you'd been honest with me." She nervously adjusted the hair at the base of her neck, freeing it from its band. "I don't see the people I work for socially."

"I understand." His eyes dropped, and he looked at the table like a child being scolded.

"As long as you do, then we'll be fine."

ZACH SAT QUIETLY, trying not to upset Regan with any more questions. Obviously, she wasn't someone who believed in crossing the line between employer and friend, like Mary Ellen had. He didn't subscribe to the policy of no romance in the workplace. When two people were attracted, that was their business as long as they behaved like adults on the job. But Regan was very clear she would never date him, so he needed to let go the thought of her on his lap, quickly.

But that didn't sit well with him. Maybe she'd recently gotten out of a relationship and wasn't interested in starting a new one. He just needed to give her time.

Zach's attention veered from Regan when a doctor in green scrubs burst through the door looking for someone. The frantic look on the doctor's face settled, and he headed right toward Zach.

"Regan?"

He spoke and she turned her head toward him. A smile instantly formed on her lips.

She stood and easily fell into his arms. Zach's breath caught. Maybe he was wrong. She seemed plenty comfortable in this man's arms. Maybe it was just him she didn't like.

"What are you doing here? I was scared," the doctor said, looking her over, touching her hair, and finally resting his hands on her shoulders in a possessive grip.

"My coworker went into labor. How did you know I was here?"

Zach looked for an ID badge to see the name of the man holding the woman who'd captivated him, but it was turned backward.

"Carlos went by your office to pick you up. They said you'd left for the hospital. He was worried."

Zach watched the man's eyes scan over her again. His hands were sturdy on her shoulders, and her hands rested comfortably on his chest. When she kissed him on the cheek and hugged him tightly, Zach's stomach knotted.

"I'll call him and tell him I'm fine." She patted the doctor's chest with her hand.

"Do you have a ride home? I'm here for another twelve," he said, looking at his watch.

"I can take her home. It wouldn't be a problem." Zach stood from his seat.

The doctor turned his eyes back to Regan and raised his brows.

Regan gave the man a nod as through to calm him before she introduced him to Zach. "Curtis, may I introduce my new employer, Zachary Benson."

Curtis shook his hand. "Benson? Benson, Benson, and Hart? Audrey Benson's son?"

"Yes, that would be me," he said, feeling his shoulders go back and his spine straighten as he slipped into the role of benefactor.

"It's nice to meet you. Your family has been very generous with the hospital."

"Good fortune should be shared."

Curtis smiled and turned his head back toward Regan. "You're in good hands." He kissed her on the forehead and hugged her tightly. "Dinner, Sunday night?"

"I wouldn't miss it." She was still smiling as Curtis pulled his beeping pager from his waist.

"Have to go." He kissed her again. "I love you."

"I love you, too."

Her affection for him shone in her eyes, and Zach realized this woman, who had his stomach tied in knots, was still a stranger, a complete mystery.

A working relationship, he reminded himself. That's all it could be, much to his disappointment.

CHAPTER 6

*Z*ach kept his distance as they walked to the parking garage, and she was okay with that. She knew what he was thinking, and she was okay with that too. There were times when having a good-looking doctor for your brother was a benefit.

She'd seen Zach's eyes when Curtis told her he loved her. Yes, he thought she was in love with the tall, handsome doctor who had sought her out in a panic. Let him think that. It served him right for not being up front about his own identity.

She'd do a good job for him. She was good at what she did. But never again would she be manipulated—or careless enough to fall in love with—the man she worked for. No, never again. The risk to her life and the lives of her family wasn't worth it. If Zach Benson pursued her, she'd just have to leave.

"Thank you for coming with me," he said as he started the car.

"My pleasure. But you would have been fine."

"No, I don't think I would have been. Mary Ellen takes care of me. Not the other way around." He backed out of the parking space. "I was scared. I was really scared. I can negotiate million-dollar real estate deals. I can face historical societies and tell them

I'm tearing down an old building, or head to court and face down a contractor who took off with the money for a job and didn't finish it. I can do all that without even a bead of sweat rolling down my back, but seeing Mary Ellen like that—that scared me to death."

"You handled yourself very well, Mr. Benson. I never would have known." Even when things became complicated and out of his control, he hadn't lost his composure. He'd stayed even tempered. He'd taken care of Mary Ellen.

He glanced her way. "I guess I'll be in good hands, then."

"That's what I was hired to do."

"It's too late to go back in and finish your work. Would you mind coming in a few minutes early tomorrow? I know I toyed with your first day, and I'm not sure how much training you got. I wasn't really expecting Mary Ellen to take her leave already." He blew out a breath. "I'm going to stay there tonight and finish up what I should have done today. If we get started early, that'll help us both out."

"No problem." She guided him through the streets of Nashville until they came upon her house.

"Nice place." He pulled up in front of the old brick row house.

"It's my sister's. She's in New York doing an off-Broadway play."

"Really?"

Regan nodded. "I've seen it. It's horrible, but she's fabulous and she's happy. So I get the run of the place until July."

"Then what?"

She shrugged. "I guess I have to find my own place."

"I know a company putting up some great condos downtown." He laughed.

"Well, maybe if she strikes it rich, she can buy me one."

"What about the doctor? Not ready to move in with him?" She saw the pulsing in his jaw and watched him shift in his seat.

With a smile, she shook her head. "No, he's a slob, really. I'm not ready to be his maid. Besides he has a roommate and a big black lab who hogs the bed."

Regan stepped out of the car and looked up at the front door of the house as it opened. Carlos, another of her brothers, walked out onto the front step, and she smiled and gave him a wave before she turned her attention back to Zach. "Thank you for the ride. I'll see you in the morning."

She shut the car door and hurried up the steps to the house without giving Zach a chance to ask about the man who awaited her there.

Inside, Regan threw her purse on the desk by the door and fell into the overstuffed chair in the living room. She kicked her shoes off and rested her feet on the table. Arianna would have been yelling at her already, but it was Regan's home until July, and she'd put her feet up if she wanted to.

The smile on Carlos's face must mean he had the same thought. He handed her a beer, sat down in the opposite chair, and kicked his feet up too.

"You had me scared to death. They couldn't tell me why you were at the hospital, just that you darted out in an emergency."

She caught the tone in his voice. There was reason for him to worry, and she knew it. Once upon a time they'd had to race to the hospital to find her. And what had they found but her near death at the hands of some man she'd thought she loved.

"Some first day, huh?" he added.

"Some first day." She took a long sip of the cold beer and tossed her head back.

"Sorry I couldn't get here this morning to take you."

"It's okay. I may blame you later, but it turned out to be a very interesting ride." She raised her eyebrows and finally smiled, thinking about it.

"Do tell." He sipped his own beer.

"I rode to work on the lap of a very handsome man."

"On his lap?"

"Yep, fell right into his lap and couldn't move. I rode to work that way. He even took me to lunch."

"Well then, I'm glad I didn't make it. Sounds like a Regan Keller recovery plan of sorts." Carlos smiled, tipping his beer toward her in a salute. "So do you have dinner plans now?"

"No, I'm pretty sure he assumes I'm dating Curtis, and now his mind is spinning because you met me at the door."

"He was the one in the car?"

"Uh-huh." She sipped. "Come to find out he's my boss."

"Oh." His voice dropped and he grew still.

"Yeah. Oh." She drank down her beer, hoping it would remove his face from her memory, but it had frozen there.

Zach drove back to the office and sat in his parking space for a moment, collecting his thoughts. It had been quite a day. Who would have known that when a beautiful woman was dropped in your lap, it would consume you?

He laughed it off as he rode the elevator up to his office. It seemed quiet, compared to the rush they had left it in. In their race out the door, he hadn't even noticed they'd knocked papers off the table, and the small plant Mary Ellen had brought him. He knelt to pick up the plant and place it on the windowsill. He fed it a few drops of water he found in a forgotten cup.

As his gaze shifted out the window over Nashville, he again thought of Regan Keller. Her image remained in his mind. There were two sides to her, he'd realized. There was the professional that had fallen onto his lap. Her suit pristine, even in a rainstorm, and her hair pulled back and out of the way. But when she'd gathered Mary Ellen up and started for the hospital without another thought, he saw the compassionate side to her. Her eyes had softened, and when she'd let her hair free there was peace in her.

Of course, there were the embraces with the other men. He felt his stomach knot again as he thought of the doctor. He wondered if the doctor knew about the dark man who waited for her at her home.

Zack pulled his tie from his neck and tossed it on the desk. He loosened the buttons on his shirt and sat back in his desk chair. In time, he was sure Regan Keller would be a loyal and perfect employee. God, how he wished that was how he'd first seen her. Instead, the thought of her seated on his lap, her long neck exposed with that beautiful brown hair pulled back and her eyelashes dripping raindrops, wouldn't go away.

CHAPTER 7

*R*egan, pleased that Carlos had gotten her car running, parked it in the garage of the Benson, Benson, and Hart building. The old lady on the bus would have been more than she could handle at seven in the morning.

Zachary Benson hadn't been exact on what time he considered early, but she figured showing up an hour before the official beginning of the workday was a good start.

The lobby was almost deserted, but the coffee kiosk was open. She bought herself and Zach each a coffee and headed toward the bank of elevators.

The ride up was quiet. There weren't multiple conversations and office gossip going on. When the doors opened, she stepped out onto the floor and walked to her desk first. Laying the tray of two gourmet coffees atop it, she shoved her bag in the bottom drawer.

Pulling the lint roller out of her bag, she rolled it over her suit coat, which she'd worn with a straight skirt and her favorite Italian pumps. Her white blouse was plain, but she'd dressed it up with a silver chain necklace. It had been a personal splurge in Hawaii. One of the items she had saved for herself and not gotten rid of in her attempt to eradicate the hurtful memories of her last relationship.

Regan slipped the roller in the bottom drawer with her purse, picked up the coffees and turned to Zach's office. She tapped lightly on the door, but there was no answer. She stood for a moment longer and tapped again. When he didn't answer, she let herself in.

A laugh escaped her throat when she noticed the pristine office of the CEO of Benson, Benson, and Hart looked like a college dorm room. A flat-screen television protruded from a cabinet in the corner, which she'd never have noticed, just like the elevator in the corner that went directly to the parking garage. The Murphy bed was down, and the sheets were rumpled. There was a pizza box on the table and three cans of soda. His desk was a mass of paper, and an acrid smell made her look around for the coffee that was burning in the pot.

With a shake of her head, she set the coffees on the table and turned off the coffeemaker. The door to the bathroom was open, but Zach wasn't there. He didn't seem to have stuck around after having made such a mess.

Well, executive assistant didn't mean glorified secretary. Sometimes it meant caretaker, handler, and maid. She started to pick up the remnants of his dinner and throw them away. She straightened the sheets on the bed up and tucked them in tightly to the mattress. Zach's scent lingered on them. She tried not to let it wash over her, but it had been so long since the cologne of a man tantalized her. Quickly she shook off any crazy notion that her boss smelled good or that she cared if he did.

Regan pushed the bed back up into the wall. The remote to the television was on the table, and she picked it up and aimed it at the TV, studying the mass of buttons.

"Second button on the right lowers it." Zachary's voice boomed from behind her, and she jumped, placing her hand on her heart.

"Oh, so you are here?" Her voice was cool and steady, but her heart rate wasn't.

He was in shorts and a T-shirt. His tall frame was muscular and toned, and his sandy hair was damp with sweat. Zach kept a straight face, but his eyes shimmered with laughter.

Regan forced herself to look away from him and lowered the TV by pushing the button he'd told her to. "Took a run?"

"Had to ward off the pizza I ordered."

"You left your coffeepot on," she said as she moved to the bar sink and emptied the last of the soda cans, and then tossed them into the recycle bin.

"Yeah, can't remember to turn it off."

She was aware of his eyes on her as she tidied his office. "I brought you coffee. I didn't know how you like it." She walked to the table and took his cup from the tray, offering it to him.

He accepted the cup and sipped. "This is perfect. Did you get your car fixed?" He tore the band holding his iPhone from his arm and laid it in a drawer.

"Yes."

"Well, I guess I'll grab a shower. That stack on my desk needs to be organized, and the three bids on the top need to be entered into the system."

"Not a problem, Mr. Benson," she said, moving quickly to gather the papers.

"Regan."

"Yes?" She looked up at him as he walked toward the bathroom. His legs were toned and tan, and she quickly averted her eyes to keep from examining his body. But she looked back up and caught his smile. Her breath hitched. He'd obviously noticed her reaction to him.

His smile broadened to a grin. "Just call me Zach."

.   .   .

Forty-five minutes later, Zach, clad in a suit and ready for business, opened his office door and watched Regan work. She had on the headset Mary Ellen usually wore, and she murmured, "Mm-hmm," as she jotted notes on the pad before her. He noticed that the bids he'd needed written up were printed and on the edge of her desk. His agenda was on her computer screen. He noted she'd added a meeting at one and blocked out time to meet with her to go over "items," it said.

When Regan pushed the button to disconnect her call, she turned as though she'd sensed him.

"Emerson Amelia Rothchild, born at three twenty-three yesterday. She weighed seven pounds, six ounces and has a full head of dark hair and her mother's nose." She smiled as she read the note to Zach. Her eyes had gone soft, and he longed to hold her. "You sent flowers with a little stuffed bear attached to them, and will visit when they get home tomorrow."

"How thoughtful of me." He raised his eyebrows.

Regan stood and handed him the bids she'd printed out for him. Their fingers brushed, and he noticed how quickly she pulled away.

"Here are your messages. You're a very popular man at eight in the morning."

"How many times did my mother call?"

"Four in the last forty minutes."

"You'll become close friends," he warned as he looked through the papers Regan had handed him.

"Well, Curtis likes her. I guess I'll find out."

Zach found his jaw clenched when she mentioned the doctor's name.

His eyes shifted to the office. It had started to come to life. Most of the staff would trickle in within the next half hour. He looked back at Regan, who had taken her seat behind the computer. She looked right at home.

"When you find Peterson, tell him I'm looking for him. I need an update on that conference call from yesterday." He watched her grab her note pad and make notes. "Call John Forrester and make arrangements for us to visit the site sometime this week."

She nodded as she kept writing as he continued the list. "And I need a suggestion on where to get tiramisu before Saturday to take to my mother's." That caused her to smile. "I don't know where to begin."

"I'll take care of that." She kept her eyes on her pad.

"Thank you. Chinese for lunch?"

Finally, she looked up at him. "Do you have a place you order from, or should I just take care of that?"

"No, just be ready at twelve thirty. We go out for Chinese food. We'll take your office meeting when we get back." He stepped back into his office and closed the door, delighted in the look of surprise that had lit her face. But there was also something troubling in her expression. Though it was enjoyable to throw Regan Keller off her game, it worried him that someone had made her so distrusting of men.

CHAPTER 8

*R*egan didn't find Peterson. He found her.

Kirk Peterson sat down on the edge of her desk as if it were a bar stool and introduced himself with a handshake that included an unabashed attempt to peek down her blouse. He was a stocky man in his early forties. He'd been married long enough that the wedding band on his finger looked to have grown into place, but by his casual way, it didn't seem to matter to him that there was a ring on his finger at all. While she told him what Zach wanted, he touched everything on her desk. Through her annoyance, she smiled professionally.

She managed the phone and let Zach know Peterson was there if he was available.

"Can you come in here first?" he asked.

"I'll be right in." She picked up the note pad and her pen. "I'll be right back. He'll be ready in a moment."

She hurried from her desk and skimmed through Zach's door, keeping an eye on Kirk Peterson. Though she was glad to be away from him, it distressed her to think he'd touch everything she owned while she was away. He was probably the kind of man to go through drawers and files.

Zach watched her from behind his desk, leaning back in his chair, with his arms crossed in front of him. When she rolled her eyes the moment the door closed, he laughed.

"Okay, that's all."

"What?" She snapped her head up. "Why are you laughing?"

"I really just wanted to see what your impression of him was. Mary Ellen turned green when he came around. You don't look much different."

She shook her head and flung open the door. "He's ready for you," she said as Peterson winked at her, which made her stomach churn.

Zach understood the reaction Kirk Peterson received from the women in the office. There were times even Zach was uncomfortable with the man. Somehow the creepiness of him had never landed the man in HR. He was a smooth talker and had a tendency to let you know he knew everything. But Peterson was a hell of a project manager.

Peterson's meeting and the two that followed were quick. Before Zach left his office to collect Regan for lunch, he gathered his notes to have her add them to the files.

She nodded when Zach handed them to her and told her what he needed her to do.

"Perhaps I should get these done now."

"No, they can wait. My stomach can't."

Zach wasn't sure if Regan was even aware that she cringed. He shook it off, waited for her to tuck everything away, and collect her purse.

"We'll take my car," he said as he turned back to the office and she followed.

Zach escorted Regan to the elevator, and down to the parking garage where his car waited a few feet from the door.

Regan let out a chuckle as they neared his car. "You know, it takes me fifteen minutes to get from the parking garage to the office. This took three."

"Well I'll have to look into giving you an executive parking space and a key for the private elevator."

"I'll be fine," she said as he opened the car door for her. "Thank you."

"Fifteen minutes? Really?" he asked, revisiting the subject as he walked around the car and climbed in.

"Today I'm on level four. I paid two dollars, as an employee of the building without a monthly parking pass," she informed him. "Then I had to walk down four ramps to the front of the building because there was maintenance going on in the elevator shaft. And this was on the day I showed up at seven. I'm thinking it will not be as quick a process tomorrow when I come in later."

"I'll make sure you get that key."

"No, but thank you." She shook her head as she buckled her seatbelt. "You said you ride the bus to keep one more car off the roads."

"Yes, and I only drive if I'm rushing to the hospital, going to my mother's, or am very, very hungry." He backed out of the space.

"I could have had your lunch called in."

"Yes, but then you wouldn't go with me and wouldn't be a captive audience."

Regan clasped her hands together. Zach knew she was only going to lunch with him because he was her boss. And, he knew, she wouldn't do it often—because he was her boss.

What would it take for her to relax around him? Who made it impossible for her to be calm around men?

The restaurant was thirty minutes away, and Regan wondered when the pleasantries of the job would end. He couldn't get so little done on a regular basis. And they couldn't take two hour lunches every day.

Inside the restaurant, ornate Chinese collectibles lined the walls. Lanterns hung over each tall booth. It was secluded, private, and dark.

Zach was going to be a challenge. She found herself pinching the bridge of her nose. Was each powerful man the same? They had to have certain characteristics in common. Confidence, the ability to dominate people and situations. It was just a job, but Regan felt as if she owed it to Mary Ellen to see it through. She wouldn't fall for the charm of a rich, good looking man—not this time.

Zach stepped up closer to her as they walked through the restaurant. "Are you okay?"

She dropped her hand. "Sorry, I just feel a headache coming on."

"You're hungry. See, it was good I got you out of the office." His hand hovered over the small of her back and guided her to a booth. The man behind the bar raised his hand in a welcome gesture.

Zach waited until Regan sat. "I'm going to go say hello to Mr. Lee. He's the owner."

She watched him shake the man's hand and then grasp his upper forearm. A sign of superiority, Regan had learned. The man rested his other hand on Zach's shoulder, which made her laugh to herself. Yes, Mr. Lee knew what he was doing too by showing more superiority.

They hadn't ordered, but as soon as Zach returned, food began to appear at the table, compliments of the chef.

She sipped her green tea and looked at the amount of food that had accumulated.

"Everything looks wonderful. You certainly don't eat like this every day."

"No. They've been begging me to come in for a month now. I figured it was time." Zach picked up an egg roll and bit into it. "So what is the usual fare for Regan Keller?"

"Ah, more interviewing?"

"Just getting to know you. Remember, Mary Ellen was around for ten years. I had a lot of time to ask these annoying questions."

He lifted his eggroll to his mouth and took another bite as he raised his eyebrows as a cue for her to answer.

"Let's see." She bit into a dumpling and tried to will herself to be comfortable around Zach. "I wouldn't be a southern girl if I didn't love my mama's fried chicken."

"Now that does sound good. My mother can't find her way around a kitchen with a map."

Regan laughed, then shoved the rest of the dumpling into her mouth to stifle it.

"You think that's funny?" he asked, humored. "You wouldn't if had to eat her cooking. That is why she caters all events and makes me bring desserts."

"She sounds classy." And she loved that he could joke about his mother with his mouth full, but she saw how he dealt with people around the office, with a no-nonsense approach. There were two sides to the man before her. And she was finding she enjoyed both sides, which scared the hell out of her.

"Well, we'll switch. Your mom can cook for me, and I'll let mine cater for you," he said with a nod and a smile.

CHAPTER 9

*A*fter lunch, they returned to the office. As Zach got situated, Regan went to her desk and gathered the items she wanted to discuss.

She returned with a stack of files under her arm, which she laid on Zach's desk. He sorted through them. They were all projects he personally looked after.

He walked her through the building contracts, building times, estimates, and subcontractor contacts, giving her an idea of who and what she was working with.

"This is the condo project I was telling you about yesterday." He reminded her of her future housing options when he opened the next file.

"John Forrester?"

"Man in charge." He showed her the drawings and the plans for the building.

She gazed over the concept drawings from the. "Zach, these are going to be gorgeous."

"This one is my favorite." He pulled a drawing from the pile and watched again as her eyes widened.

"Yes, that one is wonderful."

"I designed it."

She looked up at him "You're amazing."

His eyes zeroed in on hers and softened. "I was hoping you'd tell me that someday."

"Mr. Benson..." her tone was threatening.

"I'm kidding." He gathered up the pictures. "You'll have to think about city living. Nice view, roomy living accommodations, ample room for entertaining..."

"More money than I will ever make in my life," she quipped as she gathered her notes and the files.

"So what is your ideal home?" He sat back in his chair and watched her.

Regan let out a little hum. "Oh, Tennessee sprawling land. A few horses, bank of trees, a porch wrapped around the house with rockers for me and..." She stopped and shook her head. "Well let's just say not here in town."

"That does sound nice."

"I'd better get these filed. I'll call on the project in Kansas City tomorrow, and I'll check your itinerary for Monday morning." Regan stood and quickly left the office.

Zach turned his chair toward the windows. He could see the condo project from where he sat. It would be over a year before the first residents could move in. When building large buildings, there had to be patience, and he'd always had that. That was, until the moment he met Regan Keller.

Since the moment she'd landed in his lap, he couldn't clear his head of her.

For the rest of the week Zach kept his distance from Regan. There were no more lunches out or coffees in the morning. He'd heard Mr. Benson more times than he'd have liked.

They had a meeting scheduled with John Forrester at the condo project, which was less than a mile down the river. Regan suggested they walk to the site, and he looked at her high heels and laughed. But just to get the opportunity to spend a few moments, with her he agreed.

She excused herself, and a minute later, walked back into his office wearing tennis shoes.

"You're one of those women who plan for everything, aren't you?" he asked, enjoying the subtle difference in the way her calves looked in flat shoes as they walked out of the building.

Her hand brushed the silver necklace she wore. "Not really, but I thought it best not to wear my good shoes on a site."

"Mary Ellen only thought of that once we were on site and she was falling over rocks and construction debris."

Regan wasn't like Mary Ellen at all. She took care of him, but she didn't coddle him. She was prepared for anything, and he appreciated that. Then again, he found there wasn't much about Regan Keller that he didn't appreciate, except for her emotional distance. Then again, he hadn't known her but a few days.

Regan carried a notebook against her chest with items they would need to address with John. Zach walked a step behind her to watch her walk. The way the ponytail she wore at the base of her neck swung from side to side made him want to loosen it and run his fingers through her hair. But when she talked he'd catch up to her and hope she didn't notice him ogling.

"Until this week I never noticed how many job sites have your company name on them. I must have seen three on my way to work this morning." She clutched the notebook closer to her chest.

"I have twenty of them in five states, but I personally oversee four of them. They're the four I designed and acquired. I'm meeting next week with an investor for a new project in Los Angeles." He adjusted the hard hats he carried under his arm and thought how proud his grandfather would be to see what he'd done with the company.

"Where do you live? In a high-rise condo that you designed?" She shook her head when she said it. He knew the reaction well.

Just because his name was on the side of the building, everyone assumed he had to live the lavish life. Then again, he always had. But even in adulthood he was judged.

"Would it disappoint you if I told you I don't live all that far from you in a condo that I rent?" He handed her a hard hat and put on his.

"Thank you" she said, taking the hat and putting it on. "You rent a condo?"

"See, I did shock you."

"Yes you did." She smiled. He didn't want her to think he was above the men and women that worked for him, but the world thought differently when you had money.

They entered the work site. Dust kicked up, and they both shielded their faces until the breeze died down. He breathed in the thick scents of dirt and sawdust. The sounds of progress embraced him. Cranes, forklifts, drills, saws, and the vivid curses of men working hard. This was his project, and seeing it physically standing before him, he couldn't think of a better feeling.

"Just so you don't go home disappointed, I get the suite on the top floor of this building, but that'll be a year away." They both looked up at the top floor of the building, which was only a structural skeleton.

"Now that makes more sense. You deserve the top floor." She smiled and headed toward the offices that were located in a temporary trailer on the edge of the lot.

Zach stood a moment longer, still in awe of her. Maybe she'd be the first person in the world who understood how hard he worked to keep his name on the letterhead on which those lengthy contracts were written.

When they entered the trailer, John Forrester stood from behind the old metal desk, his hand already extended toward Zach. "Finally, you grace us with your presence."

"Funny, very funny." Zach took the stab with the humor John intended. He'd been on site every three days, sometimes more often than that just to check in, even if he didn't go through the building every time. This particular structure had been the last one his father had overseen before his retirement. Zach had promised himself he'd never take it all so seriously that it would take three heart attacks to get him out from behind the desk. However, even as he had promised, he knew he was lying. He loved what he did.

"You must be Regan." John extended his hand toward her.

"It's nice to meet you, Mr. Forrester."

"Manners. You've got yourself a prize." He smiled at Zach, who nodded and gave her a grateful glance, but she quickly looked away. "Please, call me John. Mary Ellen said you'd fit right in. You look like you do." He shifted his glance back to Zach. "Well, let's head up."

"Up?" The quiver in Regan's voice put humor on John's face.

"Yes, the work isn't all here on the ground." John headed walked the the door and opened it.

They followed him toward an orange cage that hung to the side of the half-finished building.

Zach reached for her arm, but when she took a quick step back, he dropped his hand. "If you'd rather stay down here, I can go through the notes," he offered, hating the fear that he saw in her eyes. He couldn't help but wonder if the fear was of him or the climb to the top of the building. Regan shook her head.

"If the job is up, then I go up."

CHAPTER 10

*A*s they rode to the top, Zach watched Regan carefully. She was pale, and her knuckles were white where she gripped her fingers around the notebook in her hands. What was it that drove him to want to wrap his arms around her and let her bury her face in his chest as they rode higher and higher? Did Mary Ellen fear heights that bad? Why had he never noticed?

When the elevator jarred to a stop, he laid a gentle hand on her back to steady her and ease her out of the cage. His father had done it to him as a child. The wind at the top raced through the space with its open walls. She didn't flinch this time, but he heard her suck in a breath when she saw the view for the first time.

Nashville lay below them like a colorful map of trees, streets, and buildings. The child in him wanted to take her to the edge so she could see how small humanity could be from such a height.

John began showing Regan around. "We've got six units on each floor."

Zach kept his eyes on her. The color was returning to her cheeks, and she'd released the grip on the notebook so that she could open it and begin to take notes. Finally she was comfortable. One thing he was learning about Regan Keller was she would adapt to any situation, but she wouldn't give in to others.

John continued his tour. "So far each floor looks much like this. We have the interior walls framed up, and the electrical and plumbing have been run throughout the building. The glasswork will be done floor by floor. We'll get to this floor next week."

"And when John Forrester says it'll be done next week, it will be," Zach added.

"Damn straight. I've never gone over on budget or on time with a project. I run my crews tight. There is no screwing around on my site." He tucked his thumbs into the front pockets of his jeans and rocked back on his heels.

"And that's why I use and abuse him like I do."

Regan looked up from her notebook. "Electrical inspections?"

"Scheduled for a week from Wednesday," John answered, and she jotted the answer down.

"Structural inspection?"

"You sure are on top of it," John said with a smile when she looked up at him. "In a few days. They want to get a look at the penthouses."

Regan nodded. She fired off a few more questions about budget and scheduling, and John answered even her simplest questions with enthusiasm, which was why Zach liked to work with him. He lived for his work.

When they'd returned to the trailer and finished their meeting, John leaned back in his chair. "Regan, it was a pleasure having you visit today. You should come in with this slob every time." Zach caught his eye and narrowed his stare. John gave a silent nod. It was understood that Zach had eyes for Regan, though he'd never assume John would venture toward a relationship, he now knew better.

"Thank you." She stood and so did John. "It was nice to meet you. We'll touch base in a few days." Regan extended her hand, shook his hand again, and turned to Zach.

Zach gave her a nod. "Go ahead and start back. I'll be right behind you."

Regan let herself out of the trailer, and both men watched as the door closed behind her..

John rested his hand on Zach's shoulder as they watched her walk away through the small, clouded window. "She's a keeper."

"She's very efficient."

"That's not what I mean and you know it. That's one very sexy, very confident woman you have manning your office. Are you man enough to handle that?"

Zach gave a snort. "She's not much into the workplace relationship."

"This is the one you let ride to work on your lap?" John slapped him on the shoulder then walked back around his desk. "Mary Ellen mentioned it. I went to see the baby."

"Fairly efficient yourself," Zach joked, and then watched the sway of Regan's hips as she turned the corner from the site to the street. "Yeah, she's the one."

"Just remember you have to work with her, and she's the one with all the inside knowledge to screw you over."

"Thanks for the warning."

"Though I don't think she's like that."

"No, I don't either." As tight-lipped as he'd found Regan to be, he couldn't imagine she'd be the kind of woman to ruffle anyone's feathers.

John sat back in his chair and kicked his feet up on the desk. "Good luck with all of that. I have to say, I like her."

Zach liked her too—and wasn't that cause for serious concern.

"I'll catch up with her. I'll talk to you soon," Zach said as he let himself out of the trailer.

She'd taken off the hard hat and freed her hair from the band that had held it in place. She was running her fingers through her hair when Zach caught up with her.

Like a schoolgirl with a stack of books, Regan clutched her note pad and the hard hat close to her chest as she walked. She looked innocent and happy. But just from the way she usually reacted to him, he knew she was protective against men.

Without looking at him, she acknowledged him by speaking. "I've never ridden that far up in a construction elevator before."

"I thought you were an executive's assistant in real estate. "

"Sure, but he didn't build buildings. He had buildings built for clients. By the time I rode the elevators, they were inside the building, and so were the walls."

"It can be a little unnerving the first time."

"To say the least. How old were you the first time you walked twenty stories in the air with no walls?"

"I was six, and as excited as any boy could have been seeing the big machines that built buildings." Even as a grown man, the thought made his stomach bubble with excitement. "My father had his finger looped through my belt buckle the entire time. I think he knew I would try to run from one side to the other and not stop."

She laughed, and it unleashed that need for her that she wouldn't release to him. Her laugh would haunt him in his dreams if he let it.

Regan kept her eyes forward as they walked. "So what are your big plans for the weekend?"

"Well, of course the luncheon at my mother's. Then I have tickets to the symphony on Sunday."

"Symphony? Oh, that sounds nice. Well you'll enjoy yourself. I haven't been in years." She sighed with a smile. "Sunday I have dinner plans that include pie."

"Ah." He wondered if she'd added that quickly so that he wouldn't be tempted to ask her to attend the symphony with him, which he'd intended to do. "Dinner with the doctor?"

"Yes, as a matter of fact." She lowered her head and bit down on her lip. Zach wondered if there was a problem with the doctor. Perhaps the other man who'd answered her door.

"I guess I won't see you until I get back from Los Angeles."

As they neared the office building, she swung her arms freely, the notebook still in her hands. "Your suitcase is by your elevator. Your folder with your tickets and itinerary are on your desk. A car will be waiting for you at the airport. And the tiramisu is in the fridge in your office. I cut it into servable slices. She just needs to put it on an elegant tray."

"You got the tiramisu?" He stopped and she turned to him.

"Yes. It's in the fridge."

"I'd forgotten about it. I just threw that in the mix, never assuming..."

"If you say you need it, I get it done. That is my job." She lifted her brows, smiled, and started to walk again.

He jogged to catch up to her. "Let me know where you bought it. She'll expect me to come up with it again."

"I didn't buy it, I made it. I'll bill you," she said on an airy laugh as she walked through the revolving door and toward the bank of elevators while he stood on the sidewalk wondering how on earth he was going to prove to her she could trust him.

CHAPTER 11

*C*arlos threw bags of barbecue on the table then turned and grabbed two forks. He handed one to Regan and sat down across from her.

Regan opened one of the takeout trays and stuck her fork into the potato salad. "Since you started sleeping on the couch, I swear it's started to sag. Not to mention, you're going to make me fat by bringing in all this beer and takeout every night."

"Mom wouldn't want me starving you on my time off." He set down two glasses filled with ice and split a can of soda between them.

"Speaking of time off, haven't found a job?"

"No. No one wants a Puerto Rican dancer with a receding hairline."

She covered her mouth to keep the food from flying out. "Puerto Rican dancer? Is that your new talent?"

"No, but hell of a way to pick up ladies," he said spooning potato salad into his mouth.

"Didn't think you were interested in the ladies right now."

"I got divorced, Regan. I didn't die." He grabbed a rib from another container and began to pull the meat from the bone with his teeth. "I think I should be thinking of other women. It's healthy. At least if I'm thinking of other women, I'm not thinking of Madeline and that man."

"It's been two years," she said softly, resting her hand on his.

"Two years to just give up, is that what you're saying?"

"Carlos…"

"Sorry. I'm just in a bad mood about it all. You share your life with someone, and then one day it's over. Worse, she runs to your best friend for support and now he's married to her."

"She didn't run off with him."

"I know. It just makes me feel better about being so mad." He wiped his hands on a napkin, and picked up his soda, taking a sip. "Anyway, I'm just looking for that silver lining that Mom's always talking about. Single and sleeping on my sister's couch is not a positive in my life, no offense."

"None taken. It isn't really my couch." She smiled.

"It's just that Eduardo needs braces. Christen needs a new uniform for football, and now Clara wants to dance. Money's too tight to let them do everything they want to do, but I don't want to turn them down. Just because Madeline and I couldn't see eye to eye doesn't mean they should suffer. So the job thing's just got me down. I got passed over for another one today."

"The private school in Memphis?"

"Yeah."

"I'm sorry."

"No big." He shrugged.

"Well, I was thinking, if you were interested, I think I could get you a job on a site. One right here in Nashville."

"You mean on one of your building sites?" He sat up straighter in his seat.

"Yes, that's what I mean." Regan shook her head. Carlos was a brilliant man, but he kept that in check by acting the imbecile most of the time.

"Sure, college, graduate school. Yeah, I've reached the level I could pound nails into wood." He stood, walked to the refrigerator, retrieved a beer from the fridge, and twisted the top off.

"I didn't mean to insult you. I just wanted to help."

"I know," he said as he sat back down. "I've applied to eight schools in three districts. I've already gotten the thanks but no thanks from three of them."

"Well then, there are five who need to decide you'd be the best for their kids."

He nodded. "I've got three months to do something. My savings is almost depleted, and if Arianna comes back in July and sees the dent in her couch, I'll have one in my head."

"You don't think she already knows you're sleeping on the couch?"

"No, or she would have had something to say about it by now."

Regan covered her brother's hand with hers before he could lift another bite to his mouth. " I propose if neither of us is on our feet, like we want to be, by the time she comes back and claims back her house, I'll spring for the cardboard box, and we'll live together by the river."

"Sounds like a fantasy fulfilled." He lifted the beer in a salute. "So what's the job?"

ZACH PARKED his car around the side of his mother's house near her front rose garden, knowing he'd want to make a quick exit. This would save the hassle of having his car penned in by the guests that would soon be arriving. The grounds were green and manicured. The white pillars on the front porch and the large arched windows welcomed him. He appreciated southern architecture. Wouldn't it be nice to build a large building with white pillars and arches like the grand old houses had? But steel and glass were the way of it.

He strolled to the front door, the tiramisu carefully balanced in the crook of his arm, and a bouquet of roses for his mother in his other hand.

She had gardens of roses of every shape and color, but she loved when they came through the door in tissue paper.

Audrey Benson answered the door in her white flowered sundress. A lavish wide-brimmed hat, which matched her dress, adorned her head like a crown. She kissed Zach's cheeks and smiled.

"Are those for me?" She took the roses and cradled them in her arms. "They are lovely."

"And your dessert, ma'am," he said, shutting the door with his elbow as he watched his mother's eyes widened with delight.

"You got the tiramisu?"

"You asked me to."

"It's beautiful, where did you order it from?"

"Ah, I was going to keep this a secret, but I figure when I fly out on Monday you'll be on Regan's phone begging her for contacts."

"How is it you know me so well?" She headed toward the kitchen, and he followed.

As it had always been, the enormous kitchen, with its miles of dark granite counters, was spotless and clutter free. She had trays of appetizers on the island still covered to keep his father's fingers from digging into them.

"I have to taste it," she said as she laid her roses on the counter and pulled out two small plates from the cupboard.

Zach set down the tray. Toting that dessert around, he'd done nothing but think of Regan. She'd taken the time to prepare something so lavish for a woman she didn't even know. Thinking of her mixing it together and cutting it into perfect servable squares made him wonder what else she took her time with. Did she keep house as precisely as she kept her desk? Did she sip tea and make cupcakes? Did she make love with the same passion she made desserts?

He shook the thought from his head. Images of Regan licking tiramisu from her fingers nearly had him needing to leave his mother's presence.

He had desperately wanted to invite her to join him, but she was very straightforward with her attitude about seeing him socially. He didn't think of the luncheon as a social event—it was more a torture session for Zach. But since it didn't have to do with business, he knew she would have turned him down flat. Much like the symphony he'd attend the next night. It had seemed like fun when he'd received the tickets, but he'd really wanted to take her. Instead, he'd be taking Madison Fitzpatrick with him.

Nothing against Madison Fitzpatrick. However, her white-blonde hair in its tight knot on the top of her head wasn't quite the style he looked for when he chose a date. He wanted the dark beauty who sat outside his office to accompany him. Alas, he'd be spending the evening with his mother's grannyish best friend.

He didn't blame Regan for not wanting to date her boss, but he couldn't think of much else. The faces of the two men she'd embraced on Monday still filtered through his mind regularly. Maybe he should ask his mother about Dr. Curtis, but then he didn't have a last name to go along with his inquiry. Besides, when his mother gave her time and money, she didn't do a lot of socializing with people beyond the board of directors.

There was no one but Regan that he could ask about the dark man who'd answered her door. Though the doctor had mentioned another man was worried about her when he'd gone to pick her up from work. His mind was in overdrive. Did the men know about each other? Regan didn't seem like the kind of woman who would string along lovers.

That thought alone had his head spinning.

A week away from her face would benefit him greatly. As long as hearing her voice on the phone didn't make him think of her too much, he'd be okay.

"Oh, this is delightful." Audrey sighed, bringing Zach back to the present. "Taste." She shoved a spoonful of the tiramisu in his mouth and he nodded. The creamy texture of coffee and mocha melted on his tongue.

"That is really good. Let me have another bite," he said with his mouth still full.

"Where?"

"Where what?" He dug the spoon into the piece of dessert Audrey was sampling.

"Where did you get it?"

"I don't think I should tell you. I think I should keep it my secret."

"Zachary Tyler Benson, I'm your mother and you'll tell me, or you're right—Regan will have me on her phone bright and early Monday morning."

He shook his head. She actually would do it. "Don't hound her. Promise?" He raised his eyebrows, waiting for her confirmation.

"Would I do that?" She stuck her bottom lip out.

"Mother."

"Fine." She smiled and folded her hands before her like a good girl.

"Regan made that just for your party."

"She made it?" Audrey's eyes widened just as they had when she'd seen him walk through with the delectable dessert.

"Yes. She said she'd bill me later." Unable to help himself, he took another spoonful.

"She really won't bill you, will she?" she a whispered.

Zach laughed and kissed his mother's cheek. She might have been born to money and lived life lavishly, but she loved anything that was cheap, or better yet, free.

Tyler Benson strolled into the kitchen in his swimming

trunks, leaving a trail of water across the tiled floor. His eyes lit when he saw Zach, but the tapping of his wife's foot put him quickly in his place.

Audrey crossed her arms in front of her. "People will be here in less than thirty minutes. Why are you standing here dripping in my kitchen?"

"I'm sorry, ma'am," Zach's father joked and kissed her cheek. "Nice to see you, Zach." He held out his hand, and Zach shook it at a distance, not wishing to get wet. "Oh, God! Is that a tiramisu?" His dad made a move toward it, but his mom's hand smacking his arm stopped him.

"Don't you dare! You are restricted from such things."

The very mention of his restrictions drew Zach's attention to the scar that ran down the center of his dad's chest. How could a man who enjoyed his life, business, and was physically active be forced into retirement because his heart couldn't keep up?

His father leaned in closer to his mother. "Then why do I have to be at your luncheon?"

"Because you love me, dammit. Now get a shower." She tried her best to shoo him out of the kitchen, but not before he ran his finger through the slice of dessert on her plate.

"Damn, good. You make that yourself, Zachary?"

"No, sir. My new assistant seems to have many skills. One being desserts."

"Better keep her around then."

I certainly intend to, Zach thought as his father dug his finger in one more time before heading upstairs to become presentable.

CHAPTER 12

The party was just as Zach had imagined. Dull. He knew it was one more attempt for his mother to flaunt him in front of her friends and their lonely daughters.

"Zachary, this is Marsha Livingston," she introduced him to the blonde at her side. "Remember the Livingston Care Estates that we built in the Hamptons?"

"Yes, a very nice facility." He smiled politely.

"Marsha, I'll find you an iced tea," his mother said, excusing herself.

His mother left them alone, and Marsha, who was probably all of twenty-two, looked up at him. "My father was very impressed with your company. He hopes to build more facilities in the future. He'd certainly use your company, I'm sure."

Zach nodded and accepted a glass of champagne from a tray that passed by him on the hand of one of his mother's caterers. "That would be a very welcomed opportunity."

Looking around the room, he simply wasn't interested in the guests his mother had gathered. He knew all the names. Many of them had been engraved on plaques on the sides of buildings he'd cut his teeth on when he joined his father and grandfather in the business. Their daughters were elegant, educated, and beautiful. They were young and hopeful. They were bait for his mother to marry him off. But none of them could measure up to the quiet determination he'd found in Regan.

The party hadn't yet died down when Zach cornered his mother. He'd graciously diverted Marsha Livingston's attention to another young man, and Sylvia Astor had found herself all alone in the rose garden after he'd excused himself to take a phone call he decided he needed to attend to right away. He kissed his mother on the cheek.

"I really have to be going," he said to her displeasure. "I have a lot of things to do before I leave on Monday."

"Where are you going?"

"I'll be in Los Angeles. I have a big prospect."

"I wish you had someone to go with you. I could make arrangements." She looked around the room. "At thirty-seven you shouldn't be alone. It is killing me."

"I'll be fine. This is one of those clients that like things personal. I'm not taking John Forrester or Regan either."

"Well, fine then." She straightened his shirt collar. "Please call me. I miss you so much."

"Mom, I'm here once a week, and you talk to me three times a day."

"I talk to Mary Ellen and…"

"Regan."

"Yes, Regan, more than I talk to you."

"I'm a busy man."

"I know, dear." She grasped his hands in hers. "Don't be too busy to remember what's important."

Zach kissed both of her cheeks, made his way through the guests, and away from the few that were steering his way for conversation, and slid out the side door.

The long drive was filled with cars, and he was glad he'd parked where he had. He climbed into his Lexus and started away from the estate in which he'd lived his whole life, when he hadn't been away at school, that was. There was no southern drawl to his voice. A fried chicken had never landed on his plate either, but he was blessed and he knew that. He had parents that doted on him. He'd never needed nor wanted for anything, and his family business was a legacy he was proud to carry on.

As he turned from the gated drive, and headed back toward downtown Nashville, he looked around. He realized he was in the middle of Regan's dream. Tennessee sprawling land, horses, and houses with large porches. What kept her from her dream of living in the country and having a family, he wondered. What was going to keep her from him? Nothing, if he could help it. He couldn't remember when a woman consumed his every thought. Zach Benson wasn't one to let go of something he wanted. And he wanted Regan Keller. He was just going to have to get her to trust him. He'd never hurt her. He'd never let anyone else hurt her. It was time he showed her what a great partnership they could have.

CHAPTER 13

onday was lonely. Regan arrived at work early and took the opportunity to get to know her surroundings and other coworkers, knowing Zach wasn't there. Before she sat to answer the weekend's e-mails and return Audrey's second phone call, she'd taken out the plans for the Nashville building and looked over the designs. She needed to schedule meetings with three different departments on the build and wanted to familiarize herself with it better.

She looked over the plans for the penthouse suites. What would Zach's penthouse apartment would look like when he was part of it? Would it be streamlined, with dark cherry wood and tones of beige? Or would he be an eclectic type with bold colors and priceless works of art? What did his rented condo look like? His car was a simple black Lexus, nothing too fancy or flashy, but classy. The suits he wore were tailored to him, but again, not flashy. He had millions, she assumed, tucked away in banks and trust funds—but he ate from the hot dog cart next to his office, where he spent twelve or more hours a day designing and financing the next big build in Nashville, or wherever he and his company were needed.

She kept telling herself it didn't really matter what his life away from the office would be like. It didn't matter what her handsome boss planned for his future. All that mattered was that when the building was completed and he'd moved into his new home, she'd still be the woman answering his phone calls.

But Regan couldn't help but wonder, because she was acutely aware he wasn't in his office working and leaving his coffee pot on.

She'd taken the bus to work so Carlos could use her car. He was doing her a favor as well. It was still making noise, and he'd promised to figure out what was wrong. The old lady had been on the bus, hoarding her two seats when Regan climbed on. She hadn't tried to sit. She stood with the rest of the passengers, but she couldn't help but look around as though Zach might be sitting there waiting for her to take his seat.

It was nine-thirty when he finally called, and as soon as Regan had spoken, she wished she'd kept the sound of relief out of her voice.

"How is L.A.?" She gathered her note pad and pen.

"Dark," he said flatly, and she smiled. "And the sun is up."

"Not a big fan of Los Angeles, huh?"

"Smog is not natural air."

She let out a small laugh. She couldn't agree more. It had been one of the selling points when she'd taken the job in Hawaii and left Los Angeles behind. Now she was more than grateful that she'd returned to the fresh air of Tennessee.

"Tell me, Mr. Benson, how can I assist you today?" She tried to sound professional, but it came out a bit too flirty.

"You're in a cheery mood."

"Remember? I had pie." She hoped reminding him about her dinner would take the edge off of him flirting back.

"Sounds like a good time." He cleared his throat. "Here's what I need you to do."

Zach read off a list of items he needed her to follow up on.

There were e-mails, letters, phone calls, and contracts to take care of. He needed some items emailed to him, others could wait, and some he'd need given to Peterson.

"I'll get this all taken care of," she promised.

"I know. By the way, how many times has my mother called you already?"

"Twice so far. I guess she really enjoyed my dessert."

"It was a hit."

"She wanted to take me to lunch today."

He let out a breath. "I'm sorry."

"Don't be. I have plans today, but we agreed on tomorrow. She said you wouldn't mind if I took a long lunch."

"Who am I to argue? Regan, honestly I can call her and have her cancel if you…"

"No. I look forward to it." She laughed. "I figure it will give me some insight on you."

"I don't know if I like that or not." The distress in his voice made her want to meet his mother even more.

"Do you have something to hide, Mr. Benson?"

"Not a thing."

"Then I wouldn't worry about it." The flirtatious tone crept back into her voice, and she sat taller in her chair to at least look professional.

"I won't, then." He let out a small laugh that disappeared into awkward silence. "So what plans do you have today? Never mind. Don't tell me. I shouldn't have asked."

"If there isn't anything else, Mr. Benson, I'll get to these right away."

"Thank you, Regan. By the way, I left something on my desk for you. I think you'll find it'll come in useful. I'll call you later after I meet with the investor."

Regan hung up the phone after they'd said goodbye, and went straight into his office. On the top of his desk, beside his phone, lay a key. The keychain had her name on it. When she picked up the key, she realized it matched the one he used in the elevator.

Next to the key was a permit that would allow her to park in the building without having to pay.

She'd been toying with him about the long trek from the parking garage. She certainly hoped he didn't think she was complaining.

Regan let go of her stiff professionalism and gave into a smile. Well, she'd take the permit. That would come in very useful and save her a lot of money, but she'd leave the key. It was his elevator. That was too private for her. Even though Zachary Benson continued to be on her mind, she couldn't begin to take special gifts from him, no matter what they were.

She'd remember to thank him for the parking permit.

AT NOON, Regan met John Forrester on the corner for a hot dog from Frank's cart. He was a gentleman, she decided when he offered to pay for her lunch, even though she'd invited him. They sat at one of the stone tables with the fountains to their back, and the river in front of them.

"Thank you for lunch," she said as she took her first bite of her Polish sausage. "Mmm, this is just what I wanted."

"My pleasure. It's not very often a beautiful woman asks me to lunch." He opened his soda and took a long drink. "How's it going in L.A.?"

"Zach's not a fan of smog. Other than that, he has a full day of meetings and he's working hard."

"Did he get the contract?"

"He's working on it. He is very secretive though. The investor doesn't want his name on anything. At least until it's all said and done, then Zach says he'll want all the credit."

John nodded his head. "So to what do I owe the pleasure of

your company?"

Regan liked John Forrester. He had a personality that was infectious, and you just wanted to be around him. She figured him to be in his early fifties and someone who had worked outside in the elements most of his life. His skin was tan from the sun and the lines that crossed his face showed experience, but he was strikingly handsome. She also knew he was someone Zach trusted wholeheartedly. John worked on almost all of their Nashville projects and numerous ones out of state.

"I'm here to ask a favor." She winced when she said it. She'd only had her job a week, and barely felt comfortable enough to ask him. "My brother is between jobs right now. He's a junior high school math teacher, but currently out of work."

"I see. And you want to know if I can use him?"

Regan let out a small sigh. "Yes. I probably shouldn't even ask, but…"

"Has he worked construction before?" he interrupted her before she could back out of the conversation.

"He did for a short time to earn money through college. He's not a master of any specific trade, but he's a hard worker."

"I see." John took a bite of his hot dog and wiped his mouth with his napkin. "So it could be temporary if he gets a teaching job?"

She nodded, realizing that wasn't a great asset when asking for a job.

"I can see what I can do. I have a few guys leaving the job next week. Would that be soon enough?"

"Really? You can use him?" Her voice shot up in delight.

John rested his hand on hers. "For you, I'll make sure I can."

"Oh, thank you. He'll be a good worker. I promise." Excitement bubbled inside her. She couldn't wait to tell Carlos.

"If not, he goes." He was matter-of-fact about it, and she nodded. That she understood. But Carlos wouldn't let her down, or John Forrester for that matter.

CHAPTER 14

The moment Zach stepped into his office the following Monday morning, he sighed with relief. He was home. He'd never much minded business trips, but his trip to L.A. had been tedious and drawn out. The investor was not one of his most favorite people to work with, but he brought millions to the bargaining table, which Zach couldn't ignore. But not having Regan there, with her meticulous note taking and her keen ears and eyes, he'd hoped he hadn't missed anything. Worse yet, he couldn't ask for her help on anything to do with the project for the time being. When the time was right, she'd be brought up to speed on the events of the build, and so would John Forrester. In fact, he could discuss minor things with John before he could let Regan in on his deal.

He couldn't be sure why the man always wanted to work the details out without anyone else being in on it. Obviously, he had something to hide. It only infuriated Zach that he couldn't have his people working on it.

He blew out a ragged breath. Zach had built buildings with the man before. This one would be just as successful and twice the size of all the others. It would all be fine, he reminded himself, even if he had to grit his teeth throughout the entire process.

Zach set his keys and sunglasses on his desk. There were stacks of papers neatly organized awaiting his attention.

The key to the elevator sat next to his phone with a note addressed to Mr. Benson under it. He opened it to find Regan's handwriting scrawled in it.

Thank you for the parking permit. I appreciate it. I'll leave the elevator key. Thank you, Regan.

He wasn't too surprised. A small part of him hoped she'd call and yell at him for it anyway. He'd leave it right where it was in case she changed her mind.

Zach's coffee mug was full and hot, waiting for him. He smiled when he saw the cinnamon roll on a plate next to the coffee. After the tiramisu, he was confident in assuming it was homemade.

Trying to regain control over his mind, he sat down with his coffee and scrolled through the news on his computer.

Picking up the fork that balanced on the plate, he cut into the cinnamon roll, and took a bite. As predicted, it was to die for.

Looking at his watch, he realized he'd officially stalled exactly nine minutes and twenty-seven seconds. He couldn't wait any longer. He had to see her.

He reached for the button on his phone to summon her, but that wouldn't do. Instead, he plucked a flower from the arrangement in the vase on the coffee table, and twirled it in his fingers. He opened the door only to be disappointed that she wasn't at her desk.

"A flower for me? You shouldn't have," Kirk Peterson laughed as he walked toward him.

Zach put on a smile, hoping the disappointment that he felt in the pit of his stomach didn't show on his face. He pulled the flower back casually as though he'd picked it up off the floor and he tossed it into the trash can.

Kirk waved a file at him. "I wanted to talk to you about the Memphis project."

"Yeah, why don't you come in?" Zach stepped back to let him through and gave one more look down the hall, but still there was no sign of Regan.

An hour and a half later, Kirk Peterson finally left Zach's office. He rubbed the bridge of his nose to ward off the headache he felt coming on. Regan sat at her desk just as Peterson walked out of his office. She glanced at Zach for a moment, then rose from her desk, and walked toward him with two Tylenol and a glass of water.

"Do you have anything stronger?" he joked, tossing the pills into his mouth and swallowing them with the water. "I'm going to have to fire you. You weren't here to arrange an emergency so I could get him out of my office faster."

"Well, did you eat the cinnamon roll? I was really hoping that would save me from any mistakes I might make for a week, like not being here to ward off Kirk Peterson." She batted her eyes at him. He was glad to see she'd loosened up a bit.

"Yes, and thank you." He tossed the cup into the trash. "Okay, I'll let you keep your job, but only if you have something good for me on the agenda."

"A walk around with John Forrester? They had a few inspections today, and he's afraid there will have to be some minor electrical changes."

"Great." He rubbed his temples. "What else does my day entail?"

"We need to discuss the ground breaking in Dallas, and someone called from L.A., but she wouldn't leave a name or contact information. She just said to call L.A." She shrugged. "Then you should be safe to hit the gym, the bar, or wherever you go to unwind."

With a nod, he pulled his iPad out of his desk drawer to take notes on when he met with John Forrester. "Are you coming to the meeting with John?" he called to Regan as she sat down at her desk.

"No, I have to get the plans for Memphis back from the architecture department, and I have contracts in legal. I'll be able to fill you in on..." She was talking about the Memphis project, but he realized he wasn't hearing a word she was saying. Being in her presence, for even just a few moments had his head in a fog.

His mind wandered more as she walked through his office continuing her conversation with him. There had to be a way to get her to see him, spend time with him socially, but she was very specific about that area of her life. A faint ache settled in his chest, at odds with the pressure he felt elsewhere.

"And by the way, your mother called three times." She tilted her head to look at him. "Are you okay?"

"Yes, I'm fine. Sorry." He shook off the desire that burned through him. "I'll get going. I'll be back as soon as I can."

"By the way," he said directing her attention back to him. "I'll leave the key on my desk. If you change your mind or want to use the elevator when I'm out of town, feel free."

CHAPTER 15

Zach drove to the Nashville site with the car's air-conditioning set to arctic. Maybe that would cool his thoughts about his executive assistant. He parked the car by the offices, grabbed his iPad, and put on his hard hat. John held open the door to the office.

His mind was already hot from wandering to thoughts of Regan, and the heat from the trailer that housed the office hit him like a wall. John grabbed his shoulders and sat him down, then retrieved a paper cup from the water cooler and filled it.

"Sucks, doesn't it?" John smiled as he handed him the cup.

"What is it, a hundred and fifty degrees in here?" He sipped the water and opened the collar of his shirt.

"Air is out. We'll fix it tomorrow."

"God, why wait?"

"Deadline and inspections are holding us back. That electrical contractor working in the residential units is going to cost us some time." He reached for the file on his desk and handed it to Zach. "Here's all the bad news."

Zach opened the file. He sucked in the thick air and wiped the beads of sweat from his brow. He'd have Regan call someone to fix the air for John. If John was hell bent on waiting so he could concentrate on the build site, and Zach knew he was, he'd sure as hell give him some cool air to do it in.

"Damn. It looks like they have to rerun the wiring for that whole floor."

"That's why you have the degree. I just get to walk them through and have them tell me what's wrong."

Zach studied the inspector's notes. "I'll bet if we do a few minor changes, we can get it to pass with minimal restructuring."

"Do you want to go up and look at it?"

"Yeah, I guess I'd better." He finished off the water and looked forward to the eighty-degree humidity outside.

They walked to the elevator, stepped inside, and John latched the gate. A worker walked by with metal poles balanced over each shoulder.

"Carlos!" John yelled, and the man looked up. "Find Stu. He needed your help with a fitting." The man nodded and kept walking as John started the elevator.

"Who was that?" Zach watched the man pass the pipes to another man and then hurry over to Stu, who looked to be wrestling with another pipe.

"Carlos," he said looking up, watching for the floor.

"When did he start?"

"Few days ago."

Zach kept his eyes on the ground moving farther and farther from him, watching the man nod as he took instructions from Stu and then pulled a wrench from his work belt. He looked very familiar, but Zach couldn't pinpoint why.

His walkthrough with John took longer than he had thought. In the end, the men had decided to discuss the changes over lunch and then do some rough drafting on the sight. The changes weren't hard, but it all had to be in the plans and submitted before they could start the work. He couldn't afford any delays on the project, so he'd spend all night making the changes to the plans.

By the time he made it back to the office, everyone was gone, including Regan. He couldn't help but be disappointed, but it was for the best. He needed to bunker down and start planning the changes to the wiring in the residential units.

Much of what made Benson, Benson and Hart so successful was their hands-on approach. Sure, they were a billion-dollar company. Sure, they built high-rises and condominiums in almost every state. They employed thousands of people. But they also had a hands-on approach you couldn't find anywhere else. Tyler Benson, his father, and Zachary Hart, his grandfather, had made sure Zach was just as hands-on. They'd sent him to the best college to study and learn architecture. He knew everything there was to building hi-rises and houses. Well, the technical parts. If he had to take a hammer to the wood, things might not work out so well, but he could plan every detail meticulously. What the subcontractors did with his plans, that was another story.

He changed out of his suit and found a pair of jeans and an Oxford University T-shirt that was almost fifteen-years-old in the bag he kept in the closet of his office. After hanging up his suit, he placed his shirt in the bag that would go home with him so he could have it laundered. He pulled a bottle of water out of the fridge, turned on some jazz, and headed to the conference room that adjoined his office. He set out the plans, and got to work.

Zach began to make markings and measured out other ideas. Then he began to create. Keeping within the same basic plans, he continued to design what the inspectors were looking for. He kept the reports nearby, sure not to miss any detail. It wouldn't be a Benson, Benson, and Hart building if it wasn't perfect.

It was nearly six-thirty when he heard drawers slamming and

papers flying from beyond his office. Cautiously, he stood and walked toward the door.

Regan stood over her desk lifting files, shifting papers, opening drawers, and then started digging through her trash can.

"Hi," he said softly.

"Shit!" She yelled the curse and grabbed for her chest. "Ya scared the hell outta me."

Her accent had grown thicker with that one sentence, and it had Zach's heart racing. "I could say the same thing. I thought you'd left for the day."

"I did. Then I remembered that you hadn't signed the contracts I was waiting for from the legal department. You were at your meeting with John. I have to get them to New York overnight." Her skin was pale, and he knew it wasn't the scare she'd taken. This was a different kind of panic.

"Where are they?" He kept his tone soft to calm her.

"They were right here." She kept looking around.

"Regan, would these be them?" He looked in the basket that she kept for items he needed to see.

Color filled her cheeks and made her even more adorable. "Oh, God! I can't believe I didn't get them to you. I should have walked down there. I should have found you. That's my job."

He didn't like the fear in her voice. Not one bit. "We'll take care of this." He walked over to her desk and found a pen. He signed all the areas she'd marked with red flags and sealed them in the envelope marked OVERNIGHT. He looked at the time on his Rolex watch and bit down on his lip. "The annex is only three miles from here. They're open until eight," he said with a smile. This wasn't the first time he'd gone through this. "They'll make it to New York in time," he assured her. "But we have to go now." He walked back through his office with the contracts in his hand.

"I'll take them. It was my oversight." She followed him right to the elevator.

"Fine. You take them in. I'll drive." He pulled her inside and hit the button for the parking garage. The papers in her hand shook, and he clasped his hand on them to steady them. "Really, Regan, this is going to be okay."

"No. No, this is one of those costly mistakes that loses you millions of dollars and hours of time."

He watched her intently. Perhaps the last man she'd worked for was stricter than he was. You learned from mistakes, his father and grandfather had said. He hadn't been there. Her workday was over. It wasn't as though she tucked them away in a mess. No, her desk was immaculate.

When the elevator stopped, and the doors opened, they hurried to his car. He opened the car door for her then walked around, climbed in, and stared the car. "You know. I'll be here all night. Why don't we get some dinner before we come back?"

"Zach…"

"C'mon. It's the least you could do." He played on her guilt. "Unless you have some hot date." He raised one eyebrow.

"No. No hot date tonight." She looked down at the papers in her lap and shook her head. "It's been a long while since I had one of those."

The mystery of Regan Keller had just become more intriguing.

CHAPTER 16

*R*egan had confirmed that the contracts would arrive on time when she handed them over to the courier. She was pleased that it had worked out, but she was still disappointed in herself for having to go back to the office, and now she'd been talked into having dinner with the very man she shouldn't be spending time with. Reluctantly she climbed back in Zach's car.

"We made it in time. They'll get there," she said as she latched her seatbelt.

"I had no doubt."

He drove only a few more miles and pulled into the parking lot of Steve's BBQ Pit with Beer. Even from the parking lot, she could smell the familiar scent of barbeque and smoke.

She laughed when she saw the sign and the forty motorcycles parked out front next to a few BMWs and town cars. "Is this one of your hangouts?" she asked as she slid from the car.

"Oh, yeah. Best pork sandwiches this side of the Mississippi."

The restaurant was an eclectic mix of professionals and bikers. The building looked like an old shack with its walls decorated in a myriad of garage sale items. Some still with the tags on them.

It was far from the kind of place she would think Zachary Benson would frequent. Then she had to remind herself, she'd met him on the bus. Perhaps she'd never completely figure him out.

The air was smoky with barbeque and the stench of stale beer made her crave one. Patsy Cline filled her ears with sweet dreams, as Zach led her to a booth.

"This is great." She found herself raising her voice over the noise.

"I thought you'd like it."

A waitress with skintight jeans, cropped T-shirt, and full bosom, moved to the table. She chomped on a piece of gum, and Regan was sure she'd long ago crossed her fortieth birthday.

"Zach, sweetie, it's been a while." She smiled with a wink.

"Too long, Hilary." Zach smiled back as though he were happy to see an old friend who'd known him his whole life.

"How ya doin', hon?" She looked at Regan and sized her up, then gave Zach an approving nod.

"I'm doin' fine." Regan gave her back a bit of southern hospitality in her accent.

"Whatcha up for?" She took a pen from behind her ear and her order pad from her apron pocket.

"I'll have a beer," he looked at Regan and she nodded. "Make that two. Oh and, Hilary, bring us some of that hot cornbread."

"You havin' your usual?"

"Yep, make it two."

"You're easy to please, doll," she said with a smile as she sauntered off.

Regan felt the urge to burst with laughter. When Zach had spoken of his mother catering everything, she never would have thought he frequented a barbeque joint enough to be on a first-name basis with the wait staff.

"Seems like this is a home of sorts for ya," she let her accent drawl.

He leaned back against the booth and draped his arm over the back of it. "You could say that. It was one of my dad's favorite places. Can you imagine, next to stress, why he's had three heart attacks?" He watched the crowd and then lifted his hand to wave at someone who walked by.

"Is that why he retired?"

"Yep. Couldn't stand the thought of me finding him dead behind his desk. Really, I just wanted his office, so I fired him."

Regan laughed. "Ah, motivation," she said as Hilary returned with their beers and cornbread.

Zach raised his beer glass toward Regan. "Here's to our continued success."

"To continued success with contracts signed and overnighted like they should be." She lifted her glass to his.

Regan sipped her beer immediately and let the cold taste of wheat and barley sooth her. She was relaxing around Zach again, and it felt good, but she remained cautious. It felt like their first date on the picnic blanket with hot dogs. No, she stopped herself. That wasn't a date. That was deception.

No, it was wonderful, and there was no reason to remember it any other way, even if her mystery man had ended up being her boss. He'd apologized for the "misunderstanding."

"You know, if you spoke, we could have a conversation instead of you having one in your head."

Regan looked up from her beer and noticed he was watching her. "I'm sorry. I guess I have a lot on my mind."

But she made an effort, and their conversation was casual as Hilary brought out two enormous slabs of ribs, corn, coleslaw, and biscuits. The scent of barbeque sauce filled her nose, and her mouth began to water.

"I can't eat all this." Regan laughed when she saw the platter.

"Good, I'll take it back with me. It'll keep me company all night."

"What are you working on?" She took her first bite into the ribs and moaned. "Oh, wow. I've lived in Tennessee all my life. I thought I was an expert on barbeque, but this is…"

"The best damn barbeque you've ever eaten?"

"Yes." She wiped her mouth. "Sorry. Again, what are you working on?" She washed down the bite of succulent meat with her beer and focused back on Zach.

"Just some redesigning of the condos downtown. John had some inspections that were calling for change. But I can't afford delays, so I'm pulling an all-nighter to get them done."

Her mind instantly went back to when she'd picked up after him on his last night in his office. She wondered what kind of form he'd be in the next day. There was a tingle of excitement brewing in her belly when she thought of it.

"Why don't you send the changes to the architecture department?" She took another bite.

"Because I designed this building. I should make the changes."

"You're amazing. Simply amazing."

"Thank you. My parents would appreciate the compliment. They like to tell me often how much they spent on my education, so it should be worth it."

"I hear that same argument from my father about my education and that of my brothers'."

"Yeah, they decide to put me in private school all my life and then send me to Ivy League universities, and I'm indebted." He shook his head. "Parents. What can you say?"

"Your mother is quit a character." Regan bit into her corn, trying not to shoot juice at him.

"Character," he said with a rise of his brows. "Yeah, I suppose you could call her that."

"Sorry. That sounded disrespectful."

"Not at all. Trust me. You pegged her."

"It was a slow day. I only heard from her two times today."

"One dessert, one lunch, next you'll be having a girls' weekend in Atlantic City."

"We talked about it, but our schedules are full." She laughed and sipped her beer. "I may need a few extended lunch hours though. She did mention a day at the spa."

"She would. She must be taking to you very well."

"I'm glad to hear it." But she had to wonder if it was safe to spend so much time with his mother. Where did she draw the line? She wouldn't date him, but she would spend time with his mother? It wasn't logical. It too was going to have to end.

As they stepped off the elevator into Zach's office, Regan held in her sigh. She'd thoroughly enjoyed their evening together, though she hadn't planned to. Zachary Benson was charming, and that was too bad. He just might have been a wonderful lover, but she'd never let herself find out.

"Well, back to work," he huffed.

"Why don't I make you some coffee before I go?" she offered and headed to the coffee maker.

Zach thumbed through his phone and started music on the speaker, and Pasty Cline sang. "I guess this is our song."

"What?" She turned from the bar and looked at him.

"It was playing at the restaurant when we got there." He turned it up a bit and walked across the office, taking her hand in his and pulling her to him. He slid his arm around her waist, and after a moment of hesitation, she rested her hand in his and the other on his shoulder. He spun her in circles around the office.

"You're light on your feet."

"Ballet."

"Ballroom," he offered with a wince. "Forced to do it. I swear I hated it." He laughed.

The dance died down, and their movements were slower as their bodies crept closer. His hand slid from hers and down her arm until it captured her waist. Zach looked into her eyes, and she gazed back at him without breaking free from his arms.

Regan would never be sure when his lips touched hers or when their mouths crushed against one another's. Desire blossomed, he consumed her, and she let him. His lips were strong. The sense that told her to hold him tighter won over the one that tried to force her from his arms. Her hands left his shoulders and her fingers laced in his hair. His scent washed over her, and all she wanted to feel was his body pressed against hers.

The music had changed, but she couldn't hear anything except the blood rushing in her head. God, she'd done it. She'd fallen into his arms, right where she'd longed to be. His mouth was covering hers. Their hearts were pounding against each other's, and his hands were wandering over her back. Regan's head spun with delight—and danger.

When her common sense broke through, she pushed back from him. Breathlessly she raced for the door.

CHAPTER 17

*R*egan could hear her niece and nephews playing when she arrived home and walked up the front steps. But even their laughter didn't make her feel any better about what she'd done. She slammed the front door behind her, ran up the stairs to her bedroom, and slammed that door as well. She fell onto the bed and sobbed. How could she have been so stupid to have kissed her boss, again?

The tap on the door wasn't unexpected.

"Go away!" she shouted.

Carlos obviously took it as his invitation to enter.

"I said go away!"

He let out a grunt that told her he wasn't going anywhere. "So what happened to you?"

"As if you'd care." She snapped up her head and reached for the box of tissues on her nightstand.

He crossed his arms in front of him, and leaned against the doorjamb. "You're right. I don't care, but Clara is here, and she doesn't want to see Aunt Regan all crybaby."

"You're an asshole. All men are assholes." She sat up and rubbed the tears from her cheeks.

"Yes, we have a club. Curtis and I are the founders, and I'm guessing your boss is a member."

"Oh, you're quick." She almost smiled.

"So what's the story? Did he make you write out a report in longhand? Let me guess, you had to sharpen sixty pencils? Or—wait, did he..."

"If you say beat erasers together, I'm throwing you out the window," she said, shaking her head, and finally mustering a smile. "You are a teacher down to the core, aren't you?" She laughed as she wiped the tears from her eyes.

Carlos sat down next to her on the bed. "Reg, tell me what's up."

"I kissed him." Her voice dropped, and heat filled her cheeks. "I shouldn't have, but I did."

"And how was it?" He rested his hand on her back.

"Wonderful." She looked up at him.

"Good. It sucks to waste kisses on bad ones."

"Carlos, I can't do this again. I can't fall in love with the man I work for."

"Why? Because Michael Hamilton was such a great guy?" His sarcastic tone made her straighten her spine. "He used you, Regan. You didn't do anything wrong."

"I should have known. How do you work so closely with someone, love them so much, and not know he's cut you out of his life?"

"Because he didn't want you to know."

"God, I was carrying his baby, Carlos. You'd think he could have let me in on it then." The tears were streaming down her cheeks faster.

"Don't beat yourself up for that. You did the right thing. You're an amazing woman, Regan." He gathered her in his arms and let her cry it out. "I don't know anything about Zachary Benson, but I don't think he's in the same class of men as Michael Hamilton. Not many men are."

"Daddy," a small voice spoke from the door. Regan turned her head to see Clara, her expressive eyes dark with concern. "Is Aunt Regan okay?"

"She's fine," Carlos answered. "We'll be down in a few minutes, okay?"

She nodded. "Can I call Mommy?"

"Why?"

"I can't remember the website with the games she lets me play."

"Yes, honey that's fine. Tell her I say hello." He was soft with her, and Regan admired the way he handled his children.

Regan turned her head when she heard Clara walk away. "You're a wonderful father."

"They don't deserve to have me hate their mother."

"You don't hate her," she reminded him. "It's amazing how you still care for her and take care of her."

"Lots of history there." He kissed the top of her head and stood up. "I saved you some dinner."

"I should have called. I'm sorry. I ate with Zach."

"Well, at least he fed you." He winked. "Don't dwell on the past. If you're attracted to this guy, and it sounds like he's attracted to you, maybe you should feel this out. Give it a chance."

"I don't want to get hurt."

"It seems like you're hurting right now—and the kiss was good." He smiled and left her alone.

ZACH SAT on the couch in his office and flipped through the channels on the television. Images passed by him, but he saw nothing. When his cell phone rang, he grabbed for it. There was no need to look at the ID. He knew it was his mother.

"Hello, Mother. How are you this evening?" he answered, still flipping through the channels.

"You're at your office, aren't you? Haven't I told you that's not a safe place for you to be? You're going to have a heart attack like your father," she scolded.

"I'm fine. I had to do some redesigns." He realized he hadn't been able to concentrate enough on them since Regan stormed out of the office.

"Don't let me find out you slept on that couch. I don't want you staying there when you have a perfectly good place to live."

He'd already decided he was staying the night. With all the amenities and the amount of work he had to do, it didn't make sense to go home.

"Okay, Mom. You won't find out," he said, still unable to lie to his mother.

"Uh-huh. The reason I'm calling is that I'm having a little get-together on Saturday, and I want you there."

"Mom, you had a little get-together last week. What's the occasion?" He was praying it wasn't another attempt to fix him up with socialites he just didn't care about.

"I want you to bring Regan out here."

He sighed and turned off the television. "Then call and invite her to lunch. You know you can find her in the office after eight."

"Don't get sassy with me, young man. You heard me. I want you to bring Regan on Saturday."

"So I'm supposed to ask her to lunch?"

"You're such a smart boy. I like her, Zachary. She's a wonderful girl. Did you know her mother used to own a bakery? That's why she's such a genius with desserts."

"Yes, I knew that."

"We talked a lot at our lunch date last week."

"I'm sure you did." He'd forgotten about their luncheon. Regan hadn't mentioned it again.

"I don't like your tone. What's wrong with you?"

"Let's just say Regan and I aren't seeing eye to eye right now." But they had been. She'd been as involved in that kiss as he had.

"Then pull it together. Eleven sharp, and I won't accept any excuses from either of you."

"Fine, Mother. I'll tell her."

"You'd better. You're not too old for me to turn over my knee," she said, and he couldn't help but laugh. She'd been threatening him with that since he was six, and she'd never done it.

"Okay. I love you. Tell Dad hello."

"I will. He's out swimming. I'd better go down to the kitchen before he eats something he's not supposed to. I love you, Zachary. I'll see you on Saturday."

"I love you too," he said and then ended the call.

Zach shook his head as he turned off his phone. The women in his life exhausted him.

CHAPTER 18

When Regan sat at her desk the next morning, her heart was already pounding. She'd thought all night about what to tell Zach when she saw him. There were apologies and groveling. There were accusations and anger. She wasn't sure which road to take. Maybe if she acted as though she'd forgotten all about it, he would too.

The intercom on her phone lit up. "Can I see you, please?" His voice was serious and dull.

She gathered her notepad, pen, and courage, then walked into his office.

He looked particularly stern this morning in his black suit and black tie. He offered no eye contact when she walked into the office and sat down in front of his desk.

"I need to leave for Kansas City by four this afternoon. Make that happen." She started to jot down the notes on her pad, irritated by his unpleasantness. "The plans are done and down in printing. Pick them up for me and see that they are couriered. They need to be to John this morning. Don't worry about making coffee, I've already had two pots, and I'm meeting with Simone Pierpont for breakfast."

The name had stuck in her head when she took the message her first day. Her heart flipped in her chest, and she tightened her jaw, but she kept her eyes down and her pen moving.

"Last, my mother wants you at her house at eleven on Saturday morning for lunch. Be on time," he instructed. Regan lifted her eyes and found his coldly focused on her. "That's all for today. I'll be back in a few hours," he dismissed her, and she left the office.

Well, she thought, she could see where things stood. Fine, she'd make his arrangements. She'd take the plans to John, and she'd be at his mother's house, not because he told her to be there, but because she enjoyed the woman's company.

Damn him!

Regan threw the pen down on the desk and headed to find the plans that needed to go to John Forrester.

ZACH SAT in the lobby of the Nashville Hilton Hotel and waited for Simone to come down. She was already fifteen minutes late. He figured he only had another ten to wait.

When she descended the stairs, Zach stood to greet her. She was lovely in her flowing dress, more suitable for an evening, but on the oil heiress, it seemed appropriate. Her long black hair, tied in a tail at the base of her neck, and her milky white skin shimmered like the diamonds that adorned her ears and wrist.

"*Mon ami!*" She took his extended hands in hers and kissed both of his cheeks and then his lips. "I have missed you so."

Zach smiled and took her hand. "Simone, lovely as always."

"Of course." She took his arm and he led her to the restaurant.

They were seated at a table secluded from the other diners but next to a picture window that allowed them to watch the people of Nashville pass by.

Zach watched the waiter set down their mimosas and walk away before he spoke. "So how is Monsieur Pierpont?"

"He is well, thank you," Simone confirmed as she sipped her mimosa. "He is in Greece this week on the yacht."

"That sounds nice." It had been ages since he and Simone sailed on her father's yacht. Perhaps if he landed the build in Los Angeles, that would be his reward.

Zach had a good relationship with the oil baron who often told him he was the son he wished he'd had, though Zach had never shared that information with Simone. Simone had been a handful her entire life, and her father had wished to have a son as diligent and hard working as Zach.

"He has a new wife," Simone casually said. "The trip was her gift."

"And how do you really feel about her?" He smiled, knowing exactly how she felt about it by the tone of her voice.

"Do you need to ask?" She looked around. "She is a horrible woman." Her French accent dripped with detestation. "That's why I'm here. I'd rather be stateside than in the ocean with that… that… woman!"

Zach laughed. This would be her fourth stepmother, if he'd counted correctly, but then again he hadn't been in the loop like he once had. He was sure there would be more in time.

"You and your mother are well?"

"Yes. We have a new chateau outside Paris. It is wonderful." She reached across the table for his hand. "You will come stay, oui?"

"That would be nice," he said, retrieving his hand from hers.

"What is this? You have a new woman in your life." Her eyes were wide, and her painted red lips curled into a tight smile.

He tugged at the napkin in his lap and then smoothed it back out. "What makes you say that?"

"I make you uncomfortable, and I never make you uncomfortable unless you love someone else." She swirled the mimosa in her glass like a fine wine. "Please tell me, or I'll be forced to call Madame Benson." She smiled from behind her glass.

"You would."

"*Oui*," she promised.

Zach took a deep breath. He'd confided in Simone since they were children at school together. No matter what he said, she'd see through him if he lied, as easily as his mother could.

"I can't get her out of my mind, but at the moment I don't think she's fond of me."

"I will talk to her." She pushed at a dark curl that had inched toward her face.

"No, you won't." That was the last thing he needed. If Simone showed up at Regan's desk demanding she be nice to him, Regan would come unglued. And who would blame her? "She's done all she can to keep her distance, but last night we kissed."

Simone applauded with the tips of her fingers in celebration. "That is wonderful."

"It was wonderful. But she bolted out of the office, and then this morning I was cold to her."

"*Imbecile*." She shook her head at him, then said in English, "Bastard. You must apologize. If you love this woman, you must go after her."

"Wait!" He held up his hands and shook his head. "I didn't say I love her." That might be moving too fast for even him. He liked to build big and wait it out. Zach was a patient man.

"You did not have to." Her eyes became soft behind the shield of long dark lashes. Simone eased back in her chair and tilted her head to the side as she sized him up. "Zachary Benson, I have known you too long for you to sit and lie to me."

"I didn't realize that was what I was doing."

"Well then, if not to me, to yourself." She drank down the rest of her mimosa. "What are you doing here with me? Go to her."

"No." He was cool and as the waiter returned with their food, he shifted to let him set his plate in front of him. "I'm leaving town today. This wouldn't be the time to get into it with her."

"You are leaving town on business?"

"Yes, I'll do some business while I'm there."

"Ah, you are leaving town to get away from her." She stabbed a well manicured finger in his direction.

"And I thought I could sneak that past you." He laughed and she shook her head.

"Nothing passes by me." She waved a hand in the air. "Where are you going?" she asked with a raised brow.

He was already wincing. "I'm going to Kansas City."

"What?" Her eyes flew open. "Oh, you are not going to see her! That... that..."

"No," he said calmly, but he knew the mere mention of the city would receive that kind of reaction from her. "That was three years ago, Simone. I haven't seen her since you put an end to it."

"Good. Senator's daughter or not, she was using you."

"Perhaps." And Zach knew that she had. It had been his only serious relationship. It was the only time he'd let his mother choose the woman he'd been with. He'd promised himself he'd choose the next one.

Simone shook her head. "What would you do without me alleviating you of useless women?"

"I don't suppose I'll ever know."

"Correct."

Zach sipped at his mimosa. He couldn't remember a day when Simone Pierpont hadn't been his best friend. A sexy French woman as his dearest friend could come in handy when he needed it to, but he wondered what Regan would think of her.

Regan. He set down his glass. He hadn't left her on good terms that morning, and the last thing he'd mentioned to her was meeting Simone.

CHAPTER 19

*R*eluctantly Regan drove to the Benson Estate for lunch with Audrey on Saturday morning. She'd spent a restless night telling herself it didn't matter that Zach Benson had some French tart on the side. Regan wasn't seeing him. She'd done her best to let him know she wouldn't be either. But to have kissed her and then flaunted the name Simone Pierpont in her face, well, that was too much. Regan had googled the woman. She'd gotten quite a lesson on the oil heiress and her lengthy list of affairs.

Regan's breath caught as she drove down the road toward the beautiful house at the end of the tree-lined drive. She was in paradise, and the pinching between her shoulder blades from her bad attitude released.

Gardens were blooming around the circle drive at the entrance. The floral aroma filled her senses and made the bouquet of mixed flowers she'd brought for Audrey seem inadequate.

Regan parked her car and climbed out. She stood in the vast openness, and took in the view. Horses grazed in meadows on either side of the house. The leaves rustled in the light breeze, and the sounds of a rippling creek nearby calmed her instantly. She was right in the place she'd always dreamed of being. Tennessee sprawling land and rocking chairs on the porch. She was very happy to have made friends with Audrey Benson.

With the bouquet in her hands, Regan walked toward the front door and rang the bell. A handsome man, with eyes that matched Zachary's, answered the door.

"You must be Regan," he said.

"Yes."

He extended his hand. "Tyler Benson."

"It's very nice to meet you."

"Please come in," he offered, and Regan stepped into the entrance of the grand house taking it all in. "Audrey is expecting you on the patio. I'll walk you back."

Regan followed him down the hallway to an enormous kitchen and out the back door. Beyond the patio more rose bushes were in full bloom. Acreage spilled out before her with a grove of trees beyond the first field that hid the creek she could hear. Audrey awaited her next to the pool on a lounge.

"Oh, Regan, you're here!" She stood, her sunglasses hiding her eyes and the large brim of her hat shielding her face. Pulling Regan to her, she kissed both of her cheeks.

"Thank you for the invitation. These are for you." She handed her the bouquet.

"Oh, aren't you just the sweetest thing." Audrey buried her nose in the flowers and then looked around. "Where is Zachary?"

"Zachary?" Regan's jaw tightened at the mere mention of his name. "I wasn't aware he was coming to lunch."

"That little…" She cut herself off and waved a hand to clear the air. "Well, let's have some wine." She took Regan's arm and escorted her to a shaded lounge by the pool.

Audrey was easy with conversation. Her favorite topic, of

course, was her son, and that made Regan relax into the lounge and laugh effortlessly when she went into detail about his antics at boarding school, specifically when he ran naked across the school grounds.

"Mom, you tell that story like you were there." Zach voice came out of no where, and both women sat up to see him walking toward, them smiling. "How come you tell people that story? Don't you want them to like me?" He looked at Regan. "She forgot to add I was chasing the dog who ran off with my clothes after I took a dip in the river."

Audrey smiled, sipped her wine, and then let her face grow concerned. "Where have you been?" She stood and kissed him on the cheeks.

Regan stood, following protocol, unsure how she was supposed to react to him. She was still angry with him. The anger, though she'd been laughing, swelled when she realized Simone Pierpont had to have been part of the story Audrey had just shared. Just the sight of him standing there so casually with a glass of wine in his hands, as though he hadn't kissed her and then gone straight to his mistress, made her want to run.

"I told you to bring Regan to lunch. Not have her meet you here."

"I wasn't sure I'd be back from my trip on time." He shifted his eyes to Regan. "But Regan is very good with her scheduling." He smiled at her, looking so full of himself, so powerful. "How are you?"

"Fine, thank you," Regan said cordially, but her muscles had gone tense, and a headache formed at the base of her neck.

"Well, let me go check on lunch. The two of you relax." Audrey passed by Zach as Regan dropped to the lounge, kicked up her feet, and drank down her wine quickly without looking at him.

"You're going to pass out drinking that fast," he warned as he lifted the bottle from the small table and topped off her glass.

"Good."

"You're still mad at me." He sipped his wine, looking out over the pool.

"Ya think?"

Zach turned to her and smiled. "You know, your forehead wrinkles up when you're angry." She rubbed her fingers over her forehead to smooth it out. "No use." He laughed. "I can read you."

"Who do you think you are?" She stood and kept her eyes narrow. "You kiss me, after I tell you I'm not going to see you socially."

"You kissed me back."

She huffed. "Then you run though a list of things to do and run out of town, after having some intimate breakfast with some French floozy?"

"Now, she's not a floozy." His face softened. There was something deeper with Simone Pierpont than just casual sex, or whatever it might be. It twisted her gut.

"You're impossible."

"Yes, I've been told that." He smiled and eased down onto the lounge his mother had vacated.

"Why did you even tell me to be here? Did you just want to humiliate me in front of your mother?" Her hand had begun to shake. She set her glass of wine on the table between them.

"I don't think I could do that. She likes you too much."

"She was expecting you to walk through the door with me," she whispered through gritted teeth. "Why would she want you to be with me? What did you tell her?"

"I didn't tell her anything."

"I don't believe you." He was just another man who thought he could control everyone, including her and his mother. Regan folded her arms in front of her.

He shrugged. "Well then, I guess you'll have to think I'm lying."

She blew out a breath. "I think we need to talk about it." She looked out over the pool. This wasn't a conversation she wanted to have with her employer. She'd been very specific about her feelings, so why had he pushed it? Why had he kissed her? And, dammit, why had she kissed him back?

"Okay, talk."

She spun her head his direction and swung her lefts from the lounge ready to give him an earful, but Audrey appeared from the door. "Lunch is ready."

Zach stood, and reached a hand out to Regan to help her from her lounge. She pushed to her feet without taking his hand and walked to the house. She wasn't done with him.

Regan sat next to Zach, with his parents across from them. Doing her best to take an interest in what was said at the table, she focused on Audrey's gossip about the country club and even managed to force a smile when she casually spoke of Simone Pierpont.

She just wanted lunch to be over so she could go home and leave the day behind her. She wasn't happy with herself for getting so worked up over the kiss, her departure from his office, or the fact that Zach had had breakfast with that French woman whom his mother spoke of so easily. However, the heat from his body and his lingering stare made it difficult to breathe or concentrate on anything beyond getting through the meal.

When lunch was finished, Zach brought out another bottle of wine. Once the bottle was empty, Regan was sure she'd be free to go. She enjoyed the company of Zach's parents, but walking away, giving Zach the cold shoulder, would be even better than the taste of the expensive wine he'd served.

Audrey let out a loud sigh and patted her cheeks. "I think I've had too much wine and too much sun today. Tyler, would you walk me upstairs. I think I'd like to lie down."

He stood as though it were part of the protocol.

Regan also stood. "Thank you so much for having me."

"Oh, you're staying." Audrey smiled and Regan took a breath to speak. "I've bought a beautiful pie. You told me you loved pie." She winked and Regan closed her open mouth. "I won't be too long. Zachary, you show her around. Take her through the gardens and out to the stables. Run along."

CHAPTER 20

Zach stood, moved around the table, and kissed his mother's cheek before his father led her away.

Regan watched him with his mother. He was a different in her presence than he was in the office. He was gentle and loving when he was caring for someone. The executive was about the contract, the timeline, and the money. Only someone with a genuine heart cared for his mother in a way that was obvious to an onlooker, but then again she'd seen it before. The powerful man who could be vicious on the business end and on the home front act as though he were a decent and loving man.

But there was something in Zach Benson's eyes that hadn't been in Michael Hamilton's. A compassion she wanted to believe was genuine.

"C'mon," he said moving in next to her and taking hold of her hand.

"I will not." She took her hand back and looked at him. Even if she believed he was capable of separating the power of the businessman from the sincerity of a lover, she had to be true to herself.

Regan needed to leave, quickly. She'd wanted to leave him

alone, ready to console himself with his French mistress, but a little part of her wanted him to long for her after she left.

"She wants me to show you around, let's go." He gave a nod toward the door, and she could see that his executive attitude could cross the threshold of the home.

"Fine." She folded her arms to keep them closed around her. "I'll let you show me around, but you keep your hands to yourself."

"Regan." He stepped closer to her, raising his hand to her hair. "Are you sure that's what you want me to do?" He slid his fingers to her cheek.

A shudder of anticipation ran through her. No, she didn't want him to keep his hands to himself. She wanted them to roam all over her. She squeezed her eyes shut. It had to go away. Her longing for him had to go away.

"Regan." She opened her eyes and looked at him. He offered her his arm. "Let's take a walk."

They started in Audrey's rose garden, and despite Regan's best efforts to retain an icy demeanor, Zach's undemanding conversation melted her defenses.

"This is lovely." She could smell the fragrance of the roses all around her. It would be a wonderful place to spend all of her days. There was every color rose imaginable. "How does she take care of all this?"

"She sits in that lounge chair and watches someone do it for her," he whispered.

"Oh." She nodded with a smile. "So this is where you grew up?"

"When I wasn't at boarding school."

"That's right. That's why you don't have an accent?"

"What?" He looked down at her as they walked.

"I assume the schools weren't around here? You don't have a southern sound." She turned up her own accent.

"No, *mademoiselle*, my accent is French."

She swallowed back the vile reminder of Simone's voice on the phone. His accent was perfect, just like hers. The thought was unsettling.

"Tell me something in French," she said, in an attempt to rid herself of unwanted jealousy.

He spun her around to face him an stroked his hand over her hair. *"J'adore tex cheveux quand le soleil les caresse."*

"Wow." She sighed.

"I'm full of surprises."

She was sure he was. "What did you say?"

"I like your hair when the sun caresses it."

Regan sucked in a breath and let the beauty of his sentiment ease her into being with him.

With a wink, he interlaced their fingers and continued toward the stables.

Regan looked back at the house as they walked further from it. "Remember when you asked me where I'd like to live?" He nodded. "I think this is heaven."

"I could make arrangements for you to live in the house They have a room for rent," he joked as they entered the stable.

The horse on the far end of the stables pranced around in its stall as they walked closer, then moved to the gate, shaking its golden mane in a hello.

"You'd think it's been years since you saw me." He patted the nose of the horse.

"This one is yours?"

"Yes. Isn't she beautiful?" He ran his hand down her neck, giving her a hearty pat on the side.

"I don't know much about horses."

"She's a palomino quarter horse."

Regan nodded with a laugh. "Got it."

"She was mine from the moment she took her first step." His eyes settled on the horse much as she'd seen Carlos' do when he'd watch his children—full of admiration.

"Would you like to go for a ride?" He looked down at her.

The thought of sitting so high on the large animal with Zach pressed up close to her made her entire body quiver. That was too intimate.

"No." Her voice was unsteady. "Not today. I'd like to keep walking if that's okay."

"Sure. We haven't even made it to the creek yet."

Regan longed to see the creek that wandered through the land. The sound of it was bold, rolling along, not held back, but she'd yet to actually see it through the trees.

Behind the stable was path that wound its way through the tall grasses that lay before them. He looked down at her shoes. "We could go back and get the cart my dad drives out this way. Your sandals might not survive the dirt and rocks."

She had to laugh at his concern for her footwear. She reached down, holding to his arm for balance, and pulled the shoes from her feet. "Then you won't mind if I take them off. They're horribly uncomfortable."

"Now we can't race."

"Oh, I don't know about that," she said, letting go of his hand, and taking off as quickly as she could.

He followed her, running in his dress shoes until he caught her and scooped her off her feet.

She let out a squeal and laughed until he set her on her feet just as they cleared the trees that gave way to the creek.

Once she caught her breath, she took in the tranquility of the quaint spot. The large sycamore trees, with their full branches of thick green leaves, by the water's edge created a cool green hideaway. An enormous boulder sat in the middle of the water.

He pulled of his shoes and socks then rolled up his pant legs. "C'mon, we're going in."

"No we're not."

"I'm your boss. I say let's do it."

She gave him a narrow-eyed look, irritated that after he'd held her hand, and carried her through the grass, he'd even say that.

"I'll answer your phone and schedule you meetings. But I won't go into water because you tell me to."

Regan watched as Zach's shoulders dropped. "That was insensitive of me. I forget that I'm not really funny or charming."

Well, he certainly wasn't funny, but she couldn't seem to fight off the charm. Regan gathered her skirt in her hand and followed him to the bank of the creek.

Zach took her hand again, gently, and pulled her near him as they started toward the creek. "There are stones here in the shallow part to help you get to the boulder."

She stopped, searching for the stones he spoke of. "And if I fall?"

"You'll get wet." He laughed as he tugged her along.

CHAPTER 21

Once they made it to the boulder, Zach helped Regan up to the top and they sat.

They didn't speak, but she knew he watched her taking in the sights around them. Regan let herself relax and listen to the peacefulness of the area. She closed her eyes, felt the breeze blow against her, and listened to the water ripple beneath her.

When she opened her eyes, she saw Zach reclined on his elbows looking up at her. "You're beautiful."

"Please don't ruin the moment."

"You said we should talk about what's going on between us." He lay back on the rock and tucked his folded hands under his head.

"Nothing is going on between us. It was a mistake," she said smoothly. "Just a mistake. They happen."

"That's too bad."

"Yes it is." She lay back against the rock and watched the breeze rustle the leaves on the trees. Folding her hands, she rested them on her stomach.

"So, why is it that you won't see me?" he asked.

"I thought we were done talking about it."

"No, you were. I'm not." He was smiling with his eyes closed.

"I won't see you socially because that's not professional. Things happen when the assistant falls in love with the boss."

"I see. Does that mean I should fire you?"

"I'm not attracted to you that way." She hoped she was convincing.

"I don't believe you," he said opening his eyes and watching her.

Regan leaned up on her elbow and looked down at him. "Is this really important? Do you really want to see me socially? Romantically?"

"Uh-huh."

"I thought I made it clear."

"Uh-huh."

"Stop that!" Her heart was racing and her palms had grown damp. She pushed her hair back as she sat up and cradled her knees to her chest. This was the end. No matter what it led to, it was the end, not a beginning. If she saw him socially, she had to find a new job. If she refused to see him, their work relationship would be strained and she'd have to find a new job anyway. It was a no-win situation—for her—and she was going to lose everything again.

"Regan." He sat up next to her. "I haven't been able to stop thinking about you since you fell onto my lap. I look at it like a sign from above."

She shook her head and angled her body away from him. "No. It was a horrible day."

"Maybe." He reached his arm behind her and moved his body in closer to her as if to move into her territory, and lowering his head until his breath was in her ear. "I know you're involved with other men."

"Other men?" She pulled away and saw dark sadness in his eyes. The fear that he knew what she'd been through stabbed at her. What if he was the kind of man who held that against the woman and thought the man was justified in how he acted? Did he think she was still involved with the man she'd worked for before him? That she was so weak she would hold on to anyone? "What other men?" she asked and her voice cracked with the question.

"Dr. Curtis," he said holding up one finger. "And then there was the man who met you at your door." He held up another finger.

The tension released in her shoulders, and her breathing returned to normal. Regan had to smile, and the fear that he was some pompous control freak slid away, leaving her with her urge to laugh. "Mr. Benson, you are very observant. And you certainly have been spending a lot of time thinking about the other men in my life."

"I can't help it." He raised his hand to her face and caressed her cheek. His blue eyes sank into hers and held her. "Regan, you're all I think about. I want to be with you. I want to get to know you on a personal level, and I want you to want that too. Tell me why you're so guarded."

Regan turned her head and looked down at the water that rippled beneath them like the emotions that shifted inside of her. The job in Zach's office was supposed to be a fresh start and end the pain she'd endured. It wasn't supposed to be a vivid reminder. "No. I won't talk about it. If you want to see me socially, you have to fire me."

"If I did that, would you go on a date with me?"

"No." She was sharp with her answer. Regan turned and gathered her skirt, ready to climb from the boulder.

Zach let out a long breath. "You're not helping."

She turned back to him. "If you fired me, I'd be too mad to date you."

"Then you're just going to have to quit," he said before he crushed his mouth to hers.

Regan gasped as his tongue found hers. Her chest pounded

and her head spun as he laid her back on the rock. It was happening again. She was letting a powerful and handsome man manipulate her.

No, that wasn't true. His hand skimmed her side and she wrapped her arms around him, pulling him atop of her. She tunneled her fingers through his hair, wanting to be here with him, wanting to open up to him. Regan was letting Zach win her over, and it felt so good.

Zach's fingers grazed her shoulder before he tangled them into her hair and deepened the kiss. She was falling, her heart was tumbling, and there was nothing she could do about it. She'd wanted Zachary Benson since she'd fallen onto this lap. Even as he pressed against her and she pulled him even closer, she knew she was making a mistake again. She was losing the battle against herself.

Zach moved his kisses from her mouth down her throat as she ran her fingers down his back. Her breath had quickened, and she sighed as he returned to her mouth.

Regan's mouth was as hungry as his. She could make love to him right on the boulder in the creek. Regan found that she longed to touch him and have him touch her. His arms were encircling her, drawing her in, and she pressed closer. God, she craved him.

He took a sharp breath and drew back, resting his brow against hers. His entire body tensed against hers as though he fought for control and her emotions raged between gratefulness and regret.

"We'd better stop before we can't," he said as he moved off of her, but kept his arm draped over her possessively. "Thank God you came to your senses."

Her body stiffened. Regan wanted to accept her new feelings, but the old ones were too raw. "I don't think that's what happened. I think I lost all good sense."

"Fine with me." He kissed her again, gently this time. "We

should get back to the house. My mother has a keen sense when there's hanky panky being made on this rock."

She turned her head and shot him a glance. "I don't want to know." She was too worried the name Simone Pierpont might sneak into the conversation again, and she didn't think she could handle that.

"No, you don't," Zach said smiling as he sat up and looked down at her. "This isn't a one-time thing, Regan. I want you to be mine. Exclusively mine."

Every muscle in her body stiffened, and she sat up. "Like your possession."

"No, like my partner." He turned and cupped her chin with his hands. "A partner whom I care deeply for, and one who cares for me back. Regan, I don't want to run your life or ruin it. Damn the man who must have done that to you." His voice rose slightly, and anger shook it. He dropped his hands.

Tears welled in her eyes. As they fell, he brushed them from her cheeks and kissed her where the wet trail ended.

"Regan, I don't want to hurt you. But I don't want to share you either."

"Share me?"

"A woman who is as beautiful, compassionate, and smart as you always will have men who want her."

Regan's jaw tightened. "I'm not someone who passes herself around."

"I'm not saying this well, then. The other men in your life—please tell me the other men aren't important."

She lifted her eyes to him. "The other men are important to me, and if you'll have dinner with me tomorrow I'll show you why."

"Tell me now," Zach pleaded as he moved in closer to her. His eyes had grown dark, but not in anger this time, she knew. They spoke silently of his sincerity and concern.

"No. I have to show you."

"Okay." He scooted off the boulder and stood in the creek with his hand out to help her down. "Can I at least say it's a date?"

Regan swallowed the bitter taste of panic and took his hand. "It's a date," she said. But the vile feeling of regret filled her core and spoiled the moment. She'd let herself care for Zach Benson, knowing he could grow to hate her and control her, and if she managed to stay alive, she'd hate herself too.

CHAPTER 22

*R*egan wanted nothing more than to fall into bed after she returned from the Bensons' house. She'd run the gamut of every emotion she'd ever had, and it had drained her. Lunch had turned into dinner and another walk through the roses. She wondered if Audrey would notice the one missing bloom Zach had cut for her and tucked behind her ear as he kissed her in the moonlit the rose garden.

Carlos had waited up for her. He smiled when he saw her walk through the door with a smile on her lips and the rose tucked behind her ear.

"He caught you."

"Yes he did." She managed to beam through the tangle of fear that still penetrated her.

"You'll be okay." He kissed her cheek.

"It'll be different," she said as a warning and a promise to herself.

The next evening Zach arrived at exactly at six as she'd asked him to. She sat waiting on the steps as he pulled to the curb.

Regan stood as Zach climbed from the car and walked up the

front steps. "I would have come all the way to the door." He slid his arms around her waist.

"I know, but I wanted to watch for you." She loosened the tie around his neck and pulled it off. "You might be a little over-dressed."

"I see that." His eyes scanned over her.

She'd dressed casually in a sundress and sandals, and she wondered what he'd thought she meant by dinner out when he'd dressed as he did every day for the office.

Regan wrapped her arms around his neck. It felt so right when she tilted her head to kiss him. "Tomorrow is going to be very strange."

"No. I said this wouldn't get in our way. I'm taking another woman to lunch tomorrow. Hot dogs, on my blanket, under the tree." Her entire body tensed, and he held her closer. "No one but you, Regan. I promise."

There wasn't much more she could say. She only nodded, wanting the fear of rejection that riddled her to disappear, knowing it wouldn't.

"And…" He lifted her chin with his finger. "If I find your letter of resignation on my desk tomorrow, I'll know you've fallen head over heels in love with me."

She stepped back and picked up her purse and a canvas bag from the step. "We'd better get going."

Zach took the canvas bag from her. "Where are we going?"

"My surprise. Let's see how you do." She grabbed his hand and walked toward his car.

They drove only twenty minutes out of Nashville, and Zach shook his head as they drove slowly down the street as kids played ball and rode bikes. "Why do I have a strange feeling you're not taking me to a restaurant?"

"You're just observant. Okay, it's the second one on the right. The one with the flag hanging on the side."

He pulled to the curb and put the car in park. Regan already had the door open, and a dark-haired girl ran toward her.

"Aunt Regan!" She wrapped her arms around her.

"Clara, you saw me three days ago. Why are you so happy now?"

"I love to see you. Mommy says you are one of the nicest people she knows." Clara smiled as she passed along the compliment.

"You know what? I really like your mommy too. When you go home, you tell her I say hello." Clara smiled with a nod as Regan turned to wait for Zach.

Zach climbed from the car, shut the door, and walked slowly to the sidewalk. "You've brought me home to meet your family."

There was a grin on his face that said he was reading too much into the evening already. Her family was very gracious when it came to guests, but Regan feared she might be throwing him in the lion's den.

Regan tucked her lips between her teeth to keep in her smile. "Would you have come if I'd told you?"

"You'd be surprised."

"Here." She pulled a bottle of wine from her canvas bag and handed it to him. "You'll score points with this. It's my mother's favorite."

"I would have brought one of my own if I'd known I was coming."

She took his hand in hers and wrapped her other arm around her niece's shoulders as they started toward the house.

Regan's mother opened the door as they walked up the steps. Reading glasses adorned her cap of white hair, and her wide body was covered by a cherry print apron.

The chaos in the house moved from the door as her mother scattered everyone away. When Regan had called and mentioned she was bringing a friend, her mother hadn't asked whom, but Regan knew she'd be waiting to meet a man.

"Hello, Mama." Regan kissed her mother as Clara slid through the door.

"My baby." She cupped her face and smiled at her as though it had been months since she'd seen her instead of only a week. Her mother looked past her, her hands still on her face. "Who is your friend?"

"Mama, this is Zachary Benson. Zach, my mother, Emily Keller."

"Mrs. Keller, it is an honor to meet you." He handed her the bottle of wine that Regan had given him. "This is for you. I've been told it's your favorite."

"Oh, it is. Thank you. This will go wonderfully with dinner. Please, come in." She stepped back and they walked through the door.

The house smelled of fried chicken, and sounds of a baseball game on television roared from the other room.

"Come." Emily took his arm. "Alan, get up," she whispered loudly, and Regan's father stood from his recliner. "This is Regan's friend Zach."

Her father did a slow scan over Zach, and it made Regan nervous. Her family wasn't the kind to immediately judge, but she saw it in her father's eyes. She knew he wasn't so sure that a man in a nice pressed shirt and perfectly pleated slacks was what his daughter needed, again. As his expression relaxed, so did Regan.

He extended his hand to Zach. "Nice to meet you. Alan Keller."

"Thank you, sir. This is a lovely home you have," he complimented them both.

"You like baseball?" Alan ushered Zach to the couch where Regan's nephews sat comatose watching the television.

"Yes."

"Good. Yankees are winning." He nudged the boys. "Hey, we have company, say hello."

116

"Hi!" they said in unison without looking away from the game.

"These two boobs are my grandsons. Eduardo and Christian. Sit." He offered the seat. "Would you like a beer?"

"That would be great." He looked up and Regan smiled at him.

"I'll get it." She winked, relieved that he'd met her parents and was still looking at her with calm eyes. She walked with her mother to the kitchen.

"So this is your new man?" her mother asked in a hushed tone.

"Mama..."

"No. Carlos told me you've had eyes for someone, and I knew there was something going on in that brain of yours."

"You read me like a book." She kissed her mother on the cheek and then pulled open the refrigerator for a beer. "We've really only decided to see each other. It's been complicated."

"You've known him for a long time?" Emily took out the salad tongs and tossed the tomatoes into the lettuce.

"No, only a month."

"Long enough. I only knew your father one month before we were married." Her German accent sometimes mixed with her southern one. It made her very special. "Dinner will be ready in ten minutes. Let's hope those boys get here by then."

Regan walked back to the living room with Zach's beer.

He stood when she entered the room. His proper manners would have allowed him no differently, she knew. She saw her father's eyes divert from the TV and watch Zach's movements. She caught the nod as he turned his attention back to the game.

"Dinner in ten minutes," she said, handing him the bottle. Her fingers lingered on his.

"I can't wait." His thumb stroked her hand and it sent heat through her body.

"Aunt Regan, you're in the way!" Christian complained. Regan reached over to pull the Tennessee Titans cap from his head, and messed up his hair. He twisted the cap back on. "C'mon, the game is on."

"You are so like your father," she said adoringly to the ten-year-old who tried to see around her.

"No, he's just a dweeb," Eduardo, said and Regan laughed. His twelve years seemed much more mature until he said things like that.

The front door flew open and the noise of others filled the room. Regan gave Zach a pat on the arm and then left him to hang out with her nephews while she went to greet the others who walked in.

When she saw her sister walk through the door, she screamed aloud and immediately she pulled her into her arms.

"I didn't know you were coming," she squealed.

"Surprise!" Arianna Keller laughed as their mother ran from the kitchen and her father stood from his chair.

Emily wrapped her arms around her daughter and began to sob.

"Mama, don't cry," Arianna said.

"I'm so happy to see you."

"I only have time for dinner. I leave in the morning, but I wanted to be here and share my news."

"What news?" Alan scooped up his daughter and kissed her on the forehead.

"I was hoping to do this over champagne, but"—she threw her arms into the air—"I made it onto Broadway!"

CHAPTER 23

*Z*ach stayed back. Their voices were clear, but the wall and crowd of people blocked his view. He smiled. As an only child, he'd never seen siblings offer such exuberant love and compassion that they surrounded a person. They all were as thrilled with Arianna's news as she was with herself. Perhaps he had that with Simone—perhaps. He wasn't involved in their exchange, but his body warmed as he listened to them all.

"Come on. Dinner is ready, and Regan brought a friend." Their mother walked Arianna toward Zach.

"Well, she did good." Arianna winked at Regan when she saw him standing beyond the crowd. "Arianna Keller." She stuck her hand straight out and met Zach's.

"Zach Benson," he greeted her. The sisters' eyes, hair color, and smiles matched. However, he could see no restraints on Arianna as he had with Regan. He was sure she was the type of woman who went after anything she wanted and got it. "Congratulations on your move to Broadway."

"Thank you. I've worked very hard, it's about damn time." He'd heard that siblings could be different, and looking at Regan and Arianna Keller, he saw that was obvious. Regan, even in her casual sundress, was refined and put together. Arianna, on the other hand, was dressed in tight pants with a fitted shirt, and she wore heels that made her tower over her family. Long earrings dangled from her ears, and it had been a very long time since he'd seen that many rings on ten fingers. Her personality was as outward as Regan's was inward. He already enjoyed the differences.

Arianna followed Emily to the kitchen. Zach caught Regan's arm as he noticed the men who had walked in with Arianna. He pulled her to his side and shook his head. The doctor she'd hugged at the hospital and the stranger from Regan's house stood before him, casting suspicious glances over him.

"Zach, right?" Curtis held out his hand to him.

He pushed back his shoulders and cleared his throat. "That's right."

"Curtis Keller." He shook his hand, and Zach nodded when he heard the name the man had in common with Regan. She'd let him think the handsome doctor was her lover, but in fact he was her brother. She'd been very careful with what she wanted him to know.

Regan curled herself around Zach's arm. "This is my other brother, Carlos."

He was the man he'd recognized at the Nashville site. "You work for me."

"Guilty. Thank you for the job."

"My pleasure. John is a great man to work for."

"He sure is." Carlos looked around them. "Did I leave my children here?"

Carlos slapped Zach's shoulder as he slid past them and found his kids still on the couch. Clara had found her way to them and held tight to her father. It was an exchange that tugged at him. A man that picked up his daughter and held her as if it was the last time he'd see her. Had his parents felt that way when he returned from school after months of being away?

"That's why you brought me here," he whispered in her ear. "Those are the men in your life."

That flash of fear stole into her eyes again as she bit on her lip, and his chest ached at her pain. Someone had hurt her deeply, and it had her hiding and holding onto her family. It was as if she'd wanted to protect them from him in case—he didn't know what she'd protect them from. But he was sure, by the sizing up he'd had done, they were there to protect her from him.

"I told you, they were serious, but no worries."

"No worries? So they won't beat me up?"

"Oh, I didn't promise that." She kissed him quickly as they walked to the dining room to gather for dinner.

Zach watched them all assemble. For a family they were an eclectic mix. The parents were older than he'd imagined. Both had white hair, were fair skinned, and had crystal blue eyes. Curtis looked like his father, but neither of the girls looked like either Emily or Alan. Their complexions were much darker and their eyes were brown. Carlos, he assumed, wasn't blood related. But then again, what did he know about families beyond his own?

"Zach, where are you from?" Emily asked as she passed the plate of fried chicken.

"I'm from Nashville. But I spent most of my childhood in France."

"Oh, my." Emily raised a hand to her chest. "France. I haven't been to France... well since I too was a child."

"So Carlos is working on one of those enormous buildings downtown?" Alan interjected.

"Yes, I saw him there with my own eyes," he said then shifted his eyes to Regan, who averted her stare to her plate.

"Pop, it's just temporary," Carlos assured his father. "I have applications into five more schools that haven't gotten back to me."

"They should call me," Alan said with his mouth full of biscuit.

"I'll give them a reference. Then I'll show them my checkbook." Carlos shook his head.

Zach recognized the argument. He'd had it many times with his own father and grandfather.

"Carlos, what do you teach?" Zach tried to save him from the beating he saw coming.

"Math. Junior high."

"That takes a very special person." He lifted his glass to him.

"Oh, that's my Carlos." Emily patted Carlos' hand.

"They don't care what my family thinks."

"Well, you're safely employed until then." Zach nodded, and Regan's hand slid to his knee beneath the table to give a gentle squeeze. He covered her hand with his. He hoped she knew he'd do anything for her, including employ her entire family if needed.

When dinner was over, Emily pushed Zach and Regan from the house, sending them to the front porch. They were guests for the night and exempt from cleanup. Carlos let him know that next time things would be different. Eduardo, Christian, and even Arianna all set forth their complaints about being guests as well, but Emily would not hear them.

CHAPTER 24

*R*egan sat down on the porch swing and pulled Zach down next to her.

He draped his arm around her shoulders and with his other hand caressed her face before he pulled her to him in a kiss intended to melt away any doubt she might have left about his feelings for her.

"I've waited all day to do that." He nipped at her lips again.

"I'm still scared," she admitted, resting her hand over his on her cheek.

"What are you scared of?"

She dropped her head. "I don't want to be hurt again, and I don't want my family hurt either."

"I would never hurt you." He lifted her face with a finger under her chin. "Why would someone hurt you and your family?"

Regan shook her head and shifted her eyes to the ground. "I'm not going to talk about it. I just don't want to have it happen again. I don't want this to be the catalyst for it to happen again."

He sat back slightly. "Just because I'm your boss?"

"Yes." She turned her head. "I'm sorry."

"Don't be. Now I know that I'm the only man in your life

kissing you like this." He dipped his head down again, engaging her tongue in a dance that was sure to send her pulse racing. "Come home with me tonight."

Regan sat up straighter, pulling from his embrace. "I'm not ready."

He sucked in a breath to calm the anger he felt rising in him—it wasn't geared toward her, but to the SOB who'd hurt her. "I can wait. Regan, I'm not going to rush you or hurt you."

"I know." She took his fingers and interlaced them with her own. "I just need some time."

He hated the fear in her eyes and the way her body stiffened when he'd mention anything about them taking things to the next level. "I'll give you time." Zach pulled her close so that her head rested on his shoulder.

He was used to his projects taking years. He could wait out Regan's fear. If she needed to trust him, then he'd be the man she could trust. And if she needed his protection, he'd certainly do that too. But Zach hoped Regan would fall in love with him and realize they were much more than employee and employer. They were already in a partnership.

Arianna backed out the front door, her arms loaded with plates of pie.

Zach stood quickly. "Let me help you with that." He took two of the plates and handed one to Regan.

He sat back down on the swing and took a bite. "Oh, God, this is wonderful!"

"I told you pie makes me happy." Regan took a bite for herself.

"Got it!" Sensing he should keep the mood light, he shoved another piece in his mouth. "How embarrassing for my mother! She bought you a pie." He laughed as he took yet another bite.

"It was very nice of her."

Yes, his mother could buy her a pie. She could wine and dine her like she was the one in a relationship with Regan. But Zach now understood that pie was so much more than dessert to

Regan. It was family time and family dinners. It was her father wanting her brother to succeed. It was a hug from little girl who missed her daddy. It was the excitement everyone shared when you came home with news that you'd succeeded. Pie was what he wanted with Regan—every piece and every crumb.

He let his eyes wander from his plate to her. "I assume you bake pie like this too, then?"

"I'd say we all have some very profound pie-making experience."

"You could say that again." Arianna laughed at her sister's comment.

"We all had our share of working in Mom's bakery. So yes, I certainly can turn out any baked good you might need."

"Tiramisu?"

"Or a tiramisu." She laughed.

"Lucky me."

Arianna watched them. "So, how long have you two been together?"

"Since about two o'clock yesterday," Zach answered and Regan jabbed him in the ribs.

"I work for Zach," Regan said, her voice very serious and her tone threatening.

Adrianna nodded, as if Regan had spoken in code. Then her lips turned up into a wide smile. "You both will have to make a trip to New York to see me. You know, on Broadway," she sang the word and wiggled in her seat like an anxious child waiting for a gift. "I guess you get to keep the house a bit longer. Unless Carlos has kicked you out completely." She broke off the crust to her pie and popped it into her mouth.

Regan grinned. "He told you he's been staying?"

"Clara." They both laughed. "C'mon, Mama wants to open that wine you brought." She nodded toward the house.

They opened the wine and all sat down in the living room with their glasses.

At eight thirty, the doorbell rang and Carlos moved for the door with Clara close in tow. Soon Eduardo and Christian gathered their belongings and left the room. Regan patted Zach on the knee. "I'll be right back."

A few minutes later Regan sat back down and Carlos sauntered back to the room, alone. "I'm gonna head out. Mama, thanks for dinner."

Emily rose to kiss him. "I love you, son."

Regan and Arianna kissed him as well, and Zach shook his hand. "It was nice to meet you and your children."

"I'll see ya on the site." He waved to them all and left the house.

Arianna sipped her wine. "He'll get over it soon enough."

"It's been two years. It's time," Alan said pragmatically, still focused on the television.

"I suppose we should go." Regan stood and took Zach's wine glass to the kitchen. Emily followed.

Zach stood, meaning to follow too, but he heard Emily questioning Regan. He stopped just outside the door, unsure whether he would be intruding. "You're careful?"

"Mama, I'm fine. Nothing like that has happened. Besides, I'm thirty-three years old. I'm not a teenager."

"I know. I don't want your heart broken again… or anything to happen to you."

"Neither do I."

Zach backed away from the door. They were all watching out for her, and it was his job to make sure they were satisfied that she was happy and safe. Eventually she'd need to tell him what had happened. It wasn't just a relationship that had ended badly. There was obviously much more.

CHAPTER 25

*R*egan was quiet on the way home, but Zach took solace in the fact that her fingers remained laced with his. Perhaps this was fulfillment to her. She'd been surrounded by the people who meant the most to her.

"So, while you were around"—he smiled—"I was looking at the pictures on the wall. Is Carlos adopted?"

She laughed and turned her head to look at him. "Huh, what would give you that idea?"

"Curtis is the only one who looks like either one of your parents. You and your sister look exactly alike, only she's about two inches taller than you even without those shoes on." He looked at her, and her eyes were smiling from behind the curtain of dark lashes. Even when he spoke of her family, it made her happy. "Then there's a picture of just you and your sister when you're really little, and other family pictures of the two of you and your parents. Then another where Arianna is holding Curtis as a baby. Then there is a family picture of you all, and Carlos is right in the middle. I don't know, maybe he was six or seven. Spill the story."

"Mama and Papa were married fifteen years before they had

children. What they got was me and Arianna. She was two and I was three months old when we came to live with them."

"You're adopted?" She nodded with a smile. He shook his head and let out a quick laugh. "I should have guessed that. You are all so wonderfully different."

"They were our foster parents. We were born to a young couple and the state took us away. They placed us with the Kellers and we never left," she said with a warmth in her voice. "Mama was told she couldn't have any children, but the day our adoption went through—I was already two—was the day she found out she was pregnant with Curtis. She was forty."

The reality that he was almost forty hit him. Family. It was something he'd always thought he'd wanted, and after dinner with her family, he was sure of it.

"So what about Carlos?"

"Ah, Carlos became my brother when we were seven. He's two months older than I am."

Zach couldn't even begin to imagine sharing everything with others. He had no cousins or siblings. No one was ever in his space, and he never had to vie for his parent's attention. Even at school he'd had his own room. "How does that work when your family is already established?"

"You adapt," she said. "He just blended. His parents had brought him here from Puerto Rico when he was four. They belonged to our church, and we were friends. His family was very poor and the church helped them a lot. Mama helped by giving Carlos' mother work in the bakery and around the house. His father worked odd jobs fixing things." She adjusted in her seat and looked out the window.

Regan let out a breath before she continued. "They were in a car accident going home one night. The roads were slick. Carlos was the only survivor. Mama stayed with him at the hospital for days while he cried for his mother. When he was ready, they released him to my parents. They were still foster parents and they took him in. And just like me and my sister, Carlos never left."

He gave her hand a squeeze then lifted it to kiss her fingers.

Family. How amazing it was that everyone's family could be so different. He'd always appreciated his parents, but sitting among Regan's family, there'd been a different kind of acceptance. Among the different eye colors and backgrounds, beyond the mismatched china and glassware was a family that valued each person.

He wanted that. He could marry, have a child, and no expense would be too much to shower his child with anything they wanted. But he'd finally seen where that wasn't important. If Regan was the other part of his fantasy, a house full of children and a marriage full of love, he knew there would be a perfect balance in their home, just as there had been in the Keller house each time a new child came to live there.

"Carlos is the only one with children?" he asked.

"Yes. He married very young. He and Madeline were sweethearts in high school. Eduardo came when they were only twenty. A couple of years ago, they got divorced and she married his best friend."

"That had to have been quite a blow to Carlos."

"It was. She didn't have an affair with him, though Carlos accused her of it. Truth is, times were tough. He was out of work a lot and going to graduate school, she was working two jobs, the bills were piling up, and the kids were little. It wore on them. Really, it's too bad. Madeline is a wonderful woman, and Carlos loves her so much."

How could someone love someone and just walk away from their marriage? Was that what it all came down to? Walk away if it became too hard?

He wondered how Regan felt about that. She'd been very forward about how she felt about dating her boss. Would she walk away if it became too hard? "Why didn't they just stay married?"

She shrugged. "I'm not sure they know. But she's married now and they share the kids. And the kids are wonderful!"

"They love you a lot."

"They are my world," she said, and Zach could hear the sincerity of it in her voice. She loved them as much as they loved her.

"Ask me in." He looked at her, covered in shadows.

"No." She was firm. "Let's see how it goes for a while."

He couldn't hide his disappointment, but he reminded himself he had time. "You're killing me."

"I know. But it's for the best."

He nodded in agreement. She needed that space, and he'd give it to her. But everything inside of him wanted to take her up those stairs, close the door behind them, and please her in every physical way he could. "I'll walk you to the door." He opened his car door and she shook her head.

"No. If you do, I'll want to pull you in. I need to be very strong." She leaned over and kissed him hard, then pulled away leaving him wanting more. "Tomorrow we go about our day as though nothing has changed. Between eight and five, we are coworkers only. No special treatment, no secret kisses." He dropped his shoulders and let out a ragged, long breath. Her mouth tightened. "I'm serious. If this is going to work…"

He didn't like the fear in her eyes. It took over every time he thought they'd taken a few steps forward. "Regan, it's going to work." He nipped her lip with his teeth then kissed it gently. It was going to take more than seduction to prove to her that he was the man for her. He pressed his forehead to hers and sucked in a deep breath. "Go before I carry you into the house."

She smiled as she climbed out of the car and walked up the steps without looking back.

The house was dark, but she knew Carlos was there when she shut and locked the door.

The couch squeaked. "You didn't invite him in?"

"No. I'm not there yet. What are you doing in the dark?"

"Sulking."

She walked to the couch and sat down next to him. "You're okay too."

"I love her. I can't let her out of my heart, and I need to."

She knew he was crying, but she stayed close without touching him. "Do you think it would help if you told her how you feel?"

"No. We made our decision. She married him. The kids seem fine. I have to let it go."

"It's been two years. How are you going to let it go?"

"I don't know. It's killing me," he said. His voice sounded wet, and after a while he sniffed hard.

Regan kissed her brother on the head, stood from the couch, and walked up the stairs. It seemed like they both hurt when it came to love. She wondered how long her new affair would last. Perhaps she should look for a new job just in case the one with Zachary Benson should come to a crashing, lying, cheating, hateful end.

It wasn't very positive of her. How was it going to work if she was so pessimistic?

Regan undressed and slipped on her nightgown. She brushed her hair before climbing into bed. As she rested her head against the pillow, she sighed. She still couldn't help but wonder what she was doing. Her stomach was twitching with nerves, and she pressed her hand over it to soothe it. Then, absentmindedly, she traced her fingertips over the scar that would always remind her she was making another big mistake.

CHAPTER 26

*R*egan hadn't been as nervous about going to work since her first day at Benson, Benson, and Hart. Now that she and Zach were an item outside the office, her nerves were making her sick to her stomach. She'd tossed and turned all night long and fought with makeup to conceal the black circles under her eyes. Now it was time to face the decision she'd made and walk into that building sure that what she was doing was the right thing. Even if she wasn't sure it was.

Regan hurried to the office, stored her things under her desk, and then went right into Zach's office, but it was empty. She walked back to her desk only to find an enormous stack of contracts and plans on it. The note on top said please see to this ASAP.

This was what they'd agreed on. No special treatment—and there was none. So why did it feel so much like he was rejecting her?

Regan sat right down at her desk and started sifting through the piles. As the office began to fill, people stopped by her desk to say hello or to drop off messages for Zach and reports that were due on other builds. Audrey—not Zach—had called her at least four times, and so had Simone Pierpont. Daily conversations with Audrey she could handle. Simone Pierpont—that was another story.

It was ten o'clock before Zach called. "Hello, darling."

"Don't." She kept her voice hushed as the anxiety over his absence weighed her belly. "Not only are we between eight and five, but where are you?" Her voice trembled with the surge of anger that'd hit her the moment she heard his voice. "This isn't what I had in mind by us keeping it professional. I thought you'd at least have the courtesy to come into the office."

"Regan, calm down," he said. "I'm in L.A."

"L.A.? What are you doing there? I've only been gone from you a few hours."

"I know. When I got home, I had seven messages from the investor, so I went into the office and there were four more. This deal is too big for the firm to lose. I got on the next plane out here. I've had to buy new clothes and shoes." He laughed. "I'm so sorry. I didn't want to bother you in the middle of the night."

She blew out a breath and calmed. "I'm sorry."

"No need. Did you get the pile I left you on your desk?"

"Yes. I'm almost to the bottom of it."

"Well you'll be happier when you get to the bottom." His voice smiled even through the phone. "I'll call you if I get the chance. I'm hoping to get out of here by tomorrow. This guy—never mind. Oh, and we need to make plans to be at the ground breaking in Dallas. It's only a week away."

"I have your itinerary already scheduled and your ticket—"

"Regan." Her pulse quickened when he said her name. "I want you there. Get on that flight."

"Are you sure that…"

"Regan, don't worry about it." His voice was tense and sharp, not in anger but with the sense of sensual urgency. "And I know you booked a room with a king bed. You wouldn't have done any less. Don't you dare go booking yourself a separate room."

The tantalizing sound of his voice made her breath catch in her chest. The very image of sharing a room—a bed—with him had her body heat rising. She put her hand to her chest and sucked in a breath to calm her racing thoughts.

"I miss you," he said right before he hung up.

Regan disconnected her headset and let her nerves calm. Then she began to sort through the pile of papers, wondering what was at the end. There she found a drawing of a rose just like the one Zach had tucked into her hair. He'd signed it, *Love, Zach.* She smiled as she slipped it into her purse. How quickly things could change. She missed him desperately. They'd moved beyond a causal relationship, and it was time she was intimate with someone.

Everything about Zach indicated she could trust him. She knew that instinctively. But it was so difficult to know whether she could trust her instincts.

Then she thought of Carlos. He mourned his failed marriage, and Regan wallowed in the pain of a mistake. They both needed to move on and stop living in the past. Zach was not Michael Hamilton. She was going to take her first step. She was going to go to Dallas with Zachary Benson. She was going to hold hands with him in public and kiss him senseless. She was going to share his bed, and for the time being, his life. Yes, that's what she was going to do.

Zach's trip to L.A. had extended three more days and had drained every ounce of energy from him. He flew from there to Kansas City, where weather had caused extensive delays. The overcast skies had dampened his mood, and the only person who could have lifted it was a state away. Certainly he'd much rather spend his time with her wrapped in his arms than linger here dealing with the rain and an angry construction foreman.

"Rearrange my itinerary," he called to tell Regan. "I'll have to meet you in Dallas."

She sighed, and he felt her disappointment. "Zach, maybe this isn't the right trip for me to go on."

"Don't be silly. I want you there more than ever. I miss you." He lay in the hotel bed with the late shows on and her voice in his ear, his body aching because she was so far away.

"Okay, then. I'll meet you there. You promise to be there, right?"

Zach didn't like the tension in her voice. "I'll be there." He let out a breath. "Do you realize I only got in a few minutes of good kisses last weekend? Not a very good start for a new relationship. I'd like to have had a few more hours of it by now."

"Well then, I'll make it worth your wait." There was a playfulness in her voice now, and he was more comfortable with that. He was also in agony that he couldn't just touch her, kiss her, or make love to her whenever he wanted to—like right now.

"Get some rest. I'll call you in the morning with details. I was hoping to get John out to L.A. to work on that project, but if Kansas City falls much further behind, I'll have to ship him out here."

"He'll do whatever you need him to."

"I know. Good night, Regan." He hung up the phone and folded his arms under his head. A few more days and he'd have her in his arms and in his bed. He couldn't help but wonder how she'd react to that. There was still something she hid from him; her whole family had kept a guarded eye on him. Someone had hurt her badly, and they were all sure he'd do the same, including Regan.

Zach had no intentions of hurting her. For the first time in his life he knew he loved someone, and it was killing him not to be with her. He couldn't tell her over the phone. He wasn't even sure he could tell her in person yet, but the love was there. It was real. And it wasn't going to fade, ever.

Zach picked up the remote to the TV and changed the channel. He'd never lost a bid on a build, and he'd never lost a battle in business. He certainly wasn't going to lose the woman he loved over some other man's mistakes. Regan Keller was his, forever.

CHAPTER 27

*R*egan heard Carlos tapping his foot on the wood floor of the entryway, then he pounded his hand against the wall. The sound resonated up to her bedroom and made her jump.

"If you want a ride you'd better hurry!" he called up to her. "Just because you're off to sleep with the boss doesn't mean he'll tolerate me being late!"

"That's not funny." She walked out of her bedroom with her suitcase.

"You look lovely, now let's go." He hurried up the stairs and took the suitcase from her.

Regan looked down at the outfit she'd put on. "I don't know if I like this suit. Maybe I…"

Carlos turned and gave her an icy stare. "If you change one more time, I'm leaving your ass here. Now c'mon!" He strode out the door and to the car with her suitcase as she tried to lock the door and hurry down the stairs in her high heels.

They climbed into the car after Carlos chucked her suitcase in the back, and as he drove, she rummaged through her bag and did a verbal last-minute check of her carry-on bag for the tickets, contracts, reservations, and everything else she would need to do business in Dallas.

"You're making me nervous," Carlos said, "and all I have to do is push you out of the car."

"I just want it all to be perfect. He doesn't need anything to go wrong just because I'm by his side and not at the desk in his office."

"What is it with women? You worry too much."

When they reached the terminal, he pulled to the curb. He gathered her bags and set them on the sidewalk.

"Now, call if you need anything. Say no if you have to." He gave her a supportive glance. "And dammit, Regan, let go a little and have some fun. The man is crazy about you, and you're crazy about him."

"I'm scared to death." Her heart was racing and her hands shook. It would only take a word and Carlos would take her back home. But she wanted to do this.

"I know. You'll be fine." He kissed her on the cheek. "See you in a few days."

When Regan's plane landed in Dallas, she was giddy with anticipation and drenched in anxiety. It had been a week since she'd seen Zach, touched him, or kissed him. Within hours, he'd wrap her in his arms and make love to her.

She let out a steady breath as the plane taxied to the gate. So much for promises she'd made to herself. Regan was falling head over heels in love with her boss. Again.

Regan followed the signs toward the baggage claim area, and there he was. Her suitcase already rested at his feet, a bouquet of daisies filled one hand.

She kissed him first. "What is this?"

"Reminiscent of our first date. It's just missing a hot dog." He smiled. "Are you hungry?"

"I'm starving."

He handed her the daisies, wrapped one arm around her as

they walked away from the carousel, and pulled her luggage out to the limo that waited for them.

"This isn't the car I booked."

The driver opened the door for them. Regan climbed into the car, and Zach followed before the driver shut the door and put her luggage in the trunk.

She laughed as it pulled from the curb and Zach wrapped his arms around her and covered her mouth with his.

"I've been known to do a few things on my own." Their tongues met and their breath quickened as he leaned her back on the seat.

"I thought we'd wait to get to the hotel." Panic rose in her, fighting past the pleasure she felt as his lips slid over her throat and his hands explored her rib cage under her shirt.

"Appetizer." He smiled as he caught her lip in his teeth, and she gasped.

When the car slowed, they gathered themselves back up. Regan did her best to straighten the blouse she wore and rake her fingers through her tousled hair.

He skimmed her cheek with his finger. "You're beautiful."

"Nothing like a teenage romp in the back of the limo on date night."

"This was a romp? It's been a while since you've had one, then." His smile was seductive, and his laugh was damn sexy, even if he was laughing at her.

The door opened and the driver helped her out. She stood outside of a restaurant whose windows and doors were etched in gold trim and reflected the midday sun. Patrons in business suits walked in and out, busy on cell phones or talking to one another.

"We're meeting clients. So, I promise to keep my hands and manners in check." He touched her arm and pulled her closer to whisper in her ear. "But before the night is over, you're mine."

The sudden twinge in her chest made her want to run. Was it

a promise or a threat? She told herself she had to stop worrying. He wasn't going to hurt her.

There were four others at the table waiting for them. Regan hoped to God she looked okay and their little *romp* in the back-seat hadn't stolen all her professionalism.

"Zachary, how nice of you to join us." The first man stood. He was tall, gangly, and as old as her father. He shook Zach's hand and then hers before introducing the others at the table.

Regan sat next to Rebecca, the older gentleman's assistant and only other woman at the table. Rebecca graciously made conversation while the men bantered about business.

"So you're Zach's new assistant?" she asked.

"Yes, I've been with him a little over a month."

The woman nodded. "Mary Ellen had her baby, then?"

"Yes, that was on my first day. Her water broke right in the office." She reached for a breadstick from the basket on the table. "She had a little girl. Cute as a button."

With meals ordered, business went on around them. Regan caught a few names she recognized, and they filled her in on the plans for the ground breaking. All the while, Rebecca watched her with a thoughtful eye.

When the meal had ended, Regan excused herself to the ladies' room. When she walked out to the sinks, Rebecca was there.

"They are such bores. I tell you, if I wasn't getting paid to pay attention, I think I'd die of boredom," she said as she fixed her lipstick.

Regan only smiled, but Rebecca still watched her in the mirror. "I just can't get over the feeling I've met you," she said.

"I don't think so. This is the first trip I've made with Mr. Benson." She was careful to keep her professionalism by not calling him Zach.

Rebecca tilted her head, and her brows drew closer together. "Where did you work before?"

"I was in Hawaii before. I didn't make it away from the islands for a few years. I'm sure I resemble someone."

"Perhaps." She continued to stare.

When they returned to the table, Regan was relieved to find the men standing at the table shaking hands ready to leave the restaurant. They said their goodbyes and walked outside.

The car waited for them. Zach let Regan in and then followed. She kept her eyes focused out the window. She didn't want to look at him, afraid that he'd see she was hiding something. She'd never thought anyone would remember her, but they did. Rebecca was proof that her past was still there.

Zach touched her arm gently. "Everything okay?"

"Yes, just fine." But it wasn't fine. She'd recognized Rebecca as well, though she wouldn't have been able to call her by name before they were introduced. They had met. It seemed like a lifetime ago. Regan had been prominently displayed on the arm of Michael Hamilton. It had been one of the very few times he'd taken her into public with him when she was pregnant. She let out a jagged breath, hoping Zach wasn't watching as he took a call on his cell phone. Seeing the woman at lunch had made her worry that she would eventually run into others who knew her, and she didn't want to risk that. As far as she knew, Michael Hamilton lived his happy life with his wife in a plush villa in Italy, and he thought Regan was dead.

She'd assumed their paths wouldn't cross again—until today. Now she was scared for her life again. And not only for herself, but for Zach too.

Regan was bigger than her past was, she reminded herself with a deep breath. Her fresh start of a new life had happened the morning her car wouldn't start and she fell into Zachary Benson's lap. She wasn't going to let that go.

CHAPTER 28

Zach had upgraded his room to a suite to impress her. During the ride to the hotel, she hadn't smiled once and had barely said a word, but when she saw the suite, a cool smile formed on her lips.

"Zach, this is beautiful." She spun around in the entry.

"I'll fix you a drink." He walked to the stocked bar and poured her a glass of wine and himself a whiskey and Coke.

She was staring out over Dallas when he handed her drink to her. She'd tilted her head when he moved behind her, exposing her neck. It was long, slender, and his need to kiss it grew irresistible. His lips skimmed her skin and her pulse quickened under his lips. Regan turned into him, and he slid his free hand around her waist to the small of her back, pulling her closer to him. She felt small in his arms, fragile, and feminine. He took their drinks and set them aside then gathered her back into his arms.

He pulled her blouse from the waist of her skirt. She shuddered. "Zach..."

He didn't like the fear that clouded her eyes when he touched her, and her body tensed. Zach drew back. "I won't hurt you."

"I know, but I'm afraid."

"Of what?"

"Of you rejecting me later." Her words were sharp, and they stabbed at him. The pain in them made him bitter toward every man who came before him. But he wanted to be the last, and in order for that to happen, he had to find a way to break through that wall she kept between them.

Zach shook his head and then rested it against hers. "Let me show you what it's like to have a man who truly loves you touch you." He lifted his head and looked into her eyes. Their color shifted and he could see the battle brew beneath them.

Finally she nodded.

He skimmed his finger down her neck and to the first button of her shirt. He unfastened it, and she sucked in a breath. "I'll go slow," he promised as he unbuttoned the second button. "I'll treat you as you should have been treated. Regan..." He focused on her eyes. "I love you. I will never hurt you."

A faint smile formed on her lips, and she nodded again.

Zach locked his eyes with hers. "Let me taste you."

Regan closed her eyes and let her head fall back. The moan she let free from her throat gave him the permission he'd sought out.

He skimmed his tongue down her neck toward the generous opening in her blouse. One by one he released the tiny buttons until her skin was beneath his fingers. He licked and nipped down her neck and chest to the swell of her breasts. Unhooking her bra, she quivered in his hands as he cupped her breasts and sampled each nipple with his tongue.

Her hands were in his hair, her head thrown back, exposing the delicate skin of her throat which he feasted on again.

"I'm ready," she whispered. "Make love to me, Zach."

An excitement he'd never felt before pulsed through him when she said she was ready. She was surrendering more than her body to him. She was giving him her heart.

Every muscle in his body tensed as he brushed a kiss over her lips, scooped her legs from beneath her, and carried her to the bedroom. Laying her down, he looked at her, as he unbuttoned his shirt.

Regan sat up and began to unbutton his slacks. She met his chest and stomach with gentle kisses as she pulled away the fabric and let his pants fall to the floor.

Zach pushed her back to the bed and pulled the skirt from her hips. He didn't look down at her naked body. He only met her eyes.

She reached, pulling him atop of her, wrapping her legs around him, and he couldn't wait any longer, but he couldn't just take her. He had to protect her and that meant taking the moment to leave her body and find the condom he'd put in the drawer.

"I hadn't thought of that," she said breathlessly.

"I promised I'd take care of you." He rolled on the condom, and then gathered her back into his arms and kissed her as he entered her. A faint gasp escaped her as he rocked himself inside of her.

The slowness of the moment was over. Heat and desire took over. She met his pace as he dug to be deeper and deeper inside of her. Her hands clung to his back. Her fingernails clawed at his flesh. She quivered her acceptance of him inside of her, which took him to the edge.

Pleasure burned inside him. His body pressed hard to hers as he released. His mouth consumed hers. It had gone quickly, but he couldn't have waited. He'd never wanted to touch and feel another person as much as he had with Regan.

"I love you, Reagan. I love you so much," he said with his weight still on top of her, keeping her still.

Tears welled in her eyes, and he moved to her side, his arm still draped over her.

"I didn't mean to make you cry. I only meant..."

"I'm sorry. It's been a very long time." She wiped the tears from her cheeks as fast as she could. "I've broken every promise to myself," she said with her voice quivering. "I shouldn't be here now. I shouldn't be wrapped in your arms with you telling me things like this."

She rolled from him and gathered her discarded clothing.

He touched her back. "Don't run from me. No more running." But she wouldn't face him. Zach sat up and gripped her shoulders, resting his cheek to her back. "Tell me why this frightens you. Tell me why I can't get close enough to you to love you. Tell me what happened."

She shook her head and then let out a cry. "All you need to know is I fell in love with a man I worked for, and he hurt me."

"Did he hit you?" Every instinct urged him to grip her tightly and hold her, but he didn't want to scare her. He pulled back his hand.

"I'm not fragile," she said, but really hadn't answered his question.

"Regan, you have to open up to me. I love you, and you're shutting yourself away from me. There is nothing you could tell me that would change how I feel for you."

She turned to look at him. "I've only had three lovers before you. I thought I was in love with each of them. I know now I was wrong. I was young with the first two. But I gave myself to them wholeheartedly. With the last, the one who... well, the one who hurt me, I surrendered completely." She clenched her jaw and shook her head. The tears had stopped, but he could see she was now angry. "He could say all the right things. Do all the right things and make me believe things I never would have believed in. I left a good job for him. I followed him. He was rich, handsome, and persuasive. I was his assistant. We traveled the world, but I was to stand by his side with my notebook open and my mouth shut, and I knew how it was."

She looked away and took a deep breath. Her hands had

clutched into fists, and she shoved back her shoulders as she turned to look at him. "What I didn't know was that he was abusing me. Mentally. He was tearing down my defenses and building walls with rules and gifts. In the end the walls were so tall I didn't see the bulldozer. I didn't see he was keeping me and loving another. That with his influence, charm, and money he had chosen someone else for his wife. In my insecurities I never noticed that I had even helped plan some of the events." Tears began to fall, and she wiped them quickly.

"He married his woman. The woman chosen for him by his parents and their money, a woman that he'd been sleeping with as long as he was with me. My heart was ripped in two. He was my boss. He used me, betrayed me, and left me. And yes," she started, then paused, and swallowed hard. "He hit me."

Zach's entire body tensed, and he took her hand and gripped it tight. She covered it with her other hand, which was cold and shaking. "I returned to Nashville, lived on my savings, worked small jobs to keep sane, and I survived. Fate brought me to your door, and now I'm afraid it'll happen all over again."

He eased back and looked at her. "I'm sorry, Regan." He skimmed her hair with his hand. If only he knew who the man was, he'd see to him. He'd make him pay for his mistakes. Every part of him wanted to rip him apart for hurting the woman Zach loved and keeping her from loving him. "I cannot promise you that through all this I won't hurt you at some time. It's human to make mistakes. But I will promise that I will never lie to you. I will never do wrong by you or harm you. If you or I choose to go our separate ways, we do so honestly. And just for the record, I'm not ashamed of what we have. You're not just my assistant. You are a vital part of my life at the office and away. I meant what I said. I love you."

She fell into his arms and nestled her face in his neck. "I haven't decided if you're the most wonderful man to walk the earth or the craziest."

"A fine line between the two." He smiled, but his it felt like his heart was being wrung by the hands of the man who'd hurt Regan and kept her from trusting him. "What I am is crazy about you. And if I have to fire you to love you, I'll do it." He pulled back and looked into her eyes. "But I don't want that. I want us to love each other and to work side by side. I think we make a good team."

She watched him as she let her shoulders fall, and a smile formed on her lips. "So do I."

CHAPTER 29

*R*egan stood to the side and watched Zach, along with twenty others in hard hats and suits, lift dirt with shiny silver shovels in the ground breaking ceremony of the Dallas Empire Building. She couldn't help but scan the crowd and look for faces that were familiar to her. It wasn't the first time she'd stood to the side and watched the man she loved bask in the glory of something he was building.

No one looked familiar, except for Rebecca, who still kept an eye on her as though she knew all her secrets.

Among those who attended, there were introductions and handshakes. Zach kept his professionalism, as did Regan. Both wanted the same thing—success for Benson, Benson, and Hart and a speedy trip back to the hotel.

They spent one more day in Dallas as tourists and lovers before returning to work. And work was what they did.

The Dallas project was officially underway. The Kansas City project had almost caught up to schedule without going over budget, and John Forrester was making things easy in Nashville so he could be relocated to Los Angeles for the project there. The build was going to take Zach's very best man, and that man was John Forrester.

~

ON THURSDAY, Regan and Zach drove to the Memphis site, holding hands in the car the entire way, and she sang old country songs that made Zach laugh.

"This is a great work day." Regan smiled as the wind blew through her hair in Audrey's convertible. "I'm glad your mother thought of this."

"She likes you. She wants you to like me so she can marry me off," he said with a hint of laughter in his voice, but Regan turned her head. Every time she thought she had the man figured out, something else told her to beware. His mother was planning her future.

Zach touched her arm. "Regan, I didn't mean anything by that. All I meant to say was she really likes you." Regan looked back at him. The crease between his brows told her he was sorry for hurting her with his words, and it killed her that she was so sensitive to every word he spoke.

"I like her too."

"She would like to think you would be the one I marry. She's suddenly desperate for a huge wedding at the house and grand-children." The conversation wasn't getting any better. Why was it she couldn't accept the fact that Audrey Benson was genuinely kind and liked her for the person she was? Everything inside her said that it was happening again. That she was being controlled. However, if she replayed the past few weeks in her head, there was no evidence to back that up. She was scaring herself and she didn't know how to stop.

She remained silent for the remainder of the trip and so did he. When Zach parked at the site, Regan grabbed her bag and took out her notebook. She checked to make sure she had her digital camera for visual notes.

Zach walked around the car and touched her hand. She jerked back, but he grabbed her arm. "Listen, this is all new to me. I chose you. My mother didn't. I want to see where this goes with or without her blessing. We just happen to have it right now." She was still looking away. "Dammit, Regan, I'm not him. Whoever the bastard is that made you so afraid of commitment, love, and family, I'm not him. I'm not going to break your heart and plan out your life. If you're going to be part of my life, you're going to choose that."

She knew she was being petty, but the pain was still there. Furthermore, she hadn't been completely up front with him. There was so much more to the story. He'd promised not to lie to her, but she couldn't be up front with him. She bit her lip and looked up at him.

"I'm sorry I picked a fight. Really, what you said wasn't so bad. I… I guess I'm just gun-shy."

"I would be too." He moved closer to her as she swung her bag onto her shoulder. "I love you. Really, that's all that matters." His hands were on her arms, and he dipped down and kissed her lightly on her lips. As his mouth lingered on hers, someone called his name from behind him.

Roger Byers was headed toward them. Zach lifted his head, composed himself, and extended his hand to him.

"Damn hot day." Roger's shirt was sweat stained, and even as he spoke, a bead of sweat ran down his temple.

"That's why we drove with the top down." Zach smiled. "Roger, I want you to meet Regan Keller."

"Oh, so you're the pretty voice on the phone," he mused, and she felt her stomach churn.

"Thank you."

"Well c'mon back. We got sweet tea in the fridge and a ton of paperwork for you to look at." He started toward the offices and they followed.

Regan sat uncomfortably in the office as the two men went over paperwork and plans. She couldn't help but feel physically threatened by the way Roger would look her way when Zach turned his head. There was a hate in his eyes. She'd seen it in Michael Hamiliton's eyes the day he struck her and meant to kill.

They went through the items in the office that needed attention. Zach asked questions. Roger answered them with "um" and "well." Regan took explicit notes. She was very familiar with the fact that they were close to completion, and the job was going to go over on both time and budget.

Zach's impatience with Roger was becoming obvious to her by the way he paced the floor and raked his fingers through his hair. She was sure it was showing to Roger as well. Roger Byers met Zach's well-mannered questions and concerns with half answers and stories, things she was finding Zach didn't like.

When Zach excused himself to the bathroom, Roger sat in his chair, kicked up his feet, and scanned his eyes over her. "Some cushy job you have."

"I beg your pardon."

"I'll bet you do your share of begging. I'll bet you do your share of a lot of things." He dropped his feet just as Zach walked back into the office.

Regan looked down at her notes and breathed through the hurt his words had caused.

Zach picked up his notebook and handed it to Regan. "Roger, I'm not happy about all this. You should have this building completed in less than two months, and we over budgeted, so to have gone over that is unacceptable. Your labor costs are higher than any other project."

"C'mon, Zach. We both know how this is business is. Turnover rate, materials, weather, it's all unpredictable. When have you ever known a building not to go over on time and budget?"

"When it was built by Benson, Benson and Hart. I'll be back in a week for the walkthrough. I'm too angry to go in now," he said. He gave Regan a nod. She stood and headed for the door.

Regan walked toward the car as Zach turned back again. "If I don't see improvements, I'll find someone else to finish the build." He let the door shut behind him, and they could hear the curses that Roger Byers flung at him as he walked away.

Regan couldn't help but keep looking back at the trailer to see if the man was going to come after them.

Zach opened her door to the car and waited for her to climb in. When she had, he slowly walked to the other side, got in, and started the engine. He gripped the steering wheel and sat.

"Are you okay?" She wanted to touch him, but she wasn't sure his reaction would be one she'd welcome.

"I'm just cooling down." His teeth were clenched as he talked, and he wrung the steering wheel with his hands. "One thing about Benson, Benson and Hart, we get what we want." He sucked in a deep breath. "That building will be done in my time frame, or he'll be out on his ass and John Forrester will finish it before he goes to L.A. John has the Nashville project, which is still in its infancy, so we have time. I have to send him to Kansas City to do some damage control and now here. It's all just an awful lot to chew on."

Finally, he put the car in reverse and they left the lot.

Not one foul word had slipped through Zach's lips as he drove away from the building site. Even though his sunglasses shielded his eyes, she knew he was deep in thought. A man who could breathe through his anger, and not use abusive words or fists to change the direction of things, was a special man. "Why don't you send someone else out here?"

"I have lots of foremen on lots of jobs. Unfortunately, some of them are like our friend Roger Byers. But when you need it done right, you send John. Even if he's only there a few weeks and then turns it over, you'll be amazed at what gets done." He gave a thoughtful nod and his shoulders relaxed. "I trust John."

"I believe that." Finally, she reached for his hand, and he interlaced his fingers with hers. Whatever anger he'd had over Roger Byers had melted away, and as his thumb grazed over her skin, she knew he'd never take that anger out on her. A giddy burst of joy filled her. "This has been a crazy afternoon. What do you say we finish up at the office and go back to my place? Let me cook you dinner. I have a claw foot tub that fits two and a king-sized bed that's lonely when I'm in it by myself."

Zach finally smiled and shifted his glance to her. His face had gone gentle, and he lifted his hand to caress her cheek. Even though he'd been angry, she didn't feel the need to jerk away from him. She was comforted by his touch.

He reached for her hand, pulled it across to his lips, and pressed a lingering kiss on her knuckles. "I'm not one to turn down a free meal."

"Good. Carlos is away tonight. No one will interrupt us." She lifted his fingers to her lips and kissed them. "But there is one stipulation."

He gave her a quick glance then shifted his attention back to the road. "What's that?"

"We have to stop by the store. If I'm keeping you for the night, I'm not letting you go until after breakfast."

He gave her hand a squeeze. "You're sure about this?"

Couldn't he see it resonate through her whole body? She was claiming back her life one piece at a time. With Zachary Benson, she was claiming back her heart, which had been torn into a million pieces. She was reclaiming the confidence that had been torn away with deceit and lies. And having watched his demeanor change on the ride back to Nashville, she realized she was letting that wall she'd built to protect herself physically crumble to the ground. There was nothing she wanted more than to keep Zach busy and wrapped in her arms all night long. She was now in charge. "That's my executive decision."

CHAPTER 30

*R*egan was completely aware of Zach's stare was on her as she stirred the filling for the pie she planned to serve with dinner. With every stir, she let her body sway a bit. She liked the way the hem of his shirt, which she'd ripped from him the moment they'd walked through her front door, skimmed her bare thighs. From the few groans echoing into his wine glass as he drank, she was sure he liked the way it looked.

Zach cleared his throat. "You're sure Carlos isn't coming home tonight, or your sister won't be here for some surprise visit?" he asked as he set his glass on the table and walked up behind her, still barefoot and clad in only his jeans after they'd made love all afternoon.

"I'm sure." She tossed back her hair, revealing her neck to him. Taking the subtle hint, he trailed kisses from her collarbone to her ear while slipping his hands up under the shirt she'd stolen, and cupping her breasts.

"You're going to make me spill the filling," she sighed.

"Sorry for distracting you." He dropped his hands slowly, skimming his fingertips over her sensitive skin. "You're sexy when you bake."

"I've never had that compliment. Thank you."

Zach wrapped his arms around her and nuzzled his chin against her shoulder. Regan dipped her finger into the chocolate pie filling and lifted it to his mouth. His breath was warm against her cheek as he sucked the filling from her finger, and it sent tingles through her core. She closed her eyes and rested against him. His hands wandered back up her shirt as she laid the spoon against the side of the mixing bowl.

Her skin under his touch was hot, and her breath had quickened. Zach slid his hands to her hips, hooked his fingers into the band of her panties, and pushed them down. She braced her hands against the counter, and he pushed his hard body against her. Zach dipped his finger into the pie filling and ran a line of chocolate down her neck. When she sighed, he licked the trail with his tongue. Regan felt her knees go weak.

Zach spun her around and pressed her back against the counter. He pulled her up to him, wrapped her legs around him, and turned her toward the kitchen table. She buried her face in his neck as he set her on the table.

Turning back to the counter, he brought the bowl of filling to the table. The sexy smile on his lips and smoldering darkness in his eyes told her he was going to devour her.

He dipped his finger into the filling and fed it to her. Regan sucked the chocolate from his skin. He let out a groan and pushed closer to her. She set a firm hand on his bare chest and pushed him back.

Regan reached for the first button on his shirt she'd borrowed and released it. His eyes sparked. She unbuttoned the second, and Zach bit down on his lip. He was putty in her hands now, and she was in charge. When she had opened the entire shirt, she sat before him on the table naked, enjoying the pain she was causing him. She dipped her finger into the pie filling and ran it from her neck, down between her breasts to the top of her stomach.

Zach swallowed hard, but didn't move until she reached for

him. Regan pulled him to her, kissing him thoroughly, tasting the chocolate and wine. She intoxicated herself with him and let a moan slip from her throat as his hand moved up the inside of her thigh.

He broke free from her mouth and slowly licked the chocolate from her body. Every flick of his tongue sent a shiver through her. Her desire for him grew more intense as he made his way to her stomach and lower.

Unable to stand it any longer, she grabbed for his hips and unzipped the already unbuttoned jeans that kept him from her. Zach slid them to floor and Regan wrapped her legs back around him. He gripped her waist and pulled her to the edge of the table. Her arms flew around his neck as he pushed inside her with a passion, a heat.

She stroked him with her body, gripping him, until she drove him with her to the edge and they spilled over together.

Their bodies were damp. Their heartbeats rapid and their breath only in gasps.

"God, what you do to me..." He rested his head on her shoulder.

"I've never been touched like that. You handle me with finesse and care when I need it." She ran her hand up his chest. "And when you know I'm relaxed with you, you turn up the heat."

"Oh, honey, I think you turned up the heat this time. Watching you let go and unbutton my shirt..." He lifted his head, looked down at her, and blew out a satisfied breath.

Zach brought out something inside of her no other man had ever been able to do. Not only was she comfortable with him, she was comfortable with herself. She wanted to release the passion, the need, the love she'd bottled up inside for so long.

She looked up at him with hazed eyes and smiled. Then his eyes changed, and a sudden anguished look crossed over his face. "I'm sorry. I wasn't thinking." He took a step back.

"Neither was I. That was the nice part." Regan reached for him, but he was out of her grasp.

"No. I just took you. I didn't think about protection." He raked his fingers through his hair.

"I take care of myself." She pulled the shirt closed around her.

He stepped closer to her and reached for her hand, which still gripped the shirt closed. "You know I'd take care of you if anything ever happened."

She hopped down from the table. "I said I can take care of myself."

The tone in her voice had changed. The entire mood had changed. He was treading somewhere she didn't want him to go.

He wrapped his arms around her waist. "I love you, Regan." She rested her head on his chest, and he pulled her against him tighter. "I could really get used to this."

"Me in your arms?"

"Well, that too," he teased, and she looked up at him and smiled. "Can't you see it? Sex on the table and then dessert? What a way to end a day." He kissed the tip of her nose. "But never when company is around." He wrinkled up his nose, and it made her laugh.

"I've had sex now twice in an hour. I'm feeling lightheaded." She wrapped her arms around his neck. "I'm not used to this kind of attention."

"I like it in the light. I can see your face."

"Yours isn't too bad either." She patted it and then looked at the floor. "Where are my panties?"

"Here." He gathered them from the floor then knelt down before her. "Let me."

She laughed as he held them out for her to step into then he slowly slid them up her legs, pressing lingering kisses to her calves and thighs.

She tucked in her bottom lip and bit down on it as his kisses rose. Then he stopped.

"What is that from?" He accentuated his question with a kiss, and her heart stopped as he ran his finger over the scar on her stomach.

"Nothing." She pulled her panties from his fingers and hiked them the rest of the way up. Hastily she began buttoning the shirt and turned from him.

"I didn't mean to upset you." He grabbed her arm and turned her toward him. "What happened? What is that scar from?"

"I said it's nothing," she said again and went back to her preparation of dessert.

Zach picked up his wine and took a long drink. In a few short weeks, he'd made her forget her promise to herself not to fall for her boss. Thank goodness for that. He'd decided she was the woman with whom he wanted to share his life, but there were still too many walls between them. There were still secrets, and it was killing him. He could wring the neck of the man who had made her so timid around him.

He loved her. He'd said he loved her, even though she'd yet to return the words. In time she'd tell him what it was she was keeping buried inside.

CHAPTER 31

*E*ven though Zach kept his promise to remain professional in the office, he always found a way to sneak in a little romance. He'd leave her a note in her drawer or even on his desk in the morning, knowing she'd find it when she laid items on it for him to tend to. He'd call her from a job site on her cell phone at lunchtime. Without those around her knowing, he'd speak sweetly to her. Certainly, on the other end her cheeks were flushed and her head hung to hide her emotions. This came through in her voice as she giggled and returned sweet thoughts in a soft whisper.

Whenever they got the chance, they spent the night in one another's arms. He wondered when she'd open to him and accept him as more than just her boss and more than just her current lover.

"My mother wants us to come for dinner on the weekend." He intertwined their fingers in the darkness.

"I was hoping we could go to New York and see my sister. She opens this weekend." She kissed the fingers he'd intertwined with hers. Though her body had tensed beside his, she didn't sound afraid when she suggested changing their plans to what she wanted. That was a step in the right direction, he decided.

"I'll tell my mother we'll have dinner another time."

"Thank you." Regan moved in closer to him, and her body was pliant. She was comfortable with him, and he couldn't have been more pleased to feel that wall she kept between them crumble.

In his bedroom, with moonlight casting a glow over the room, she was comfortable in Zach's arms. But she was beginning to worry the feeling would go away. She'd felt that way in Michael's arms too—at first.

Michael Hamilton and Zachary Benson were so different. Michael bullied his employees into doing what he wanted them to do. Zach took care of them, and in turn, they took care of him.

She'd never met Michael's family, and until the day he came looking for her in the hospital, in which he'd put her, he'd never met her family. Already, she'd spent time alone with Zach's mother, and she adored his father.

Michael had whispered things about trips and jewelry. There were promises of riches and houses. It wasn't like that with Zach. He spoke of his family with love, and he cherished hers. There was talk of travel, but it wasn't just a job. There was talk of vacations and destinations for them and only them. He'd spoken of marriage, though it was what his mother had wanted, but he'd said it aloud. Audrey wanted a big wedding to plan and grandchildren running through her home. Could it be that Zach was the man she could do these things with?

What happened to the promise she'd made to herself? Fear settled into her. Perhaps if things were as serious as they seemed, she should think about finding a job away from him.

No, that would be silly. She loved working with him. She loved being with him, and Regan was quickly realizing she was head over heels in love with him.

Regan turned to him in the moonlight and studied the lines of his face. His eyes were still bright as he looked back at her. He hadn't asked about her scar again. He didn't ask about the relationship she'd told him she'd had. He'd let her be. Perhaps it was time to tell him everything. Confide in him her travels into corporate America though the law offices in Los Angeles. She could continue about how the tall, dark, and handsome Michael Hamilton had swept her off her feet. Would it discourage Zach to find out that he wasn't the first to turn her head in a matter of a few weeks? With Michael, she left a perfectly good job and moved to Hawaii. She'd given up the connection she had with her family, just to be with the man she'd thought she loved.

Her heart rate picked up. She'd had a ring. She'd had a condo. She'd been pregnant with a child that she loved.

Zach would have to know these things. She had to confide in him. She had to…

She opened her mouth to speak, to tell him everything that had happened to her before she'd fallen onto his lap. But she thought better of it and closed her mouth.

Zach touched her face gently. "What were you going to say?"

"Nothing," she said and cuddled closer to him. She was a coward.

Regan's family chose to travel to New York together. However, they kept it a secret from Arianna. Regan knew when she saw them all, she'd flood them with tears. Though she was a professional, there was no reason to tempt her fate as an actress. As far as she knew, only Regan and Zach would be there to see her debut.

"You look beautiful, Mama." Regan kissed her mother in the lobby of the theater, then she turned to her father and kissed him too. "And don't you clean up good?"

"You brought him with you?" he asked softly in her ear as his gaze transferred to Zach, who stood at the bar.

"Yes, I brought him."

Alan Keller nodded his head, keeping his lips close to his daughter's ear. "He's treating you okay? Everything is okay with you working with him?" And there was the hesitation she'd known would arrive.

"We're doing fine, Daddy." She moved even closer to him where no one could hear. "I love him."

He kissed her cheek, and she knew he already understood how she felt.

"I'm going to get your mama a drink," he said with a wink. He took Emily's arm and walked across the lobby to the bar.

"I find it amazing that there hasn't been one murmur of an affair on the job site," Carlos whispered as he moved to her side.

"Oh, Carlos." She gritted her teeth. She was tiring of the inquisition even if she understood their concern.

"Hey, I know he makes you happy. I live on the couch." He raised his eyebrows, and heat rose in her cheeks. "They're just worried about you. You can't blame them."

She turned sharply. "Listen, I love the man. I can't help myself. But he knows nothing of what I've gone through."

"You can't keep that from him if you plan to make this work."

"Maybe not, but it's too early." She felt tears forming in her eyes as Curtis walked up to them. "You all have to help me keep my secrets. And you all have to trust me that I know what I'm doing."

"I ran into his mother at the hospital last week," Curtis said softly. "She's got high hopes for the two of you."

"I've heard." She gripped the clutch in her hands tighter.

"Are you ready for that? The Bensons don't exactly fly under the media's radar. What about Michael?"

"What about him? He tossed me to the curb. He's no threat to me anymore," she said, but last week's lunch meeting in Dallas had renewed the doubt in her mind. Was Rebecca still in contact with him? Had she recognized Regan, and if she had, would she say something to Michael? Her knees felt weak beneath her. She straightened her shoulders and tried to push away the feeling of fear, which was always so quick to take over.

"Okay, what about the…" When Regan threatened him with her stare, he stopped. "Fine, but you know Michael and Zach run in the same circles. With wealth and power like the Bensons have, your paths are sure to cross."

Leave it to Curtis to turn over every rock. No. There was no need to get worked up over it. She had regained her life by sheer determination. Michael Hamilton could no longer do her harm.

When Regan saw Zach walk toward her with a glass of wine, she stepped back from the tight circle she and her brothers had made.

Zach handed her the glass. "I love New York. So many wonderful buildings."

Curtis gave him a nod. "How many of them have had a sign with your name out front?"

"More than I know." Zach gave a self-deprecatory shrug. "My grandfather was partial to New York."

"Makes for a nice trust fund," Carlos added, and Regan jabbed his ribs with her elbow. "Hey!"

The lights in the lobby flashed, and the crowd that lingered scurried toward the theater doors to take their seats.

Zach touched the small of her back as they walked through the door. "Everything okay?"

"Yes. I guess that since you don't have any siblings, you wouldn't know how nosy and pushy they can be. They mean well, though."

"You forget, I don't have brothers or sisters, but I do have my mother. I know nosy and pushy." He gave her back a warm rub. "They're that way because they love us. No matter how crazy they make us."

CHAPTER 32

$\mathcal{A}$fter the performance, Arianna had arranged for Regan and Zach to visit her backstage. Regan tapped on the dressing room door and heard her sister's voice giving her permission to enter the room.

"I'll be out in a moment. I'm changing. But I'm decent, so Zach can come in." Her voice was muffled behind a screen and racks of costumes.

"You're sure you're decent enough?" She held in a laugh as she motioned for the family to enter.

"God, I'm not a prude."

Regan looked around the room. Props and costumes from the night's show filled every corner. It had all moved so effortlessly, she'd never realized that her sister had changed so many times.

Bouquets of roses and other flower arrangements filled her counter. They gave a feminine smell to the room that also smelled like hot, sweaty bodies—an odor she was sure was from the heavy costumes her sister must have sweltered in.

"That's better." Arianna pulled her robe closed and tied her hair in a tail atop her head before she turned and noticed her entire family standing before her. She let out a scream of joy.

"Oh, God!" She pulled the crowd into her arms and kissed each of them.

"Mama, Papa, I didn't know you were coming." Tears streamed down her cheeks. "But thank God I didn't know. I'd have forgotten every line."

"I wouldn't have missed this for the world." Alan kissed her, and Emily dabbed at her eyes.

"Carlos, the kids. This is your weekend. You said…"

"I lied. I was coming all along." He kissed her and held her face in his hands. "You are amazing."

"Thank you."

Arianna pulled Curtis into her arms and he hauled her off her feet. "You… you…" He set her back on the ground and looked her over. "Well, you didn't suck."

She punched him the shoulder then kissed him.

Arianna turned back to Regan. "What did you think?"

Zach stood to the side, Regan's shawl over his arm. "She was bawling like a baby," he said, saving Regan from giving her opinion.

"Zach." She crossed to him and kissed him on the cheek. "Thank you so much for coming."

"They're right. You're amazing."

"You're a keeper." She turned back to her family. "Let's go to dinner. All of us. And then, Daddy, maybe you can spin us all across a dance floor."

They dined and danced together well into the night. Regan was thrilled to have the man she loved enjoying the company of her family. He fit. He wasn't supposed to, but he did.

When Carlos bought him a drink and Arianna danced with him and laughed as he dipped her, her nerves unraveled. They had accepted him.

Zach pulled Regan from the table by her hand. "C'mon. You owe me a spin on the dance floor before they close."

"I'm tired. I don't want to dance."

"Your father is out there spinning your mother in circles. I can't be shown up like this," he said, tugging again, and she laughed.

Regan's parents danced as though they were forty years younger. It was a sight she would never tire of.

Zach led her next to them, and her father gave a nod. "Ready? Trade!" her father called out as each of them spun his partner off and collected the one that danced toward him.

"Well, Zachary, you sure do know your dancing," Emily said on a laugh as Zach dipped her and pulled her back into his arms.

"Like I told your daughter, I was forced into it."

"I doubt that." She laughed again. "Men say that, but then when it comes time for them to show off on a dance floor, they are glad they know what they are doing."

He removed his hand from around her waist and rested it over his heart with a nod. "My secret is no longer safe."

Alan spun Regan away from her mother and Zach, and spun her until she was dizzy and began to protest.

He slowed down. "That is for all the times you stepped on my feet."

"You told me to step on your feet." She laughed as he spun her again.

"I like him."

Regan tripped on his foot and had to work to regain her balance. "What?"

"I like this new man of yours. He wants to take care of you. I can tell."

"I think you're right, Daddy. He's not like the other one."

"This, I already know." When he spoke from the heart, his German accent came through strong. "You never brought the other one around. You let him hide you away."

Her movements became jerky, and it was hard to focus as she tried to keep her composure. "You're right. I was wrong to do that. I'm sorry I hurt you and Mama by staying away."

The music stopped, and the musicians began to put their instruments away. The dancers cleared the floor—all but Regan and her father.

"You are a smart girl. You did what was right." He patted her cheek. "Don't ever think I'm disappointed in you or that your mama is either. We love you." He looked up and over at his wife and Zach watching them. "You take care of him too."

CHAPTER 33

Zach pushed the button for the elevator as Regan's family gathered around. An awkward silence followed them. Their rooms were scattered throughout the hotel. Carlos and Curtis got off the elevator on the tenth floor, kissing their mother good night as the doors opened.

Zach stood to one side of her parents and Regan on the other as they rode to the fifteenth floor. The heat in the small elevator felt as though it was climbing when Zach noticed both Emily's and Alan's eyes on him. He shifted his gaze to the escalating numbers over the door, and the elevator finally came to a stop.

"Good night, Mama." She kissed her mother as the elevator door opened. "Good night, Papa. I love you both."

Zach shook her father's hand and did not let the gentle squeeze of a warning go unnoticed. When the elevator door closed, and they were alone in the elevator, he leaned against the wall with a huff.

"What's wrong?" Regan made her move toward him.

"How old is your father?"

"He's seventy-six. Why?"

"He's very old-fashioned."

Regan wrapped her arms around his waist and placed a kiss against his throat. "Yes he is. Why do you say that?"

"He's not very keen on us sleeping together."

"What did he say?" She stepped back and looked up at him. Her face had grown concerned.

"Not one word. But the looks. The body language. The handshake." He cleared his throat. "I'm not kidding, Regan, I think I'll go down and see if they have another room available. If not, I'll just bunk with Curtis and Carlos."

"You'll do no such thing." She laughed as she took his hand and pulled him out of the elevator as the doors opened. "You'll sleep in my room, in my bed. And by God you'll make love to me tonight."

"If you insist." He smiled broadly as he adjusted his suit jacket and brushed his hands down his sleeves.

"Oh, tonight I'm the boss." She winked at him as she slid the key card into the door.

Regan opened the door and quickly found herself pressed up against the back of it, Zach's hands roaming over her. His mouth covered hers. His teeth nipped her lips. The dress she wore melted to a puddle on the floor.

She slid her fingers through his hair and down to the tie around his neck. Giving it a tug, she pulled at it until it lost its form and fell to the floor with her dress. The buttons on his custom-made shirt flew open when she pulled at them hurriedly, exposing his hard, sculpted chest beneath her fingers. The scent of his musky cologne washed over her and aroused every sensual nerve in her body.

Their bodies, tangled together, slid down the door to the floor. He ripped her panties from her hips, and her bare skin rubbed against the harsh carpet beneath her. They both fought the belt that cinched his slacks. Finally, he was free of them and he kicked them away.

Zach positioned himself between her legs as she wrapped

them tightly around his waist, and he plunged into her, filling her completely.

Regan met him thrust for thrust as her fingers dug into his back, urging him to take her over the slippery edge of control. Her body grew damp beneath his as his teeth trailed down her jaw to her neck and ended with a bite above her collarbone, sending a shock that pulled every muscle in her body.

She breathed his name as she crossed the border from clear sight to that hazy cloud of ecstasy. His body shook against hers before he fell atop her. His weight limp on hers as they both fought for air.

"I don't know why my father wouldn't approve of us sleeping in the same room." The statement was light with laughter as she gasped for breath.

"If he knew what I did to his little girl…" He trailed off and kissed her before rolling to the floor beside her.

"He'd probably kill you. But only after Carlos and Curtis beat you up."

"Oh, yes. The wrath of the older brothers." He propped himself up on his elbow and looked down on her. He traced her collarbone with his finger. "Perhaps I can bribe them."

"Hum, now there's an option." She took a deep breath, trying to slow her heart rate back to normal.

"Tell me, Ms. Keller, what do your brothers like?" He ran the pendant around her neck back and forth on the chain.

"Carlos would be easy. He's very open to matters of money." She smiled as he nodded. "He could easily be bought off with a car. Nothing cheap either. Something expensive and fast."

"Got it. A Ferrari would do the trick."

"Uh-huh." She nodded. "And red wouldn't hurt."

"I'm a man. I totally understand that need."

"Now, Dr. Curtis would be a bit more difficult. He works so hard he hardly has time to enjoy the pleasantries of material things. What the doctor needs is a woman."

"Easily done."

"Oh, no. His tastes are specific." She smiled again. "He prefers blondes. He feels their tempers are more controlled. He likes them as tall as he is, so that means over six feet tall. They must have a college education and understand how important his job is."

"Doesn't seem like he's asking for much."

"Oh, I'm not done." She rolled closer to him and skimmed her finger over his jaw. "She must love children and want eight of them."

"Eight?"

"Yes, no less. She must make rhubarb pie, and she must—and this is the most important—" She raised her eyebrows to emphasize. "She must speak Spanish, Italian, French, and I think he said Chinese, but that one might be negotiable."

With a burst of laugher, he rolled to his back, grasping her hand to his chest. "I'm so sorry, Regan. I thought this would work. Your father will have to kill me."

"I thought the mighty Zachary Benson could do anything."

"Dr. Curtis may have just proven me wrong."

"That's too bad. I was really beginning to like you." She traced the line of his muscles down his chest with her finger.

Zach grabbed her hand and rolled back to meet her eyes. "Like me? Oh, Regan, I so hoped you'd be falling in love with me by now."

"Zach…" Her eyes dropped from his stare.

"Don't use the excuse you've done this before." He lifted her chin with his finger until she shifted her eyes back to his. "You fell in love with the wrong man. So he happened to be your boss, and so do I. That's only coincidence. I'm not him," he said with a shake of his head and anger brewing in his eyes.

"No you're not."

"Then tell me. Tell me you love me."

"Zach…"

"I see it in your eyes, Regan. You love me. I know it's true."

She sat up, gathered her dress from the floor, and held it to her chest.

Zach sat up next to her and touched her bare shoulder. "Please, Regan. If you don't love, me tell me that." His hand was warm and gentle as he rubbed his thumb over her sensitive skin.

"I can't."

He stood and pulled her to her feet. "I'll settle for that."

Suddenly she was no longer worried that he'd break her heart. Her fear had changed course. Now she was afraid that she would break his.

CHAPTER 34

$\mathcal{E}$very building site was a bustle of workers doing as much work as they could from sunup to sundown. Completion dates neared. New sites were acquired. New investors were found. And Zach was pleased with how business was going.

The Nashville project was ahead of schedule, even with the changes that Zach had made. He'd sent John Forrester to Kansas City to get the site up to speed, which he had done skillfully.

"I'm sending John to Memphis at the end of the week," he told Regan. "I want you to go with him because you were there for the meeting with Byers. We should have been there three weeks ago." He didn't like not keeping his word. He had threatened Roger Byers that he'd be back in a week and he'd let his schedule slip. It wasn't something he'd say aloud, but his diligence to business hadn't been as important since he'd fallen head over heels in love. Every task was harder to accomplish knowing Regan was right outside his office door. "I need to get to L.A. by the end of the week and see to it that the loose ends are being tied up so we can get that project rolling. If we can finish up Nashville, Memphis, and Kansas City enough to do interior work during the winter, it would be a good time to get L.A. underway."

He watched as Regan took down every word in her notepad. He leaned his arms on the pile of papers on his desk and inched closer to her. "Once I return from L.A., I'll need you to set up accommodations at the Ritz Carlton in New York City. First-class airline tickets for two. My mother enjoys the opera, but see what your sister can do to get her tickets to her show." Regan's glance finally shifted up to him. "It's their fortieth wedding anniversary," he explained.

A warm smile lit her face. "I'll get those arrangements taken care of," she said, sitting up straighter and looking across at him. "Is there anything else, Mr. Benson?"

"Yes." He stood and walked around the desk. He took her hands in his and pulled her to her feet.

She looked very much like the day he'd met her. The day she'd fallen from heaven and landed on his lap. All tucked up in her professionalism, she was damn sexy. She'd pulled back her hair, exposing her soft neck. He caressed her cheek, gliding his thumb over her cheekbone.

Regan lifted her hand to pull his from her. "Zach…"

"I'm the boss." He took her mouth with his, driving her into a deep kiss that left her swaying against him.

"We had an agreement," she reminded him as she lifted her hand to his chest to push him away.

"Yes, but we didn't sign a contract. I only work with contracts."

She bit down on her lip. "Yes. And the only way I'll get fired is if I lose you a contract." Her eyes hazed with something dark, but it wasn't pleasure or seduction. A tautness around her mouth told him it was anger.

"Where did you hear that?"

"Mary Ellen on my first day. She said you were a softy, but if someone lost you a contract, you'd fire them on the spot."

He pulled her closer to him, willing the haze in her eyes to turn smoky with lust. "We'd better not sign a contract about kissing at work, then. I'll have to fire myself for breaking it. I can't keep myself from you. I love you."

She stiffened and stepped back from him. But he moved closer. "While my parents are in New York, you and I are going to spend the weekend at their house. Let's see if you really like Tennessee sprawling land."

She took a breath, but a knock at the door stopped her. For that he was grateful. He didn't want excuses, he wanted her.

They had just enough time to step back from each other and look professional before Kirk Peterson pushed open the door and walked in uninvited. "We've got troubles in Memphis."

He held a report in his hands. For the first time in months, he bypassed his normal sleaziness and looked past Regan to Zach.

The Memphis project had been red flagged and could be shut down if inspectors returned and didn't see changes ASAP. There had never been a Benson, Benson, and Hart project shut down. He sure as hell wasn't going to let Roger Byers bring down his record.

He'd have to get John Forrester on the project sooner than he'd though. He'd go himself if he didn't have to focus on the project in Los Angeles. It was worth too much money to let it slip through his fingers. But his current builds were in need of his attention too.

Teleconferences were scheduled with the foreman of each build. Zachary usually ran a tight organization, and he was going to make sure it stayed that way. Somewhere he'd let his watchful eye close and he couldn't afford to do it again.

Regan had been an invaluable asset in the twenty-four hours since Kirk Peterson had delivered the report to him. She'd arranged his flights, made sure he'd eaten, brought him a clean shirt before his meeting with John, and fielded phone calls from his mother and Simone when his nerves and his time were stretched to the limit.

Exhausted, Zach leaned against the doorjamb of his office,

watching Regan as she gathered her things to leave for the day. He'd spent the afternoon with John going over the Memphis project. He wasn't sure if it was a good sign that his mind kept wandering back to thoughts of making love with Regan while he was making plans for John to fire Roger Byers and take over the build. He wished to God that he didn't have to be on a flight for L.A. in just a few hours.

Regan swung her bag over her shoulder and turned off the monitor on her computer. Whatever she was thinking of put an alluring curve in her lips.

"You have the sexiest smile," he said.

She turned with her hand to her chest, then caught her breath and stomped her foot. "I thought Mary Ellen said you weren't to sneak up on us."

"I never listen."

"I thought you were still meeting with John."

"He left while you were away from your desk." He looked around the office and noticed they were alone, so he clasped her hand and led her through the door, then shut it behind them. "Come here for a moment."

Quickly he gathered her in his arms before she could realize what he had in mind and push him away. His mouth found hers, and it was soft and warm. He drank her in before pulling back.

"I hate having to go to L.A." He brushed her jaw with a kiss as she tipped her head back. "I might not be able to survive without my"—he nipped at her lower lip and enjoyed the shiver he produced in her—"wonderful assistant."

"Well, Mr. Benson, not everyone can have such a wonderful assistant as you have. You really should give her a raise since she's so good for you."

His fingers were in her hair, sending a tingle down his spine. "You really think she's worth it?"

"She'd do anything for you." The words were breathless as they escaped her mouth.

He held her tight, knowing she'd want to break free after such an admission. "Would she tell me she loves me?"

She looked down. "Zach..."

"Mr. Benson," he joked, taking her mouth again. "I guess I'll get a bite to eat at the airport before I go. I'd much rather ravage you on your kitchen table again, though," he offered with his brow pressed to hers.

"The kids are there."

"Well then, I guess I'll just go to L.A." He kissed her again, lingering, absorbing her into memory. "I wish I could take you with me. You'll go the next time, that's for damn sure." He stroked his thumb down her jaw. "Can I give you a ride home?"

"I have my car."

Trying not to feel like he'd been turned down, he gave her a light hug. "Let me walk you down."

CHAPTER 35

When Regan arrived home, there were three slices of pizza in the fridge with a note that said *We love you, Aunt Regan*. They had gone to a movie. She had the evening and the house to herself—and no Zach.

Maybe it was for the best.

She ran a bath and dined on her pizza and wine, neck deep in bubbles. Candles flickered all around her, giving the room a golden glow. Bach played on the speaker, and the smell of lavender filled the room. It was exactly what she needed.

When she laid her head back into the water, she thought of Zach. He was on his way to L.A. She trembled when she thought of him being so far away. Could she already miss him so much? Yes.

What was she thinking? She should have cut the ties with him. She should be basking in the thought that the boss was out of town and for the next two days she could play solitaire on the computer. But it wasn't like that.

While her boss was away, she waited. She waited for the phone to ring. She waited for that special e-mail, and as always, she waited for the delivery of flowers to arrive at her home before he returned. They had a routine.

A routine, she thought with a shake of her head. Married couples with families had routines, not assistants having affairs with their bosses. Unless that assistant had actually fallen in love with her boss.

The lump in her throat was hard to swallow. Regan was in love with Zach. She knew that. She'd admitted that to herself. She'd admitted it to her father and her brothers. But she had yet to admit it to him. Why was it so hard? He'd told her he loved her. He'd asked her to tell him. He'd even said he could see it in her eyes, yet she hadn't said the words.

The words. Regan had said them before. She'd said them aloud to another man that she thought she loved. Correction, she had loved him. Regan had loved him with everything that she was. The kicker was she thought he had loved her too.

Didn't she have a beachfront condo in Maui? Didn't she sport a diamond on her finger that was no less than two and a half karats? Necklaces, earrings, dresses, purses, and shoes made her look like the proper woman he was grooming her to be.

When Michael Hamilton was around her, he doted on her. They shared a bed. They shared an office. They shared a life until...

God, even now, as she dipped her head into the water and held her breath, she couldn't think of how quickly it had fallen away from her. She'd stood before him, her stomach stretched with pregnancy, expecting his child, and he'd told her he was through with her right before the first punch threw her back, crashing through a glass table.

As she surfaced for air and gasped to fill her lungs, she ran her hand over her stomach and the scar that Zach had asked about. Tears spilled down her cheeks.

Michael had set up a nursery. He'd bought her maternity clothes and a necklace with a baby bootie embedded with a blue sapphire to mark the due date of their child. At night, he'd laid by her side with his hand on her stomach, rubbing it so gently. Michael Jonathon Hamilton III would be his son's name. She could still see the glimmer in his eyes when he said it.

Regan's head began to pound. The wine had made her light-headed, and she thought it would be best to remove herself from the water.

She slipped into her pajamas and crawled into bed. The pillow next to her smelled of Zach, and she breathed in deeply. She needed to shake off her memories and find the courage to embrace her new reality.

Then, as though she'd willed it, the telephone rang and it was Zach on the other end.

"I'm in Phoenix having my shoes shined," he told her.

"Phoenix, having yours shoes shined? Why?"

"We had to make an emergency landing. There was a sick passenger. Hence, the shoes shined. The guy next to me didn't fare as well. He has to buy a new suit."

"That's horrible. I hope the passenger is okay."

"I think the original sick one is okay. It started a chain reaction." He laughed. "But I'll be out of here in a few minutes. I just missed you and wanted to call."

"I'm glad you did." She tried to keep her voice steady, but it shook, and she knew he would notice.

"Regan, are you all right?"

"I'm fine. I just found that I was already missing you terribly." She wiped her wet eyes with the back of her hand.

"Is that all?"

"Yes," she lied.

He grumbled. "This is the last time I have to come this way alone. From now on, you'll be by my side, and dammit, if he doesn't want to deal with my people, he'll have to work with someone else. I'm tired of this jerk, and hell, I haven't even gotten to his office yet." He vented with a few choice words, which the executive rarely did, and it made her laugh. Zach groaned. "Oh, Regan, wait until you meet him. You'll understand."

"Who is he anyway? A movie star. Oh, Zach, tell me who he is." Her voice had lifted, and it felt good to share a laugh with the man she loved.

"Breach of contract," he said.

"And contracts are very important to you." She lost the edge of humor and her tone became serious.

"They are our livelihood."

"I guess you're right, then." She slid down into the bed and sighed. "The pillow still smells of you."

Zach let out a gusty breath. "I'd give anything to be there with you." He shuffled the phone. "Regan, I have to go. They just called my flight. I'll call you in the morning. I love you." The phone disconnected, and she was alone again with her thoughts.

CHAPTER 36

*R*egan and John Forrester spent most of the day with plans and contracts sprawled out over the conference table. They had to go to Memphis with a precise picture of what was supposed to be done, what hadn't been done, and what they needed to do about it. Regan typed a letter dismissing Roger Byers from his position; Zach, always gracious, had given word to the accounting department to cut Roger Byers a severance check.

They ate at Frank's for lunch and sat at the stone tables overlooking the river.

John scooped chili from his hot dog with a spoon. "You sure you know your way to the site?"

"I know the way. I have your number as well."

"Good. We'll meet there right at nine. That'll give us all day to get done what needs to be done," he said, and she nodded, looking out over the lawn toward the tree where she'd sat with Zach on her first day.

Her mind wandered to the thought of the green in his eyes and sandy hair. She'd been doomed the moment that bus jerked her off her feet.

John shoved a bite of his hot dog into his mouth. "You know you read like a book."

"Excuse me?"

He swallowed his bite and wiped his mouth. "You miss him."

"John, I…"

"Can't hide what you're thinking," he finished her sentence, then he sipped his Coke. "I told him months ago I thought you were a keeper. He is too, you know."

"I know he is. I'm just not ready to tell him that—yet."

"Why not?"

Regan shook her head. "I have my reasons. Just, please, don't say anything to him."

John reached for her hand and covered it with his. "Won't say a word. "

"Thank you. Carlos says nothing has been even whispered on the site."

"Ah, so this has been going on for a while?" He raised his eyebrows and smiled.

She felt the heat begin to rise in her cheeks. "Since Dallas. Oh, hell, since the morning I started. I was on the bus with him, it jerked, and I literally rode to work on his lap. Literally," she said again.

"That'll be something to tell your grandkids." He laughed with a wink, but she stiffened and dropped her eyes to her lunch. "I'm sorry. I didn't mean…"

"It's okay." She shook it off. "It's nothing."

"I've been around him most of his life. He's a hard worker. When he wants something, he goes after it." He took another bite of his hot dog and took a few seconds to wipe a blob of chili from his chin. "Are you ready for that? Are you ready to be the one he's gone after?"

"You make it sound like he's never gone after another woman before."

"It should sound like that, because that's the truth."

Regan put down her hot dog and looked at him. He was telling the truth, she could read it in his eyes. "He's never been in love before?"

"No, I don't think he has. Lust maybe, but never love."

"Lust?"

"Uh-huh."

"Simone Pierpont?" She had to ask. After all, it was obvious to her there was some involvement with the woman.

John just laughed and shook his head before finishing his hot dog.

She wasn't sure how to take that, but she didn't want to ask too many questions either.

"So you're not married?" She finally asked him a personal question.

"Nope. Wife walked out on me ten years ago, and I've never looked back."

"I'm sorry to hear that." She picked at her hot dog. "You haven't dated since then?"

"Oh, Audrey has tried to get me to see people. I tell you what, I'm just not interested." He finished off his soda. "Divorced people my age are cranky about the whole dating thing. Women want their equality, and I'm all for that, don't get me wrong." He threw up his hands to ward off any offensive words he might have spoken. "What I mean is it's 'I'll meet you there, I'll pay for half, I don't want any commitments except for you to wear a condom.'"

Regan choked on her soda, and he patted her back a few times.

"Women don't want to be taken care of anymore," he said in a tone that was a dead ringer for Eyeore's. "On the weekends I fish. Three weeks a year, I take a vacation. I'm happy."

"Well, if the right woman ever comes along, I'd bet you'd make one wonderful husband."

"What are you doing the rest of your life?" he teased and Regan wadded her napkin and threw it at him.

By Thursday afternoon Zach had played three rounds of golf with friends of his investor, had lunch at the country club, and met an A-list actress, who looked annoyed he hadn't drooled over her hand, but who never actually spoke to him upon introduction. What he hadn't done was meet face-to-face with the principal investor. Instead, he'd been scheduled with acquaintances of the man, more potential investors. His patience was wearing thin.

The guy was fronting over seventy percent of the build. He couldn't just ignore him and walk away from the deal. But he was a busy man and tired of games. And dammit he wanted to be with Regan.

Zach shifted from his chair in the lobby while he waited for the investor's driver to pick him up. He was surprised to see the man walk through the door himself.

"Mr. Benson, I'm so very sorry for my delays. I hope you can forgive me." He removed his arm from the waist of the sophisticated blonde at his side and shook Zach's hand. "It's our first anniversary, and I have been trying to make it very special."

"Congratulations." Zach supposed he should cut the guy some slack, since he knew what it was like to be distracted by the woman he loved. "I appreciate your taking the time to meet me."

"Yes, as we are hurrying out of town, I wanted to meet with you." He shifted his gaze to his wife. "Sit and we will return." She only nodded as her husband turned and started for the bar.

Zach stood a moment longer before following him. How could a woman just be dismissed like that and accept it? He'd never treat his wife like that. Then again, if he did, Regan would kick his ass.

He couldn't help but smile when he realized he'd melded thoughts of marriage and Regan. Regan as his wife. For him, the emotional commitment had already happened.

The investor stopped before him, his eyes narrow and hard. "Is there something funny, Mr. Benson?"

"No." He composed his features and gestured to the hotel's bar. "We should get started."

The man was studying him, his dark eyes shadowed by dark brows. He was much shorter than Zach, but he gave the impression of being bigger than he was. Of being intimidating.

"You're thinking of a woman."

"Guilty." Zach shrugged as they seated themselves at a table in the bar. "But we're here to talk about the Golden Pacific Towers."

He studied Zach for another moment. "Is she beautiful?"

"Of course."

The waitress came to the table, and Zach ordered a whisky and Coke, and his companion a glass of red wine, then he dismissed her as quickly and as sharply as he had his wife.

"How long have you been with this woman?"

The casual talk between them amused Zach. There had never been anything but business before. Perhaps the self-important investor was human after all. He'd humor him for the sake of their business relationship. "A few months. It took a while to convince her to date her boss."

"I was in love with my assistant once," the investor said. His dark eyes seemed to cloud. "But she was a nobody. I married a woman who has made my worth increase."

The waitress laid down their drinks and Zach reached for his immediately. "Your wife is very beautiful."

"She is. But…" The man sipped his wine and Zach watched him carefully. Whatever it was about the woman who'd come before his wife, it still affected him. Anyone could see that.

The man took a long sip of his wine, then set it on the table. "About the building. I've gone over all the plans. I will have them sent back to you next week. Most of the changes I have asked for are for my suite and my offices."

"I'll look them over personally." He'd expected changes. The

187

bigger a man was in his own eyes, the more finicky he'd be about a build. This guy's list was sure to be long.

"I've met with the other investors. They like you and like your style." Zach was pleased to hear that after having spent so much time with them. "I want to meet with you the first part of August. We'll finalize everything with the other investors, and we'll get this project off the ground."

"Sounds good. I can't tell you how pleased Benson, Benson, and Hart is to be working with you again."

"I only use the best."

"Thank you." His heart swelled with satisfaction. The company his father and grandfather had built, and he continued, was the best.

"August." The man swirled his wine in the glass. "It's amazing how fast a year goes by. So many things can change."

"I agree." A year ago, Zach was working eighty-hour weeks and sleeping in the office most nights to prove to himself that he could handle the company after his father left.

After he met Regan, business had become secondary. All he thought of was her. And right now, all he thought of was how much he missed her.

They quietly finished their drinks then walked back to the lobby. When the investor's wife spotted him, she rose and hurried to his side.

"We will see you in August, then." He held his hand out to Zach.

"Again, congratulations on your anniversary." Zach shook his hand and then his wife's delicate one.

He looked down at his watch. It was eleven in Nashville. Regan would be sleeping. He would go back to his room, pack, and call to make arrangements. Perhaps he could fly out earlier and surprise her. Perhaps, he'd even pass his parents in the airport on their way to New York before retrieving his love and hurrying her off to their estate and making love to her all weekend long.

On the flight Zach's mind wandered back to his investor and to the deprecatory way he spoke of the woman who had been his assistant. He'd mentioned that he'd married well. Zach didn't envy the man's former assistant or his wife.

He settled in his seat. Marrying well, isn't that what his father had done when he'd married his mother? Or his grandfather and grandmother? Not as in wealth, but as in compassion and love.

Zach pressed his head into the seat back and closed his eyes. Marrying well. It's what he'd be doing if—when—Regan agreed to marry him.

He smiled as the plane flew him closer to Nashville and Regan.

CHAPTER 37

he drive to Memphis in traffic had spoiled Regan's mood. Her stomach had been in knots all night at thoughts about the meeting with Roger Byers. When she pulled into the lot and saw John standing beside his car waiting for her, her nerves settled. On the drive she'd nearly forgotten she wouldn't be alone. John would be there and everything would be fine.

"You made it." He handed her a cup of coffee and smiled.

"I did, and thank you." She sipped from the cup. The coffee was bitter and cold. "You've been waiting a long time."

"I got here an hour ago." He rolled his shoulders. "I didn't sleep very well. This shit always makes me nervous."

"I didn't sleep well either. This doesn't look to be a wonderful day, does it?"

"That'll depend on how you look at it. When it's all over, I'm going back to a nice hotel, using their gym and pool, and having dinner brought to my room." He winked. "All charged to Zach."

Regan laughed. "That does sound good."

John put his arm around her shoulders as they walked toward the office. She was comforted by his touch, and that was a welcome feeling. A man's arm around her would usually have her flinching, but she liked John. The woman who would turn his head would be a very lucky one indeed.

"And what are your plans for the weekend?" he asked and her cheeks filled with color. "Oh, Zach is coming home tonight. You have plans."

She laughed and nipped him on the cheek with a kiss. "You are bad, John Forrester." She enjoyed his friendship immensely. He was good to have around for everyone.

Roger Byers stood at his office window and peered through the blinds. Look at that, she was cozy with the foreman too. Whore. What a cushy job she must have while he was in a hot trailer busting his ass.

He shook it off. He knew this was his last day on the job. Those goddamned workers he had were doing a shit-poor job, and he was going to pay for it. Who the hell needed Zach Benson and all his money anyway? And what the hell did that man do in a day? He fucked his assistant on the desk then sent her and his henchman to fire him? They'd all pay for that.

He watched as they started up the steps. He could almost smell her before he could see her. That floral scent she wore had stuck in his head the first time she crossed her legs in front of him and took notes from her boss.

When John opened the door, Roger wanted to punch his fist right into his face. He knew who John Forrester was. The entire organization knew who the ass-kisser was. And when he showed up on your site, your job was over—and he'd get the glory for finishing up.

Roger's blood boiled when they stepped into the trailer, but he smiled and welcomed them back.

He coolly eyed Regan in her professional attire. She was pretty. Not as pretty as he'd seen them, but she was okay. What she saw in the rich asshole boss and the old man foreman was beyond him.

"Have a seat. I don't have any fresh coffee, but we have some tea." He hardly recognized his own voice trying to sound so nice to the asshole and the whore.

"Let's just get down to business," John said directly as he set his files on the desk and then sat in the chair.

Regan sat next to John as he pulled out the reports. The muscles in her neck had instantly tensed the moment she'd seen Roger Byers standing in the doorway. The very sight of him made her sick to her stomach.

Watching him smugly sit behind his desk while John showed him every report and every violation that had been red flagged on the job made her even angrier. Regan kept notes on the meeting. Every question Roger Byers had and every answer John gave him were documented in her notes to share with Zach when he returned.

The few times she'd caught Roger's eye, he was staring at her. The uneasy feeling washed over her, and she wondered what had possessed Zach to hire a man like him. There was a prickle of fear that sank into her gut each time he spoke to her.

"Now, let's head up and take a visual." John gathered his hardhat and notebook. "Regan, you stay here and organize the reports. We'll be right back down."

After one last searing glance from Roger Byers, the men left the trailer.

Regan let out a breath and sank into the chair. The man made her skin crawl and her stomach churn. And the anger in his eyes when he'd looked at her—that was a sight in a man she'd hoped never to see again. She was pleased that John didn't want her with them up on the top floor of the building, but she wasn't too happy to know he was up there with the man either.

John and Roger were out of the trailer only thirty minutes, but when they came back and John slammed through the door, she knew there were more problems with the site than he'd thought.

"Regan, can I speak to you outside?" John held open the door for her, and she gathered her bag and followed him.

He paced for a moment, and when they both looked back at the trailer, the blinds dropped. He'd been watching them.

John took off his hardhat and wiped his brow with the back of his hand. "I'm going to let him go, and I don't want you here for it. Get back to Nashville and to the office. This place is filled with violations. Some of them weren't listed on the inspection sheet, and that bothers me. Let Zach know what's going on and that I'm on the job. I'll brief him when he gets back."

"I'm sorry this has to happen like this," she said, touching his arm.

"Oh hell, I've been doing this for thirty years. The first guy Zach's grandfather had me fire tried to push me off the side of a building. I fire people from the ground now." He smiled, but it didn't hide his nervousness. "I'll see you Monday."

John waited until Regan had driven away before going back into the musty, hot office trailer, wary that Roger Byers might be waiting for him with a heavy, blunt object in his hand. When he walked back through the door, Byers was gone. But he knew the man had made his peace. Plans and drawings were shredded and scattered among the remnants of the desk drawers. The coffeepot had been smashed against the wall, and he'd even taken the time to scrawl I quit! Bastard! Whore! on the wall in red marker.

He'd made quick work of it. John took his digital camera from his pocket and documented the mess and the wall. As far as he was concerned, Roger Byers had quit and left his letter of resignation on the wall. That was cheaper for Benson, Benson, and Hart. You didn't have to pay out as much when the man walked off the job. Especially if he said he quit, in writing no less. He knew Zach's grandfather would have been laughing too.

Zach wasn't surprised when each of her family members called her the moment she'd been released from the hospital. He'd heard Curtis on the phone with Carlos only moments before Curtis turned to him and threatened to take him out to the parking lot and kick the crap out of him if she ever got hurt again. But he found Curtis wasn't any more forthcoming with details than his sister was on their earlier conversation.

Word sped to New York as Tyler and Audrey waited to meet Arianna after her show.

Security had called Tyler Benson, since he still owned the building. He called Zach.

Zach, who had stood firm in his insistence that Regan not be alone yet, drove up the road toward his parents' house with her by his side. He adjusted his phone on his ear as he looked over at Regan. "She's fine. She got knocked around by Roger Byers."

"I never did like that man working for us," his father admitted.

"Well he doesn't anymore," Zach assured him. "John took care of that."

But now, looking at Regan, he wondered at what expense. He should have never hired that man to run the project. One slip in judgment had almost cost him everything he cherished.

CHAPTER 38

*R*egan returned to the office in the early afternoon. It had taken the better part of the drive back to Nashville to calm her nerves. Certainly, she was uncomfortable with John still being on the site. He had, however, called and told her that Roger Byers had quit and that, she decided, was why her nerves had recovered.

She thought she'd finish the items on her list and then head back to the house early to pack for the weekend Zach had conned her into. She couldn't help but smile when she thought of the boulder in the creek. Perhaps they could make use of it after all, and Audrey wouldn't know a thing.

Regan gathered items she needed to lay on Zach's desk and walked into his office. The fragrance hit her before the awareness that here were a dozen white roses in a vase in the middle of his desk. Panic struck and hit her in the gut. Who was sending him roses?

Well, really, why should she care? She hadn't promised him the world or even said she loved him. Perhaps it was for the best, but she sure as hell was going to look at the card.

Guilt plagued her when she noticed the envelope read Regan.

She shook her head and bit her lip as she pulled the card from the envelope.

Detention! You must stay at work until six o'clock! Do not leave the building! Do not try to escape! Do not go home and pack! I'll be back early. Our weekend is here.

I love you, Zach.

Regan shook her head and breathed in the fragrance of the roses.

She looked at her watch. It was four thirty. That was just enough time to get the rest of her copies made and filed. Compose the e-mails she had to finish and freshen up. She'd be ready for him all right. If he was starting their weekend with flowers, she sure was going to make him glad he did.

WHEN REGAN TURNED off her computer, the office was completely empty. She looked out into the hallway—not a soul. She shut the door to her office and walked into Zach's, unbuttoning her blouse.

Imagine the look on his face when he returned to find her waiting for him in her bra and panties on the couch. The thought of his eyes opening wide and his jaw dropping before he'd move to her warmed her to the core.

When she walked through the door to his office, it shut behind her.

She heard someone breathing.

She spun and saw Roger Byers turning the lock. Her heart slammed in her chest.

"What are you doing here?" Her voice quivered as she backed toward Zach's desk, fumbling to refasten her blouse with one hand because she was still holding the papers.

"What am I doing here? I've come to get even." He eyed her chest and spat on the carpet. "Whore."

"I...I don't know what you're talking about." Her breath

hitched as she tossed the papers onto the desk and finally managed her buttons. He walked closer to her, and her hip bumped the desk. "You really need to go. Zach—Mr. Benson will be back any moment."

An evil smile settled his lips as he stepped even closer. "That's what you think."

"He told me he'd be here." Regan scanned the room for a sign that Zach had been there. The card wasn't in his handwriting. Were they from him? Was it a setup? Her heart rate accelerated.

Roger nodded his head as he took one more step toward her and leered down her body. "You're not the only one gonna pay for this."

"Pay?" He stood so close to her she could smell onions and hard alcohol on his breath.

"You whore. You think you can fuck the boss and the foreman, and I don't get my share?" He snaked his arm behind her head and pulled her hair, yanking her head back.

She wanted to lift her head, keep her eyes on him, but he held her so tightly she could only see the ceiling. He scraped his nail down her throat, sending pain through her. "I'm getting my share. It's just not fair that they all get a share of you and I don't. You just look at me with those glossy, hateful eyes like you're so much better than me. Well, sister, now you're mine." He crushed his mouth onto hers. His teeth scraped against her lip and his fingers continued to pull at her hair. She tried to turn her head, but he kept hold of her hair, tugging sharply as he pressed his unshaven cheek to hers.

He pulled her hair again, forcing her to bend backward over Zach's desk as he released her mouth from his. His other hand clamped over her breast. When she whimpered, he tore open her shirt and clawed at her flesh.

"Stop! Stop!" she begged as he pushed his body up against hers. She tried to use her hands to force him away, struck at him with her fists, but he was like a bulldozer, ramming at her, yanking her by her hair until she couldn't defend herself.

"Bitch!" His hands were on her skirt, hiking it up. She tried to push him away again, but he hit the side of her head. Her ear rang with the force of the blow, and then he hit her once more before he pinned her legs with his own. "This will only hurt a lot." He licked her cheek and then bit her lip.

Regan's lip stung and she tasted blood in her mouth. Her eyes throbbed from the blows he'd landed, and her head swam in confusion and pain. She knew she could survive the rape he was planning. She could block it from her mind as she'd blocked so many other things, she thought as she felt her consciousness slipping. But did the man really plan to walk away from her afterward? No, that wasn't usually the case. Fear cramped her stomach. She turned her head away.

Roger gripped her chin tightly, forcing her to look at him. "Don't tell me you're thinking of him while you're with me." He slammed the back of his hand across her cheek. She staggered as he unbuttoned his pants.

Her vision had gone cloudy, and the vile metal taste of blood filled her mouth. The room around her spun, and she was going down. She felt it. Damn it, she'd been in this position before. She'd lost consciousness at the hands of a man who'd meant to kill her. She'd be damned if she did it again. She wasn't going down this time, not without a fight. As he pushed against her, she felt her way over Zach's desk with her hand. There had to be a weapon.

When her hand came across the letter opener, she knew she had one. Right next to it was the key to the elevator she'd refused to take, which would be her escape if she could make it that far. She didn't pick them up yet. When she did, she would need to take him by surprise.

When he pushed her back onto the desk, Regan casually slid

the letter opener behind her back and closed her fingers around the handle.

He stepped toward her. Leered, breathing in her face. Shoved her skirt aside and braced one arm on the desk.

When he was only a moment from taking what he'd come for, she mustered all her energy and plunged the opener into his shoulder.

Roger pushed back with a scream. A red stain spread around the wound. "Bitch! You stabbed me!"

She took the vase of flowers from the desk and hurled it at his head. The vase hit him in the side and crashed to the floor. Glass shards shot out over them both and the roses lay scattered on the floor.

Regan grabbed the key, ran for the elevator, and pushed the button, watching over her shoulder as Roger staggered to his feet. As he found balance on his knees, the door opened. Regan fell inside, pushed buttons, and turned the key trying to get the doors to close quickly. He was on his feet, the letter opener still lodged in his shoulder. He moved toward her as she pushed buttons and more buttons. Their eyes met.

"Go to hell!" she yelled as the door finally moved. An unexpected strength welled up inside her. She had won, and now his gaze was fearful and angry.

The door closed, and the elevator began to descend.

Tears burned her eyes immediately. Her breath was escaping her. She looked at her arms. They were bloody from the glass that had flown from the broken vase. Her head throbbed, her mouth bled, and her vision was growing dark.

She slid down the wall of the elevator. Her mind focused enough to know she had to crawl from the elevator. She couldn't lose consciousness. It would only be a matter of him hitting a button to have the elevator head back his way.

As the door opened, she worried that she would pass out

before she could exit, so she hit the alarm to stop it from closing and carrying her back up to the office.

She saw a man's shoes, and she crawled backward. Her vision fogged again. She had been so close to getting away. Footsteps pursued her into the elevator.

"Regan." But it was Zach's voice, not Roger's. He dropped everything in his arms and rushed to her.

"Roger... Byers. Up in your office." It was all she could say. The world slipped into darkness.

CHAPTER 39

Zach gathered Regan into his arms, carried her to the car, and called security. Even before they left the parking garage, he could hear sirens from the building and from approaching police cars. The authorities would deal with Roger Byers. He'd see to that. He'd press charges, and he'd see that she pressed her own as well. No one would ever hurt her again.

How could he have let this happen to her, he wondered as he put her in the car. He'd carelessly sent her into danger. She'd never forgive him. He'd never forgive himself.

"Regan, honey, stay with me," he said as he set her in the car and hurried to the other side. Tears stung his eyes and panic shook his hands as he started the car and backed out of the space.

She wasn't responding to him. What had that bastard done to her?

THE EMERGENCY ROOM was abuzz with chaos from an ambulance that arrived. Regan was groggy, in and out of consciousness as Zach carried her through the doors. Her eyes were swollen, her clothes a mess, and her lips were covered in dried blood. Certainly they wouldn't make her wait to see a doctor.

When Curtis walked around the corner and saw him there with his sister draped over his arms, Zach's heart leapt into his throat.

"Oh, God!" Curtis rushed to them. He called for nurses and was already pulling Zach through the secured doors toward a bed, where he laid Regan down. "Jesus Christ! What the hell happened?"

All Zach could do was watch as Curtis looked her over and nurses rushed to her. "I don't know. I found her in the elevator like this. I was just on my way to pick her up." He dragged his trembling hands through his hair as Curtis flashed a light into her eyes and she winced.

"Sweetheart, come back to me." Curtis delicately touched her face.

As Regan stirred on the bed, Zach noticed all the buttons on her blouse were torn off. He felt violently ill, and his knees went weak. God, she'd been raped.

He tried to be calm, tried to be strong for her, but the sounds of the ER retreated and he couldn't see. Curtis eased him to the floor and made him put his head between his knees.

"Are you all right?"

"What happened to her?" Zach demanded, his skin cold and clammy.

"We're going to check her out. I'm taking her to a room." Curtis motioned to a nurse. "You take care of him. We'll be in six." After he gave her the room number, Curtis pushed Regan's bed out of the ER.

It took an hour to have her examined. He hadn't gotten word on her condition, but he had received a phone call from his security force letting him know that Roger Byers had been arrested. The news gave him a grim satisfaction.

When the phone rang again and it was John Forrester, he couldn't control the fear in his voice as he had with his security guard.

"John, are you okay?"

"I'm fine. What the hell happened? What did he do to her?" John's voice trembled as much as Zach's had.

"He attacked her in my office. I don't know much more. She's beaten and barely conscious. Dammit, every button on her shirt was ripped off."

"No." The quake in John's voice made Zach sick. "That son of a bitch! I could kill him."

He looked up to see the nurse headed toward him. "I'll call you when I know more." He disconnected the call and the nurse finally led him to Regan's room. She was sleeping, and Curtis paced the floor.

"This took too long. I've made a dozen calls to get someone she'd be more comfortable with to examine her, and I'm still fucking waiting."

As worried as Zach had been that Curtis would assume the worst when he saw Zach carry her in, he was glad that at least she was beyond the lobby and Curtis was taking care of her. "Is she okay?" Zach's voice still cracked.

Curtis shot him a fierce glance. "Does she look okay to you?"

Zach looked at her. She was almost unrecognizable now that the swelling had begun. His stomach clenched.

"No." No, she looked horrible, and seeing the marks on her legs and her torn shirt on the chair next to him, he wondered just how bad things were. What had Roger Byers done to the woman he loved? Had he taken her against her will?

Regan stirred, and Curtis hissed out a breath.

"I feel lousy," she said hoarsely.

Curtis moved to her, blocking out Zach. Who'd blame him?

Zach wasn't her family, and by the look Curtis had given him when he'd seen him walk through the door, he blamed Zach for what happened to his sister. Curtis touched her face and then kissed her forehead. "I gave you something to calm you. You're fine. This was a lousy way to end my shift."

She tried to lift her head and looked around the room. "Where's Zach?"

"I'm here." He moved from behind Curtis and ventured closer to her bed. The bruises on her face were surfacing, and it wrenched his gut to think that because of him Roger Byers had used his fists on her.

She reached her hand out for him. "I'm sorry, Zach."

"Oh, sweetheart, no." He moved closer to her, tears stinging his eyes. "This isn't your fault." The sinking feeling in his chest was that it was completely his fault.

"What happened to him?"

"They have him. The police have him." He wiped at his eyes, knowing he needed to be strong for her and not to fall apart.

"John—is he all right?"

"Yes, John is fine. Byers came after you," he said. He had spoken to the arresting officer again only moments earlier. "He was making his point to John and me by hurting you. God, Regan, how bad did he hurt you?"

"I just got knocked around," she said. "I stabbed him with your letter opener." He nodded and a weak, yet proud, smile settled on his lips. They had told him Byers was injured.

Curtis stepped up to the bed. "Reg, they didn't find anything that would indicate he raped you. But did he?"

Regan folded her arms over her chest and let out a sigh. "No. He never got the chance."

Zach saw the barely contained anger in her brother's eyes—directed at him. Curtis scrubbed his hands over his face. "Dammit, Regan. I didn't want to see you like this again. How is it

I keep finding you lying in hospital rooms battered and beaten? Is this a way of life for you?"

Her eyes held fire in them as she rose in her bed. She winced. "Curtis, shut up. This is not the place or time for this."

"When is? When I have to identify you in the morgue?"

That socked the wind out of Zach, and he turned toward Curtis. "She protected herself. I don't think upsetting her is helping her."

"Let me tell you what's going to upset her and the rest of us." He pushed out his chest and met Zach's eye. "When we find her dead because of some asshole who thought he could use her for a punching bag."

"That isn't going to happen," Regan argued, her voice raspy and angry. "And Zach didn't do this. It had nothing to do with him."

"Like hell, Reg. That man was trying to get to him by hurting you. A few more minutes and you would have been raped. A moment after that you'd be dead."

"I'm neither," she argued.

"No, but you can't go through this again. Think about last time. Look at what you almost lost. Then we almost lost you. It wasn't worth it."

Regan shifted a look from her brother to Zach. The fear was back in her eyes, and Zach felt like an outsider, confused at their anger and their conversation.

Regan pushed down her sheet and pointed a stern finger at her brother. "One more word, Curtis Keller, and I walk out of this hospital."

He threw his arms in the air and stormed out of the room. Zach knew Curtis blamed him for what had happened to her. He blamed himself. But they'd been fighting about more than this attack by Roger Byers.

CHAPTER 40

Zach sat quietly by her side. He stroked her hand, the traces of blood on her skin accusing him. "I'm sure they'll let you go in a few hours. We'll head out to my parents' house, and I'll take care of you. It'll be a good place for you to rest. You need rest, Regan. In fact, I think you should take off next week. We've been working really hard. I've probably worked you harder than I ever worked Mary Ellen. I'll make arrangements for a replacement for the week and then—"

"Would you shut up too?" She lay back against the bed.

"I'm sorry." He just wanted to take care of her, more now than he ever had wanted to take care of anyone.

"Just take me home," she insisted.

"No. I'll take you with me. I'll take care of you, and you'll breathe fresh air and be safe in my arms this weekend."

She shook her head and covered her eyes with her arm.

He didn't understand why she was shutting herself away from him. "Dammit, Regan, I'm so sorry." The calm had torn away, and tears fell freely down his face. "I am so sorry this happened."

"It's not your fault."

"It is. He attacked you to get back at me for firing him. John said he trashed the office and snuck out while John was at the car with you. God, Regan, he hurt you, and that's my fault."

She sat silently for a moment shaking her head. "But he didn't get me. I'm fine. I'll be fine in a few days and no worse for the wear."

"But look at you."

"I know." Her voice was angry. Guilt filled him and he couldn't push it away.

He smoothed his hand over hers. "What was Curtis talking about earlier?"

"My big-mouthed brother talks more than he should. Don't worry about it."

"I love you, Regan. I have no intention of ever hurting you. You know that, right?" She nodded. "Then don't hurt me by lying to me."

"I'm fine." She turned away from him on the bed. "I just want to go home."

The Bensons' home was as warm and inviting as she'd remembered. Zach turned on lights as they walked through the hallway toward the kitchen. His hand was on the small of her back, and she was glad she'd come. She liked feeling him close by.

"I'll get you a drink," he offered

"Just water."

Regan rested against the counter and looked out over the darkness of the acreage behind the house. She let herself out the sliding glass doors onto the porch. The air was warm and still. Stars sparkled bright above her, and she found a moment's peace beneath them.

A house on sprawling Tennessee land with a porch that wrapped around it was calming just in thought. Being there, she felt at home. If it were her home, there would be two rocking chairs, one for her and one for her husband, and children would run about the fields laughing and playing.

She ran her hands up her arms and winced as she brushed the

cuts. A soft breeze brushed over her face, against the tender skin on her cheek. At the hospital, she'd taken a moment to look at herself, and she knew she'd look worse in the morning.

Curtis was right. She too was tired of seeing herself like this. This time it had nothing to do with her. Roger Byers was crazy. But the bruises would heal and the cuts were superficial. Nothing was lost this time.

She ran her hands over her stomach and breathed in slowly.

"Your water, my dear." Zach joined her on the porch and handed her the glass. "You're beautiful when you're looking at the stars."

"Thank you." She sipped the water and felt herself calm. "It's so pretty here. I had thought of our weekend earlier today." She moved closer to him, laying her hand on his chest.

"And what did you think?"

"I was thinking we could make love on that boulder in the creek, and your mother wouldn't know."

"Oh, she'd know." He laughed, then his eyes softened. "I had many plans too, but for tonight I want you lying beside me in my room. I want to hold you and protect you and know you'll be there when I wake."

"I'll accept your offer." She rose and kissed him gently, pulling back quickly when her lip stung from the cuts. "I'm exhausted."

"I have the pills your brother sent for you. Do you need something?"

"No. I'm okay," she lied, because she didn't want pills. She only wanted the arms of the man she loved to be wrapped around her and holding her through the night.

CHAPTER 41

Zach spent the night holding Regan and keeping her safe, as he'd promised. He woke before she did and watched her sleep for an hour before the morning sun crept through the drapes, and her eyelids finally fluttered against the light.

He brushed her lips with his and pulled her close to him as gently as he could. Her face now showed the signs of the struggle she'd had the day before, and it wrenched in his gut like a knife. There wasn't any part of what had happened that he didn't personally blame himself for. He may not have been the force that physically hurt her, but he'd been behind it just the same. She should never have gone to the site with John. He should have fired Byers months ago and not waited until the situation came to a head.

Things had never been like that before. When something needed tending to, he took care of it. He was shoveling off his duties. He was putting people in harm's way, and why? Because he'd fallen in love, and his mind wasn't focused on his business.

When she shifted in his arms, the scent of her rushed through him. He closed his eyes and enjoyed the feeling of having her close. Zach had never been in love before, never had the whole world slip from his fingers. But he had to be realistic. First, as much as he loved her and wanted to hear the words from her, they weren't coming. Second, he had the L.A. project to think about. It would be the biggest build the company had ever acquired. He needed to be focused when it came down to it. Even his love for Regan couldn't get in the way. There was too much at stake.

When Zach felt the softness of Regan's lips on his, he opened his eyes. She gazed at him solemnly, her hair curtaining her face. "It's Saturday morning, and you are thinking too hard."

"You're right. I was." He touched her hair and then ran his fingers through it. "I'm starving."

Regan lifted her head, and concern shadowed her eyes. "Please tell me your mother keeps groceries in the house."

He pushed back his shoulders and considered. He hadn't even thought about filling the house with food for the weekend after everything that had happened. "I... well, I don't know. We'll go look and see what we can find. We may be having caviar and champagne for breakfast.

Regan eased backward onto her pillow and lifted the back of her hand to her forehead. "If we must," she teased, and then she sat up and planted a warm kiss on his lips. His body temperature rose and so did other parts of him. Looking at her, her face dark with bruises, he couldn't bring himself to touch her yet. The thought of hurting her sank into his gut and burned.

He found her a robe made of silk, which would be soft against her skin. After crawling around on the floor, looking under his own bed like a dog, he found her a pair of slippers that, though unfashionable with the robe, would keep her feet warm on the cold tile floor. Then they headed toward the kitchen on an adventure to find food.

Regan seemed pleased to find that Audrey had a stocked pantry as well as the refrigerator. She pulled out a carton of eggs, a package of bacon, and a container of cream. "Oh, a big breakfast. This is just what I need."

"I swear to you, if you don't pour it into a bowl and add milk to it, I don't know what to do with it." He perched himself on the island counter and swung his feet carelessly, watching her and trying to be calm and normal around her when all he wanted to do was hold her and nurse her cuts.

"I bet if your mother saw you right now, she would put you over her knee."

She couldn't see her own face to know how it tore him apart to look at her. He watched as she moved about the kitchen, finding ingredients to make a meal as if nothing had happened. He admired her strength. "You know my mother all too well. And you know she could get away with it too."

Regan searched the cabinet under the stove for a pan. "She knew we were staying here, didn't she?" She lifted her eyebrows at him as she set the pan on the stove.

"Well, my father did. I would assume the fact that there are edible items in the kitchen was his doing."

"I love your father." She moved to the counter, opened the eggs, and began hunting for a mixing bowl.

This normalcy was such a farce. Didn't she see what she was doing to herself? Zach jumped down from where he sat and reached for her arm. "Careful, Regan. You just might stumble on something."

"What are you talking about?" She looked down at where his hand gripped her arm, and he realized he was probably hurting her. He quickly let go.

"So careless for you to use those words when you won't tell me you love me."

He knew as soon as the words slipped out of his mouth, they'd hurt her more than if he'd hit her.

"Oh, Zach, really." She turned back toward her eggs, but he spun her around again. This time he crushed his lips to her, gathered her in his arms, then deepened the kiss. How was it he could hurt and be in love? He wanted to hear the words. He needed to know that the woman he loved, loved him back.

"Tell me you love me," he pleaded, but her eyes grew dark.

"Zach..." his name was but a breath, and she pressed her fingers to her lips where his kissed her, and no doubt hurt her.

He couldn't stop. "Either you love me or you don't. You have to tell me one way or another." She said nothing and he shook his head. "It's not going to change how I feel, Regan. I love you, and I wish to hell you could tell me you love me too."

Her eyes were open wide, and he'd obviously caught her off guard with his bitterness. But he couldn't help himself. Pure, raw emotion charged through him, and he didn't know what to do with it. Never would he lash out at her physically, but because someone had, he would lose her.

Before he could hurt her again with his words or demand more from her than she could give, he turned and walked out of the house through the patio doors.

CHAPTER 42

*R*egan stood in the kitchen and watched Zach pace the patio. Her heart raced from his words, and her body ached from the strikes she'd taken the day before. She lifted her fingers to her lips, again. They stung from the cuts on them. They had swelled from the blows Roger Byers had dealt to her face. Zach's kiss should have soothed them, but it hadn't. It had made her angry with herself for not giving him what he really needed, confirmation of her love for him.

God, she did love him. She had come to grips with that. Why couldn't she tell him? She lifted a hand to her aching head and closed her eyes. Her cheeks were sore from where Roger Byers had hit her. Her arms still ached from where he'd grabbed her and bruised her. The cuts were visible reminders of what had happened only the day before. All because she loved Zachary Benson.

But nothing hurt as badly as her heart did when Zach stormed out the door. She saw him walking in the rose garden, and she took a deep, cleansing breath. It had been a year since Michael had left her for dead, just as Roger Byers had intended to do. It was time to put the pain of her past behind her.

She rested one hand on her stomach and the other on her cheek. It had been a hell of a year. She needed to move on.

A few minutes later, Regan walked to the entrance of the rose garden with a mug of coffee. Zach turned when he heard her, and she handed him the mug. "I made breakfast."

"Thanks." He took the mug and held her gaze, but he said nothing else. Finally she walked back to the house. When he followed her, a seed of hope grew inside her.

"It's only eggs, bacon, and toast. But I think it'll do." She picked up the plates she had readied and set them on the table.

They ate in silence.

When he was finished eating he gathered the plates. "I think I'll grab a shower. Feel free to make yourself at home." Then he disappeared up the stairs.

Regan cleaned up the rest of the breakfast dishes and pans. She refilled her coffee mug and headed out the back door, leaving it ajar so Zach would realize where she'd gone. It was time to show him she loved him.

She strolled down the path through the rose garden and out into the pasture, her pulse drumming faster as she headed toward the creek behind the trees. The air was already hot and thick. To sit and listen to the creek roll past her as she waited for Zach would be heaven.

Regan toed off her slippers and hiked up the robe as she stepped into the water. As it hit her ankles, a chill ran through her, but she braved it as she waded to the boulder in the center of the creek.

She sat atop the large stone and listened to the babble of the creek below her. The sun warmed her aching body and felt soothing on her face. It had almost been a year since Michael Hamilton had tried to kill her. Never in her wildest dreams would she have thought two different madmen would attack her. It made her uncomfortable in her own skin.

She wasn't weak. She wasn't fragile. But the attacks had

beaten her down. It had taken almost that entire year for her to regain who she was after Michael Hamilton had left his mark. She wasn't going to let that happen again.

She was in love with a truly decent man who wanted to take care of her for the rest of her life. There were no monetary promises. There were no one-sided conversations. Zach cared about her, and she wasn't going to let what Michael Hamilton or Roger Byers had done to her hold her back. Today was a new day, a day for her and Zach.

Regan rested her head against the stone and basked in the sun's warmth. She wasn't sure how long she'd been there when she heard the sound of footsteps among the trees. Then there he was, standing on the creek bank, looking out toward her, his hair, still wet from his shower. The T-shirt he'd pulled on was old and faded. The hems of his jeans dragged on the ground, and his feet were bare. She laughed at the fact that he'd walked through the field without any shoes on. In his parents' backyard he was absolutely at home.

He gave her a nod. "You wearing anything under that robe?" He watched her as though he were waiting for permission to touch her, and it just might kill him.

She loosened her belt. "Peeping Tom?"

"Peeping Zach," he said as he crossed the creek.

"You'd better see for yourself, then," she said, pulling one lapel down over her shoulder.

Zach climbed up the boulder and lay next to her. He gently touched her cheek and shook his head. She knew the look of guilt, and she regretted that he felt as though he'd had any part in her attack.

He slid his arm around her waist and gathered her in close. "I'm sorry for the way I acted this morning. It wasn't right. Especially after yesterday. I should have—"

"I love you, Zachary Benson." It floated from her lips like a sigh. "I love you."

His mouth opened wide, and she watched his Adam's apple move as he swallowed hard. "What?" His voice cracked like a teenager's, and Regan grinned.

"Oh, for heaven's sake. I have to repeat myself?"

Zach nodded, his mouth still open.

Tracing her fingers down his jaw, she said it again. "I love you."

He blew out a breath. "I wasn't expecting that."

"I know. I was sure things weren't going to work out. But I've decided it's time to move on. It's time to make them work out."

Zach lowered her to the rock and slid his hand beneath the robe and over her stomach, trailing his fingers to her hip. "I'm glad to hear that."

"One day at a time." She covered his mouth with hers and parted his lips with her tongue. The deeper she took the kiss, the closer he pressed his body against hers. The thickness of the robe protected her as the contours of the boulder pressed into her back. Zach lifted his hand to her hair and brushed his fingers through it.

Regan opened her eyes. When Zach's eyes locked onto hers, she cupped his face with her hands. "Make love to me here."

He pushed away the robe and his explored her with his hands. His fingertips skimmed her stomach, her sides, and breasts. Beneath his touch, her skin came to life. Blood hummed through her veins as her body heat rose. He pressed his lips to her throat as he cupped her breast in his hand, gently running his thumb over her erect nipple. Regan arched back. When he replaced his hand with his mouth, the very breath from her body released on a sigh.

She tugged the T-shirt free from his jeans and pulled it over his head. His smooth skin molded under her fingers as she traced his long, lean muscles. The sun warmed his back under her fingers.

He unbuttoned his pants and slid them off, returning quickly to her body with his lips, tongue, and touch.

He cupped her hips and pushed her legs apart with his body. Eagerly, she wrapped her legs around him, urging him closer. The thought of making love to a man had never enticed her the way it did now. Every heartbeat was too long to wait to have him inside her, on top of her, to be wrapped in his arms forever.

Then he moved into her.

She arched against him, feeling him slide against her, inside her. His lips skimmed her throat, his hands cupped her breasts, and she felt the warmth of him on her and in her. God, she loved the man.

She felt the roughness of the rock beneath her, on her back through her robe. She clung to Zach tighter, pulling him deeper inside her as he kissed her mouth with a passion that breathed new life into her. Their tongues danced, their teeth scraped, and their hands explored the wonders of one another's bodies. He trailed his fingertips over her exposed skin, and it tingled as he moved to each new area. Her heart beat rapidly, and she could feel his too as he pressed even closer to her. The sun rose higher in the sky and warmed their bodies as they melted together in unity. Every muscle in her body began to pulse as he moved against her, inside her, and his breath in her ear fed her life as she climbed toward that edge only Zach could drive her to. She held tight to him as he pushed deep inside her, and he moaned against her throat. Together they sighed and rode out the waves of their climax.

He lay heavy atop of her, and silently she willed him never to move.

Zach lifted his face and looked down at her. "I love you."

"I love you. I want to be with you always." She nuzzled her face into his neck and lay still, listening to the water move beneath them and the trees rustle in the wind.

Zach tucked a loose strand of hair behind her ear. "Are you all right?"

"Never better."

He gently brushed her lips with his. "Let's go in and take another shower." He smiled. "I have the strangest feeling my mother is going to call."

CHAPTER 43

*W*arm water ran over her already sensitive skin as Zach slathered soap over her body. She rested her back against his chest as he massaged soap over her breasts and then slid his hands down her stomach.

Regan turned and lathered her hands with the bar of soap. Slowly, she worked her hands over every inch of Zach's body, paying special attention to the parts of him begging to be touched. They washed each other, sliding their hands over one another's bodies, and making love again in the shower.

Zach tied the robe around Regan's waist. He shook his head and bit down on his bottom lip. "I've never done this in my parents' house."

Though a surge of hope lit in her, she could hardly believe a man as wealthy and handsome as Zach Benson had never taken advantage of what was at his fingertips to seduce a woman. "Liar."

"Really. Mom was always home, and we had a staff back then." The sincerity of his confession and the hours of lovemaking made her warm inside and out. There was a sense of pride in knowing she'd been the first to love Zach in a place that was so special to him. He wrapped his arms around her waist. "I wasn't allowed any privacy."

"She knew you were trouble." She could hear her cell phone beeping. Sighing, she went to find it. Zach's cell phone beeped too, and he walked to the desk in the corner of the room and opened it. Just as he dialed his voice mail, the house phone rang.

He dove across the bed and picked up the phone, laughing. "I told you. I told you. She knows when someone is messing around on that rock! You know, if I knocked you up, she'd know before I did."

Regan turned away. She didn't want him to see that when he talked like that it, tore her apart and reminded her there were so many things she hadn't been honest with him about.

She heard him answer the phone and turned to watch him. Though he was winded and knew his mother was on the other end of the phone, it didn't seem to matter to him what she'd think about it.

"Mother, how are you? How is New York?" He tugged at the robe wrapped around Regan and pulled her to the bed. He kissed her lip while covering the phone with his hand. She pushed him back and shook her head. Convincing him to make love on the boulder had turned him into a rebel. He grabbed for the tie on her robe. "I'm sorry I missed your call."

And then he stopped, sat up, and turned his attention to the conversation with his mother.

"Mother, what's wrong?" He was on his feet now, and Regan pulled the robe around her and watched his face. The intimacy slid away, as well as his color. "Oh my God."

He sat back down on the bed and pressed his fingers to his forehead. "Mom, I don't know what to say." Regan moved to his side. He shook his head as he listened to his mother. "I'll make arrangements and be out there in a few hours."

When Zach finally shifted his eyes to Regan's, she could see the tears welling up. She reached for his hand. "Mom, I can call

Arianna to sit with you." He gave Regan's fingers a squeeze, and she began to sob, not even knowing what was being said on the other side of the conversation. "I'll be there as soon as I can."

He hung up the phone and sat quietly. Regan didn't want to ask about the conversation. She'd wait until he could speak.

When he was ready, he looked her in the eye. "My father died."

His father was gone. The more he said it in his head, the worse it got. Regan pulled him to her, and then he let out his sob. Suddenly he was shaking and tears were streaming. He was a child again, he needed his mother, and his father, and neither were in his grasp.

He pulled away and went for his clothes. "I have to go to New York."

Regan stood, her shoulders shot back, and her professionalism pushed the sentimental lover aside. "I'll get arrangements made for you."

"For us." He looked at her, pleading. "God, Regan, you have to go with me."

"Zach…"

"You said on that rock you wanted to be with me always. Well, always is now." He slipped on his pants and went to her, taking her hands. "Please, my mother and I both need your cool head and way of thinking. You're part of our family. I want you with me."

She nodded. "Should I call Arianna?"

"She was with them when he died."

Regan's eyes widened and her eyebrows rose. He thought about the conversation with his mother and rubbed away the pain forming behind his forehead. "They'd met for brunch. They were laughing over mimosas and eggs Benedict. She and mom had hit it off. They were going to go shopping later. And then…" The words lodged in his chest. "He had a heart attack at the restaurant."

She raised her hand to her mouth. Tears streamed as freely from her eyes as they did from his own. He said took her face in his hands and wiped the wet trails away with his thumbs. "Regan, I need you. We are a family. My family and yours are already intertwined."

"Zach, what are you talking about?"

"You're always here when I need you most. Arianna was there for my mother. Carlos works for me and takes care of you. My mother and Curtis work together with the hospital bettering life for others. Our lives are knotted together." He took a step back and scrubbed his hands over his face. "I'm not proposing. That would be so uncalled for at this moment." He took a deep breath to try and separate the jumbled thoughts that clouded his mind. "But I feel closer to you than I ever have, and closer to you at this moment than I have been to anyone. I want us to make a life and a home together. I want you to think about it." He pulled his shirt on. "I need you," he said once more before he walked out of the room, praying she needed him too.

CHAPTER 44

*R*egan arranged their flight from Tyler's office. She booked a direct flight into New York City and arranged for a car to pick them up. She'd phoned the hospital, and Zach received the status on his father's body and was able to make arrangements to claim him and fly him back with them.

Zach knew where his father kept the important papers, and he opened the safe in the wall and handed them to Regan. Her breath caught as he entrusted her with the information and walked out of the office.

In her hands, she held Tyler's personal plans for being laid to rest. He'd thought of everything, but having had previous brushes with death, she assumed, he'd think of those things. Her cheek throbbed, reminding her that she too had had a few too many brushes with death. It wasn't something she even wanted to think about, but as she heard Zach move about the house packing for a trip he'd never wanted to take, she knew she'd better think about such things for herself. After all, she had a man who wanted to spend the rest of his life with her.

As Zach finished packing his bag, she looked over Tyler's

papers and made a list of people she would call on his mother's behalf, if Audrey would allow it. If she could help it, she wouldn't let Audrey touch any of the specifics, unless she wanted to. Something told Regan she would want to mourn her husband and would be grateful for her help.

Being Zachary Benson's executive assistant had taken on greater meaning as she made the few first phone calls to the mortuary. Giving the woman on the other end of the phone the information she had made her feel like less like an employee and more like a wife. It was a warm feeling at such a cold time.

Zach set his suitcase by the door of the office and looked at her. His eyes were hollow and his color pale. But as she discussed arrangements with the woman on the other end of the phone, a weak smile surfaced on Zach's lips. An appreciative smile. It was something no other man had made her realize before. He appreciated her for more than her organizational skills. He did need her, and she needed him.

At that very moment, she knew she was his forever.

Zach and Regan headed to Regan's house so she could pack her things. He drove faster than usual, and every thought he'd ever had regarding his father raced through his head. No matter how much he'd thought about his father's health in the past, and the times his dad had scared them with past heart attacks, Zach wasn't prepared to deal with his death.

Carlos met them at the door. Before he pulled his sister to him, he scanned a look over her. The cuts and bruises from her attack had settled in, and she looked worse than she had.

Carlos's lips grew thin and his eyes hard, but silently, Regan shook her head and his demeanor softened. He kissed his sister and then moved her aside and hugged Zach.

Zach would have expected a handshake. A slap on the back even. But the hug set him off balance.

"Zach, I can't tell you how sorry I am for your loss." Carlos pulled back and looked at them both. "Arianna called this morning." Zach nodded as Carlos stepped back. "If I can do anything, anything at all, please let me know."

"I appreciate that." Having someone there who would always catch your back, as a brother would, wasn't something he'd ever known. He'd had dear friends and employees that would be loyal to him, but Carlos wasn't acting on behalf of his boss. This was a brotherly offer, and it gave him warmth he'd never experienced.

Regan started up the stairs. "I have to pack. Our flight leaves in two hours."

"Do you need a ride?"

Zach shook his head. "No, we have my car."

"C'mon back. I just made some coffee. You look like you could use some."

Zach followed him into the kitchen and sat at the table as Carlos poured them each a cup of coffee. There was silence, but it was comfortable.

He'd never had a brother, but he assumed Carlos was being brotherly in his silence. After all, what did you say to a man you hardly knew when his father, whom you didn't know, died?

A few minutes more passed and Carlos finally spoke. "The initial shock isn't as hard as the weeks that follow." He sipped his coffee as Zach lifted his head. "Right now you still think he'll walk through the door. That he'll have something to say. But you know he's gone. Then you'll go through the arrangements, the funeral, and those who will come to pay their respects," he continued. "Then next week you'll pick up the phone to call him and he won't be there."

"You have a lot of insight." Zach said with a bit of animosity in his voice. How could Carlos know what he was going through? His parents lived twenty minutes away and...

Zach's thoughts stopped as he suddenly remembered who Carlos really was. Yes, he did know what he was talking about.

The only difference was that Carlos spoke of the pain of a seven-year-old boy. The pain was still in his eyes.

"Regan told me about your birth parents. I'm sorry about what happened." He tried to sound as sincere as the sentiment he felt.

"It was a long time ago. But you don't forget the pain." He looked up at Zach. "It will ease in time."

"Thank you."

Carlos nodded. "Regan is going to go with you?"

"I've asked her to. I've become very dependent on her."

"As your assistant?" Carlos's words had a sharp bite to them, and Zach couldn't blame him. He'd seen him look her over when they'd walked into the house. Both Carlos and Curtis blamed him, even if they didn't say so, for the marks Roger Byers had put on their sister. He blamed himself too.

Zach put down his mug and looked at him. "As the woman I love and want to spend the rest of my life with." He looked Carlos in the eyes. "I love your sister. I would never hurt her or abandon her," he promised.

"She's told you about the last man she loved?"

"Yes." He nodded. "I'm not him."

"There are many likenesses."

"And many differences. I will not let her suffer. I will take care of her. I have asked her to think about spending her life with me. When I know that's what she wants too, I will ask for her hand in marriage." He smiled. "With the consent of your father. And you and Curtis, of course."

"Of course." Carlos tilted his head and gave him a slight smile. "She loves you."

"I know."

Regan bounded into the kitchen, pulled a travel mug from the cupboard, and filled it with coffee. "I'm ready. I'll call you when I get there and let you know where I'm staying and what the return plans are. I'm sure we'll be back very soon. Audrey will probably want to get things taken care of as soon as possible."

"Then again, I do depend on my assistant. She happens to be the best at what she does," he said with a smile, and then shook Carlos's hand, and Regan kissed him on the cheek.

CHAPTER 45

*A*rianna sat in Audrey's hotel room with her and waited for Zach and Regan. She'd never witnessed such chaos as she had that morning when she'd met the Bensons for brunch. She never would have known Tyler was sick until he slid from his chair and his wife screamed.

There were no words for her to say to make Audrey feel better. She'd seen the pain on her face when she'd yelled for help and then when the paramedics arrived and she'd rattled off his medical history and medications he was on. Everything had become surreal when Audrey rode off in the back of the ambulance with her husband and Arianna followed in a cab. By the time she had arrived at the hospital, Audrey stood there, as pale as her husband had been, shaking.

It had just been instinct to pull her into her arms and hold her. There was a need to take care of her even though she'd only met the woman.

Now she waited for Zach and Regan to take her place so she could go back to her life. But her life would never be the same. She'd watched a man die. She'd watched a woman lose the love of her life. She'd witnessed love that wouldn't end even now that Tyler Benson had passed away.

Audrey sipped a small bottle of brandy from the bar. "I appreciate you giving up your day off to be with me."

"My sister loves your son very much. As far as I'm concerned, that makes us family."

"Zachary and Tyler were my family. My father died ten years ago after Zachary started with the firm." She dabbed her eyes. "I feel so alone."

Arianna moved closer to her side. "Perhaps you should lie down. You haven't had any sleep. I'm going to go down to the lobby and wait for them, and I'll be only a phone call away. You call down if you need me."

"Thank you, darling. Thank you so much." She patted Arianna's hand.

Arianna sat in the lobby and waited as she'd promised she'd do. Carlos had called, and her parents had as well. Her mother was already cooking for Mrs. Benson, and her father waited for word of something he could do to help. She'd been in the lobby forty-five minutes when Zach and Regan walked through the doors. She stood the moment she saw them and headed them off before they could go to the front desk.

Regan ran into her arms and hugged her sister. "How terrible this must have been for you. Thank you for staying with Audrey."

"It was my pleasure," she said as she watched Zach walk toward them, his face long and drawn. His eyes were sad like his mother's. "Zach, I'm so sorry for your loss." She gathered him in her arms and held him tightly. "She's okay," she whispered in his ear, and he held her tighter.

"I appreciate you being with her."

"They are wonderful people. I'm so glad I got time to be with your dad. He's so proud of you." She kissed him on the cheek. "C'mon, I'll take you up to her."

Arianna laced her arms around them both and escorted them to Audrey's room. It was dark and quiet when they entered. Regan and Arianna stood by the door while Zach moved to his mother.

"Mother," he said softly as he touched her cheek.

"Tyler?" Her voice cracked as she opened her eyes. "Zachary." She sat up into his arms

Zach stayed with her, and Arianna took her sister back to her apartment.

Arianna handed Regan a cup of coffee as she sat at the counter of her small kitchen. She watched her sister dig through her bag and pull out her notebook. Her eyes were purple and black with bruises. Red marks marred her cheek. Cuts and gashes covered her arms. And yet she sat at the counter in the kitchen going over notes she'd handwritten in regards to Zach's father's services, calling the hospital, making more notes. Arianna shook her head.

"How are you feeling?" she asked.

"I don't know. This is such a shock. I certainly wasn't prepared for..."

"Reg, I mean how are you feeling after your attack?"

"Oh." Regan laid down her pen and slowly shifted her eyes to Arianna's. "I'm sore. My face is ugly, my arms are all cut up, and I'm pissed off. Other than that..."

"You're amazing." Arianna lifted her mug to her.

"Why's that?"

"Some maniac attacks you one day and the next your making funeral arrangements for your boss' father."

"He's more than just my boss'father."

"Say it. He's who?"

Regan smiled. "Zach asked me to think about spending the rest of my life with him."

Arianna nodded her head, not shocked by the statement. "And what did you tell him?"

"I told him I love him and that's what I want too."

"That's a big step for you. This hasn't been one of your better years. Are you sure you want to commit to that?"

Regan fisted her hands on her hips and gave her a long cautious look. "I haven't decided whether you're testing me or just being a ray of sunshine in my life."

Arianna let out a snort. She knew her pretty well. Regan's problem had always been too much optimism, and she'd been the opposite, always full of pessimism. "You love him?"

"Yes."

"You want to marry him?"

"Yes."

"Michael?"

"Thinks I'm dead and so is the baby."

"And if he finds out otherwise?"

Regan waved her hands in front of her and shook her head. "There's no reason for him ever to find out." But her voice cracked, and that worried Arianna.

"And Zach knows what you went through? He understands that you gave birth to another man's baby and then your family told him she died? You told him that Curtis told him you died too? He understands that the asshole got away with almost killing both of you just so he could move on with his life and you wouldn't be any problem? He understands?" Her voice was rising because she found it highly unlikely that any man would be perfectly okay with such a thing. Even the wonderful Zachary Benson.

Regan was biting her bottom lip. "I don't think Zach is the kind of man to back away from me for any of those reasons."

"You haven't told him everything? You didn't tell him about the baby?"

"No." Regan stood and walked toward the window. "I'm not ready for that."

"You're playing with fire."

"Like I said, I don't think he's the kind of man to back away."

"You don't think he is. That's an awful lot to swallow." Arianna sipped her coffee. "I hope you're right."

They flew back to Nashville with Tyler's body the next afternoon, and Regan went back to work arranging everything for Audrey, at her request.

People began to stop by the house, and Audrey accepted the visitors graciously. She needed to be a hostess; it was what she did best. Zach followed his mother through the house, which Regan assumed he'd probably done as a young boy as well.

John Forrester stood at the door of Tyler's office and watched Regan work. His arms crossed in front of him as he leaned against the doorjamb. "You are the most amazing woman I have ever known. How do you feel about marrying older men?" He smiled as she looked up at him.

"I almost didn't recognize you." She stood and crossed the room to greet him.

"Most people are surprised to find I have clothes that require shoes without steel toes."

She laughed easily with him. "Oh, John." She threw her arms around him and kissed him on the cheek. "I feel so bad for Audrey and Zach."

"Tyler Benson was a wonderful man. I knew him for thirty years. He was like a brother to me." He held her at arm's length and gazed over her. "Dammit, that asshole did quite a job on you, didn't he?" He pushed a strand of hair from her face and looked over the bruises that still lingered three days later.

"Hell of a week." She smiled, but tears were in her eyes.

"I should never have taken you on that site." He kissed her gently on the forehead and gathered her back in his arms again. "I should have known better."

"There is no making out in my father's office." Zach stood in the doorway, his voice humorous but weary.

"I asked her to marry me." John held tight to her. "But hell, I think she likes you better."

"I hope so. I've told her to give some thought to that as well, but she's stubborn."

"Okay, okay." Regan pulled herself from John's arms and wiped away her tears. "I'll marry you both, but I want my own bathroom."

"Well at least we could design and build you one." John smiled.

"Under budget and on time," Zach added.

Regan laughed. They all did, and it felt good. Then she turned her attention back to Zach. "I've finished the funeral arrangements. Will your mother want to have a reception here afterward?"

"I'm sure she wouldn't have it any other way."

John patted Zach's back. "I'll go find Mrs. Benson." He turned back as he walked out of the office. "Hey, Regan. What's your sister's name again?"

"Arianna. Why?"

"Well, maybe if I can't coax you into marrying a man pushing fifty with both feet, I can convince her." He winked and left them alone in the office.

Zach took Regan's hands in his. "Thank you for doing all of this for her—for us. I think it's helped."

"It's my pleasure." She kissed him on the cheek. "I love you. I haven't gotten to tell you how sorry I am."

His eyes had gone sad again, and his shoulders rolled forward. Zach let out a quick breath and shook his head. "I just can't believe our children won't meet him."

Audrey was pleased that there had been over a hundred people at the funeral. The reception at the house attracted even more mourners who came to pay their respects. Her husband would have been furious with the attention, but she thought he deserved it. The Benson family filled the house, but the Keller family made it a home.

Alan and Emily Keller made food and helped serve it. Curtis and Carlos picked up glasses and coffee mugs and cycled them through the dishwasher. Arianna greeted people at the door, and Regan stood by Zach's side with their fingers interlaced. Even Carlos's ex-wife, Madeline, and their children were there helping and paying their respects to the father of the man Regan loved.

Audrey couldn't have made it through the week without the Kellers. They were an amazing family. And when she laid her head on her pillow that night, she sent a prayer to her husband and to God. *Let them stay in love and marry*, she whispered in the dark. *I pray they find the same happiness I had. They both deserve that.*

CHAPTER 46

*R*egan watched Zach nearly drive himself mad going over old plans of his father's just to make sure he'd done his own job right. He checked and double-checked every detail of every plan of every building, trying to make sure he was living up to the standards of what his father and grandfather before him had done. He was the only male Benson left, and he told her time and time again that it felt like the world weighed on his shoulders.

She watched him go from a high-powered CEO to a young man who was looking for his father's approval and wasn't getting it because there wasn't anyone left to give it to him. It broke her heart.

Regan opened his door at lunchtime, and his head snapped up. His eyes were narrow and his cheeks flushed. "I told you I didn't want to be disturbed." He ran his fingers through his already messed sandy hair. The tousled look made her want to smile, but she held it in.

"Can it, Benson. You know, I'm sorry your father passed away, but you don't have to talk to me like that." Her voice was steady and calm. She'd expected him to burst out at some point, but even if he did she knew it wouldn't be like Michael's fits of fury. There might be words, but they wouldn't be hurtful. There might be action, but it wouldn't be forceful; in fact, he was most likely to take a long run. She could address him the way she needed to and didn't have to fear him. There was a power there; a force that wasn't about who owned a company or made more money. It was a partnership and she was part of that—and so was he. Her skin warmed and peace filled her.

"If I remember correctly, you were the one who drew the line about the workday. Between the hours of eight and six, we're on company time. You're my assistant and that's that. So I told you I didn't want to be interrupted, and here you are." He stood behind his desk, trying to look professional and missing the mark terribly.

"That's right. Here I am in your office after you asked me to stay out. I guess you'll have to fire me." She laid out their lunch on the small coffee table by the couch. She fixed each of them a sandwich on a plate and opened a bottle of water as he looked on. "Even if you're behaving like an asshole, you have to eat." Regan stood with her fists on her hips and her lips tucked between her teeth.

"Don't you have any compassion for how you speak to me?" He walked toward the table, keeping his eyes to the floor.

"It's been three weeks, and I was by your side the whole damn time after your father died. And if I remember correctly, I wasn't looking my best." She knew he still felt guilt over her attack, and by God she was going to use it to shut him up. "Now sit down and eat."

He reluctantly crossed the room and sat down on the couch, shoulders hunched, and head down. She knew he was reconsidering the way he'd come across.

Zach lifted his head, and his eyes had softened. "Regan, I'm sorry."

"I know you are." She leaned closer to him and kissed him gently.

He sipped his water and sat back on the couch. "I haven't been very good company lately."

"No you haven't, but I understand." She snuggled closer to him. "It's been a hard few weeks. It'll get easier."

"I just feel like I have to do everything correctly now. I can't miss one step or he'll be disappointed. I'm afraid of messing up what he and my grandfather built together."

"You're amazing at what you do. Do it your way, and you'll be fine. John and I will be here to catch your back." She smiled and he pulled her closer.

"I know you will be."

"Just think. In another week you'll be in L.A. finalizing your biggest project. The one you brought to the company. The one you designed yourself and will see through until the end. I'm very proud of you for that."

"It will be the finest building we've ever done," he said as he pushed her back on the couch.

She forgot about his mood and the lunch that went uneaten as he pressed his lips to her neck. There wasn't anything better than breaking her own rules over lunch.

The moonlight gave the bedroom a silver hue. Zach stood in the doorway of the bathroom and watched Regan sleep. He hadn't slept well since his father had died, and this night had been no exception. It was two in the morning, and he'd had to leave the bed that the woman he loved slept so peacefully in, and take a shower to release the tension in his shoulders and neck.

Zach ran the towel over his wet hair and ambled back toward the bed. He pulled the robe from his warm skin and slid into bed next to her. He watched her and smiled. Her eyes darted beneath her lids. She was dreaming. He wondered what went on in her head when she slept.

He touched her shoulder gently, but she shrugged off his

touch and rolled away from him, still sleeping. He smiled and touched her again.

"Stop! "she said, her eyes still darting beneath her lids. "Don't touch me again!"

"I'm sorry." He pulled back and studied her.

Regan pulled her knees up, and tears squeezed from her closed eyes. "Don't touch me. No!" she repeated.

Zach took a breath to speak before he realized she wasn't talking to him. She was still dreaming. A moment later, she sat up and screamed, "Take her away! Take her away!"

"Regan, I'm here." He reached for her.

Sweat had beaded on her brown. Her pulse was racing under his fingers, and she was fighting for breath. Her eyes shot open, but he wasn't sure she even saw him for a moment. Then the haze that clouded her eyes cleared, and she stared at him.

"It's okay, sweetheart. You had a nightmare." He drew her close. "What happened?"

"I need water." She gasped, and tears continued to roll down her cheeks.

"I'll get you some."

He was back a moment later with a glass of water from the kitchen. Regan took it with both hands and sipped it slowly as Zach sat next to her. He switched on the lamp on the nightstand and watched her.

Regan took deep breaths. The water in the glass sloshed from the shaking of her hands. She sipped again and then handed it back to him.

He set the glass down on the nightstand. "What happened?"

Regan gathered the sheets up around her neck. "I just had a bad dream. It's nothing."

"I've never seen you have a dream like that. Someone was hurting you."

"No one hurt me. It was just a dream, a reaction from what happened a few weeks ago."

"Regan, someone hurt you before that." He pushed on. This wasn't about Roger Byers and he knew it. "Curtis mentioned it at the hospital. Tell me what happened." He watched her tense. "Dammit, Regan, you can't hide this from me. Not if you love me." He stood and paced by the bed. "You're holding on to too many secrets. We can't have secrets between us. Not anymore."

Regan shook her head and bit down on her bottom lip, still clinging to the bed sheet. "What happened to me before doesn't have anything to do with you."

"It does now." He turned to her, though he knew he wasn't doing a good job of concealing the frustration in his eyes. "I love you. I care for you. I want to marry you and have a family with you. But if you lie to my face, we can't have that. What are you hiding?"

Her lip was trembling now, and her eyes filled with tears. "If I tell you, you won't want to marry me. You won't want me to carry your children."

"That's not true." His voice rose, and he took a deep breath to calm himself, but it wasn't working well. He sat back on the bed and gathered her hands in his. "That is what I want. I love you." He couldn't contain what was on his mind. "Will you marry me?"

She wiped her eyes and stared at him. "Is this my proposal?"

He shook his head. "No."

"Oh."

"This is you telling me whether you would marry me. It would be nice to know before I set up a romantic evening and buy a ring and then you turn me down." He set his jaw.

Regan touched his cheek. "You really want to marry me? I wasn't brought up in a fancy house. I didn't go to school in France. In fact, the only French I know does not suggest nice things."

"You think that matters to me?" He tightened his grip on her hands. "I love you. My parents—my mother loves you. That's all that really matters to me."

"But what about children?"

"What about them?"

"I'm adopted. I don't know any history about my parents. I don't know if they carried genes for disease. I don't know if they lived to be fifty. What if I pass something on to my children that I don't even know I could?"

"Our children," he reminded her with a bite to his words, "and we would deal with it all."

"I don't know what to say."

"Yes would be good." He shook his head, frustrated with the whole conversation. "Regan Keller, please tell me you'll marry me, you'll have children with me, and you'll grow old with me."

Regan tucked her lips between her teeth and then let out a shuddered breath. "Zach, I can't promise to marry you just to calm your nerves."

There was no hiding his disappointment. Obviously, there was no more to say. He stood and walked to the foot of the bed. Picking up his robe, he put it on and pulled it tight.

"I'm going to head down to the office."

"Zach, it's three in the morning."

"I can't be here now. I'll have a cab pick you up at seven. We need to pull everything together for our trip to L.A. next week." Without another word, he pulled a suit from the closet, walked back to the bathroom, and locked the door.

CHAPTER 47

As soon as Zach left, Regan pulled herself from bed. She brewed a pot of coffee, showered, and readied herself for the day. When she looked at the clock, it was only four-thirty. There was plenty of time for her to stew in the misery she'd brought upon herself.

She sat down at the kitchen table and scrubbed her hands over her freshly made-up face. What the hell was wrong with her? She'd told her sister she didn't think Zach was the kind of man who would walk away from her, but he'd proven her wrong. That was exactly what he'd done. He'd walked away from her at three o'clock that morning.

She shook her head. That wasn't what had happened, and she knew it.

Zachary Benson loved her, and she was pushing him farther and farther away. It was only a matter of time before she lost him completely.

That was what she had wanted, wasn't it? She'd never meant to fall in love with him. She'd promised herself she'd never fall in love with the man she worked forever again, but she had. She'd broken that promise to herself.

She wiped at the corners of her eyes where tears collected, before they fell. How could she have possibly let it happen again?

Pain filled her chest and fire burned her stomach. She was furious with herself. Zach didn't deserve what she was putting him through. What could be worse—knowing she was hurting him or telling him her secret and watching him walk away from her? She wasn't sure.

Regan poured the cup of coffee down the drain and washed the mug. The coffee in the pot was still hot when she poured it down the drain too.

Regan checked her makeup in the mirror by the front door. It was now only five-fifteen. She paced awhile and then fell onto the couch. Breathing deeply, she thought about it. She would tell him. It was time Zachary Benson found out what she had gone through and what she had done. It was better for him to know now and walk away from her. John would be in L.A. with him, and everything was so organized that when he fired her, he wouldn't need an assistant for the meetings. It wasn't as if he couldn't hire a temporary assistant to take a few notes.

Regan stood and paced again.

The car he'd promised arrived promptly at seven. The traffic into Nashville was already congesting the streets, and Regan's nerves began to unravel one by one.

In the lobby of the building, she stopped by the coffee cart and ordered each of them a coffee to kill a few more moments before she made her way up to the office. She was officially sick to her stomach.

Regan tapped her fingers impatiently on the cardboard holder that held the coffees as the elevator rose. When the elevator opened, she thought about riding it back to the lobby, but got off with the other employees and walked toward her office. The door was already open, which meant Zach had no doubt retrieved the documents he would brief her and John on before they left for L.A.

Regan set the coffees on the edge of her desk, tucked her purse in her bottom drawer, and turned on her computer. She freshened up her lipstick and ran her fingers through her hair. Picking up the coffees, she turned and opened the door to his office.

The laughter hit her first and then the fragrance of expensive perfume. Regan stood stunned at the long-legged woman who sat on the edge of Zach's desk. Her legs crossed at the knees, her hand leaned back on the desk, and her long black hair cascaded down her back.

Regan grasped the tray of coffees harder, afraid she would drop them in the floor if she didn't fling them at Zach's headfirst.

He stood from behind his desk, giving the woman atop it a hand to her feet. "Regan, I didn't realize it was already eight. We were catching up."

Regan's mouth tightened, and her eyes darted to the woman who stood at Zach's side. She knew she'd lash out if she stood looking at them for one more second. As calmly as she could, she set the cups of coffee on the table to her side and turned to leave the room.

Zach hurried across the room and grabbed her arm and turned her toward him. "Regan"—he laced his arm around her waist—"I'd like to introduce you to Mademoiselle Simone Pierpont."

Simone Pierpont glided across the office and extended a lean, well-manicured hand toward Regan. "I am so pleased to meet you. Zachary has not stopped talking about you in months. Even his mother is smitten with you, as was his father. May he rest in peace." She covered her chest with her hand and sent Zach a loving look of condolence. "I would have been here for the funeral..."

"But she was busy schmoozing some sexy Italian on a yacht." Zach picked up one of the cups Regan had set on the table.

"*Tu es un idiot!*" She laughed and Zach followed suit, but Regan stood dumbfounded between them. "Monsieur Benson thinks he knows all about me, but he is wrong. I was doing business."

"I'll bet." He laughed, and her eyes widened and then shifted to Regan's.

Simone waved off Zach's comments and narrowed her eyes. "I'm glad you were not invited to go with us today!" She took the coffee from his hands and sipped, leaving her red lipstick on the lid. "We would not want you and your—your mean words."

Zach winked at Simone and Regan's muscles tensed. She was glad she'd already set the coffees down or they surely would have dropped. Zach was grinning when he turned back to Regan. "Simone is here to take you to brunch with her and my mother," he said, interrupting her mental beating of the woman standing across from her.

The stewing she'd done at the house after he'd walked out on her, and the anger she'd felt seeing Simone on his desk, rushed through her body and left her weak from the shock of what Zach was proposing. "I couldn't." She shifted her eyes to Simone, and Regan could swear she could feel her blood boil. Where did this woman get off sitting on Zach's desk, laughing at his jokes, and leaving her lipstick on his cup? "Miss Pierpont, thank you for the invitation, but Zach...Mr. Benson and I have so much work to do."

Zach touched her arms gently. "Regan, my mother won't take no for an answer."

Simone reached for her clutch. "And neither will I. Zachary will have to do without you." Zach took a step back as Simone moved toward him. She kissed him on both cheeks and then gently on the lips, leaving her trail of lipstick there as well before looking down at Regan. "I'll meet you in the lobby. I think I'd like one of those fancy American coffees." She handed Zach back his cup, strutted out of the office, and then waved without turning back.

Regan stood still, unable to speak.

He moved in to kiss her, but Regan reached her hand between them and wiped away Simone's lipstick. He began to grin then pursed his lips, but he didn't look any more serious. "You, Ms. Keller, have the day off."

"I'd rather not."

"I insist." He turned her toward the door and gave her a gentle push in its direction. "I think they have an entire day's worth of girly things planned for you."

Regan turned back around. Her palms had become damp, and she rubbed them on the sides of her skirt. He was insane to think she'd want to spend the day with her. "Zach, I don't know this woman."

"True. But she won't leave you alone until she gets to know you. Just remember to believe only half of the things she tells you about me."

She didn't care for the fact that some woman knew all about him. She wasn't ready for that. "I can't believe you're sending me off with your other woman."

Zach took a step back and then laughed, just as John had done when Regan had lunch with him and mentioned Simone Pierpont.

He gave her another gentle push toward the door. "Go. You'll have a goodtime."

"I have things I need to say to you."

"They can wait." He gathered her hands in his and kissed her fingertips. "Have fun."

"Are you sending me away because you're still mad at me?"

"Regan." He touched her hair and then ran his thumb over her lips. "My feelings were hurt. I'm not done asking you to marry me. I'm far from done asking you about what happened in your past that brought you back to Tennessee. But I love you, and as long as you love me and promise to stay in my life, then I can be patient in waiting for your answer." He kissed her again.

"So you're not mad at me?"

"No, I'm not mad."

"And you think I really should spend the day with that woman?"

"She's very important to me. It would mean a lot to me if you got to know her."

Regan bit her lip and considered the statement. "Is she an old lover?"

Again, the humor was back in his face, but he shook his head. "Simone was the first person to accept me and be my friend. There has never been anything more to our relationship."

Regan let out a breath. She'd seen the woman with her own eyes. No man could just be friends with someone like that. Could he?

Trust. She was expecting Zach to leave her past alone and just trust that she could move on from it without telling him anything. She had to trust that he was honest when he said he was only friends with the gorgeous brunette that waited downstairs for her.

CHAPTER 48

*S*imone stood in the lobby, obviously unaware of the men and women who passed and stared at her beauty. "Oh, good, he convinced you to come." She sipped her gourmet coffee. "I have a car right out front waiting for us. We'll head to Madam Benson's for brunch, and then we have spa appointments." She turned toward the door, and a man opened it for her. She glided through as though accustomed to strangers behaving as servants.

Regan hurried to follow her, thanking the man for holding open the door, but she realized he hadn't seen or heard her. He was still focused on Simone.

The driver opened the door when he saw Simone and Regan walk out of the building. He tipped his hat to Regan as she climbed in next to the French beauty.

Simone tucked her coffee into a holder, took out a mirror from her clutch, checked her makeup, and touched up the red lipstick which she'd left on Zach's coffee cup and on his lips. Thinking about the red smudge on Zach's mouth lit a fire in Regan's belly.

Simone dabbed at her face. "This heat is almost unbearable. How do you stay so put together and beautiful?"

Regan's mouth dropped open. "I beg your pardon?"

"Oh, you are so beautiful. Perhaps it's the humidity. It does wonderful things for your complexion." She tucked the mirror back into her clutch and looked Regan in the eyes. "I'm envious."

Regan could feel any composure she'd had slip away. "Of me?"

"Of course. I've never been able to get Zachary Benson to look at me as he looks at you. You've won him over, you know."

Regan settled back against the seat. She had too many secrets for a man to truly love her. "No. I don't really think I do."

"Oh, I've loved Zachary since we were seven. Poor American child thrown into a boarding school in Paris. He knew no French and he did not speak to anyone for a year." She drew a cigarette from a compartment between them and lit it. The smoke billowed around her as she crossed her ankles and rolled the down the window just a crack.

Simone took a dainty drag from the cigarette. "He was gangly and almost ugly. I was smitten." She laughed. "And since then I've gone to bed with more men trying to figure out why Zachary Benson never fell in love with me."

"And?" Regan asked realizing she was just as curious.

"I'm not his type."

"I can't imagine there is a man on this planet whose type you're not."

"You are flattering." She smiled then took another drag from her cigarette. "But Zachary Benson never thought so. He's in love with you."

"I don't know." Regan looked down at her fingernails where the polish had chipped off. Quickly she folded her hands in her lap.

"You've had an argument."

Of course they had. But she wasn't sure she was ready to talk about it with a woman who loved the man she loved.

Simone lowered the window and flicked the cigarette outside with her fingers. "Why? Why do you argue with him? What can't he offer you?"

Regan shifted her body and stiffened her shoulders. "Ms. Pierpont, I…"

"Simone."

"I'm sorry. Simone. There is nothing he can't offer. I'm not sure I can offer him what he wants."

"And what does he want?" She continued to assault her with questions.

"He wants me to marry him."

"And you've said yes?"

"No."

"No?"

"I can't marry him."

"Why not?"

"I'm not of his class. What would he do with me?"

"He would love you," Simone said sweetly and then smiled.

Regan relaxed back in her seat. "You make it sound easy."

"It is easy. Zachary Benson is not like me. He cares little about power and money. He values people."

Regan smiled when Simone said that. She was right. That was what he valued.

"I have things in my past I haven't dealt with." She heard the words spew from her mouth and then wished she hadn't. This woman was a stranger. She couldn't divulge her secrets to her and not to the man she loved.

"Deal with them," Simone said simply. "Are you who you were at twenty-one?"

"No."

"Of course not. You're not who you were six months ago, are you?"

With a sigh, Regan shook her head. "No."

"Then marry him." She reached for her hand. "He loves you.

He really loves you." She flipped her head back with a smile. "And he won't even look my way. Not the way he looks at you, anyway." Simone's eyes were soft, and Regan smiled at her new friend and admirer. "I suppose when I return to France, I will tempt fate yet again and find someone with whom I think I can share my life. Someone who will make me forget that Zachary Benson has officially left me behind."

Regan couldn't say anything. She was still amazed that the woman beside her was so candid about loving Zach, and that he was in love with her and only her.

The French woman let go of Regan's hand and examined her own perfect manicure. "My problem is I have an affinity for American men. Tell me, Regan." She turned her head back to her, puckering her red lips and tapping her finger to them. "Do you know of a handsome successful man?"

Regan laughed. "As a matter of fact, I do."

"Well, do tell."

"Six foot two, sandy blond hair, crystal-blue eyes, and of course he's a doctor."

"A doctor?" Simone's eyes grew wide.

"Yes, a very popular one at that."

She watched as Simone's eyebrows rose. "How is it that you know this handsome doctor?"

"He's my brother."

"Ah, *mon ami*! I may have to stick around a bit longer and meet this brother-doctor of yours."

CHAPTER 49

$\mathcal{A}$udrey opened the door of the house the moment Simone's car arrived. The driver opened the car doors, Simone climbed out, and the two women waved to each other. Then Regan stepped out of the car, and Audrey waved just as enthusiastically as she had when she'd seen Simone.

"Oh, Regan." She smiled as they neared the walk. "Simone said she was bringing a friend for the day. I'm so pleased it's you."

"Thank you." She watched as Audrey embraced Simone and kissed both her cheeks. Then she hugged Regan and kissed her just the same. But before she let go of her arms, she gave them a little squeeze and smiled.

"We're having brunch in the rose garden. Simone, do you remember Josepha?"

"*Oui!*" Simone placed her hand on her chest. "Tell me she is here cooking for us."

"*Oui!*" Audrey answered with a smile.

Simone touched Regan's arm. "Oh, you are in for a treat. Madame Josepha was the cook for Madame Audrey when I first visited America with Zachary. We were very young."

Regan watched Simone hurry off toward the kitchen to find

Josepha. She was sure to get a candid look into the world that Zach had grown up in by spending the day with the two women who doted on him, and Josepha too.

Audrey turned to Regan in the hallway and placed her hands on her arms. "You're doing okay? You look like you've healed well."

"I'm fine. How are you?"

"I wake up every morning thinking he's going to come in and kiss me good morning. I'm still waiting." She smiled, but her eyes were sad.

"I'm so sorry."

"It's the cycle of life. I won't be without him forever."

The comment struck Regan hard. To love like that—what an amazing gift.

Audrey looked toward the kitchen and back at Regan. "Are you okay with Simone? She's always loved Zach, but he's never thought more of her than, well, than a sister." Her voice had dropped to a whisper.

Regan nodded. "I didn't react so well when I first saw her."

"If you made it this far, you're the first woman she hasn't run off." Audrey laughed quietly. "I think you're in for the long haul."

Audrey watched as Simone filled the conversation with stories of a young Zachary from school. She always had a story, and Audrey was sure she'd never heard the same one twice.

Poor Simone had pined for her son for years, but Zachary kept her yearning. Her husband had often laughed at his son's stubbornness.

"I don't think he's human," he'd say to her. "No man would look away from her like he does."

Zachary had brought home many women over the years, and Audrey had introduced him to many more. But never had he looked at any of them the way he looked at Regan. This would be the woman she'd call daughter, someday. There was no doubt in her mind.

A smile formed on her lips when she thought she would share her grandchildren with the family who had taken her in and cared for her when her husband had died.

Simone sipped her mimosa. "What are you thinking of, Madame?"

"How happy I am that you are both here." She lifted her drink, and each woman tapped her glass. "To the women who love Zachary."

"And to the one who won his heart," Simone added as they both looked at Regan.

After brunch at Audrey's, the women, tipsy on mimosas, fell into the car laughing as the driver took them to the spa where Simone had arranged an entire day of pampering.

"I have never had a spa day," Regan confessed as she dipped her feet into the footbath filled with rose petals.

"Oh, *mon ami*, you will need to become accustomed to this." Simone sipped at a glass of wine as the manicurist massaged her feet. "This will be our very own tradition. We will start it today. When I am in town." She tipped her wine glass toward Regan. "Or when you are in France, we will spend the day being pampered by strangers and drinking champagne."

"I do feel a little guilty skipping work to be here." But she couldn't feel too guilty. Zach had sent her.

"I think you definitely should quit your job when you and Zachary are married. There are many fine things for a woman who is married to wealthy man to enjoy."

"Oh, I wouldn't dream of quitting." Regan's eyes were wide. "I love my job."

"Well, that itself I do not understand. How could anyone love working?" Simone laughed. "Well, when I am in the country you will take a holiday and spend it with me doing wonderful things like this."

"That is assuming I marry Zach." She bit down on her lip. "There is the matter that I turned down his proposal last night."

"*Stupide*! Zachary had a temper tantrum, and I'm still angry that he woke me at four in the morning." Simone set her glass down on the table and switched feet for the manicurist to massage the other.

Regan shifted in her chair uncomfortably. "He called you?"

"Of course he called me. He calls me for every damn thing." She raised her shoulders and let them drop. "He's not used to people telling him no or making him wait. When you did not accept his proposal, his feelings were hurt." Simone turned her head toward Regan and locked her eyes on hers. "Tell me you do not plan to tell him no. You do plan to marry him, don't you?"

Regan looked away as she felt the piercing in her chest of sadness and regret. "I plan on him walking away."

Zach had gotten close to other women, and he believed Simone had chased them off on purpose. But her motives were different now. He knew she had finally come to grips with the fact that he didn't love her. If anything, she was the sister he'd never had. Even better, she lived in France and only visited a few times a year.

The thought amused him as he rolled up the blueprints for the L.A. project and secured them in their tube. He laid it on his desk and opened the drawer.

The blue box from Tiffany's sat there with its glistening silver bow. It would be his secret that Simone had helped him pick out the ring. However, it would ensure Regan would love it. He envisioned giving it to her in L.A. A nice dinner, champagne, and a moonlight stroll along the beach. He'd move her with his romantic plans. He'd get down on one knee and promise to her that he'd love her forever. No matter what or who had come before him.

CHAPTER 50

Regan hurried to pack the last items in her suitcase while Carlos waited at her bedroom door. He'd offered to drive her to the office, and he'd more than once told her he was sincerely regretting it.

She'd made a list of everything she'd need for the trip and the meeting, but she'd left it at the office and was racking her brain trying to remember what was on it.

Carlos checked his watch, leaned against the doorjamb with his arms crossed, then he checked his watch again. "This is not the first business trip you've been on with the man. Why are you taking so long?"

"This one is very important. It's the biggest build he's ever taken on. He sold it, he designed it, and he's in charge of seeing it through. I want to make sure everything goes as smoothly as possible." She flew through the room gathering the last of her toiletries.

"God, you're going to walk into that boardroom and fall through the door, aren't you? Flat on your damn face." He had a crooked little smile that made him adorable, and she worried he was dooming her success.

"You're a shit." She threw a shoe at him only to have him catch it before it hit him.

"You'll be fine." He handed the shoe back to her and turned her from her suitcase. "I don't think you could ever disappoint the man. He loves you too much."

"I love him too, and that's why I'm so nervous for him."

"Love, it sucks doesn't it?"

"Yes, in the most wonderful way." She touched her brother's face. Then she turned back to the suitcase and pushed in the contents until she could zip it shut. When it was zipped, Carlos pulled it from the bed.

"God, did you forget anything?"

"You're a big, strong man. You can handle it." She passed by him, headed toward the stairs, and led the way down. "So what are your plans this weekend?"

"Christian's birthday."

"Oh, Carlos. I forgot. I've never missed his birthday."

"Damn you." He laughed as he dropped the suitcase at the foot of the stairs. "He'll get over it. Besides, I recall you missed a few when you were in Hawaii." He raised his eyebrows.

"Yes, I did. I am very sorry about that."

"You couldn't help it." He rested a hand on her arm. "There was no coming home."

"It was a year ago." She looked down at the floor, feeling ashamed. "I called in sick on Tuesday," she admitted, and her voice shook. "Audrey brought me soup, and Zach left work early to sit with me." She wiped a stray tear that ran down her face. "I didn't even have the courage to tell him why I'd stayed home."

"You deserve to mourn." His touch comforted her and his voice was soothing.

Regan shook her head and pursed her lips. "It's been a year. I shouldn't be mourning. Everyone was better off."

"Are you sure?" he asked, and Regan shot him a look. "Don't be mad. I was just asking."

Regan ground her teeth. "Look at me and Arianna and your-self. You tell me how things would have been for us had Mom and Dad not happened into our lives. I did the right thing. I will never regret that. I gave a woman like Mama a gift. I only regret loving the man and believing him."

"And now you hold that against Zach?"

Regan wanted to swing at him with her fists. She wanted to beat him to the ground for making her think about it. If Carlos wanted to make her feel bad, he was doing it. If it was his inten-tion to make her second-guess everything she did, it was work-ing. But in all their life, Carlos had never meant her harm. He'd always had her back, and that would never change. She fought back tears and nodded. "What will he think of me?"

"Oh, I don't know. Give him a chance and find out. Just remember, after you tell him, give him some time to process it." He kissed his sister's cheek. "I bet you'll be surprised."

To be surprised was exactly what she didn't want.

Zach found great enjoyment watching Regan appreciate the perks of first class. She sipped her champagne from her plastic cup and stretched her legs out far in front of her. For that reason alone, he promised himself she'd never have to fly coach again.

The trip was going to be the most successful one of his life. It would make up for the weeks he'd spent since his father had died, reevaluating everything he'd ever done. This time, he'd not only come home with signed contracts, finally, for a building he had so much pride in, but he'd have the woman he loved—and they'd be engaged.

Warmth filtered through his core, and he relaxed into his seat as Regan rested her head against his shoulder.

Zach could feel the box in his pocket, which held the ring he'd give her. The look in her eyes when she saw the sparkling diamond would be priceless. It would always be his secret, though, that Simone had been the one to pick out that ring. He'd had another in mind, but she wouldn't hear of it. Simone knew beauty, and she'd been quite frank in letting him know the ring he'd picked wasn't as brilliant as the woman who was going to wear it.

It pleased him that the women who'd meant the most in his life adored the one he loved. Love—he'd never given it much thought before, and now he'd never want to live without it.

Zach had given great consideration to the wedding and the honeymoon. Of course he would let her plan every moment of it —after all, that was what most women dreamed of—but he had ideas. He'd like her to become his wife in the rose garden at his parents' home, and perhaps a honeymoon on the yacht owned by Simone's father.

Simone's father had always been fond of him. Though he didn't know if he'd allow him to honeymoon on the yacht if he wasn't marrying his daughter. It was worth asking.

Regan cuddled closer to him, wrapping her arms around his arm. "You haven't said a word since we took off. What are you thinking?"

"Nothing." He kissed the top of her head. "How long has it been since you've been to L.A.?"

He felt her stiffen against him, but he didn't react. She didn't answer right away, but she relaxed against him again. "I left there five years ago."

"Do you miss it?" He ran his thumb over her knuckles.

"No." Her answer was definite. "It was where I landed after college, but I have no sentimental attachment to it."

"What about Hawaii? Do you miss it?"

She shook her head defiantly. "No."

Zach squeezed her hand tight. "I didn't mean to bring up anything bad. I'm sorry."

"No, it's okay."

"I'll make it up to you. I promise." He brushed her lips gently with his, and she closed her eyes and let out a low hum.

"You promise? That sounds like you have a plan." She slowly opened her eyes.

"Regan, you'll spoil my surprises if you talk about it further."

She sat up in her seat as the captain announced their descent. "I hope you didn't go out of your way."

"Oh, you have no idea." Zach rested his head against the back of his seat and closed his eyes. The moonlit walk on the beach, the ring on her finger, the lifetime ahead of them couldn't come soon enough. "You'll hate me for them. But—"

"You're a pain."

"So you've said." He smiled, his eyes still closed.

CHAPTER 51

Zach kept Regan wrapped in his arms as the elevator carried them to their floor in the hotel. He'd had their luggage sent up when they checked in, and then they'd had dinner with John. He'd spoiled Regan with champagne and dessert. Now it was time to spoil her for the rest of her life.

Zach pushed open the door to their hotel suite, and Regan walked in, still talking about how wonderful dinner had been, but then she stopped and gasped. Dozens of roses adorned the room, and their scent filled the air.

"Oh, Zach." She lifted her hand to her mouth.

"Do you like it?" He rested his hands on her shoulders and kissed the back of her neck. The floral scent of her perfume intoxicated him and the softness of her skin enticed him, but he had to pace himself. Every moment of their time in L.A. had to be perfectly executed.

"Zachary Benson, this is amazing." She turned into his arms. "Are you trying to seduce me?"

He moved his hand up her back and cupped her neck in his hand. "Is it working?" He traced a finger down her throat.

"Oh, I think it's working." Her eyes closed and her voice was airy.

Every part of him was stirring. He held her back slightly so as not to rush the moment, but his body was far ahead of him. "There's more."

"More?" Her eyes opened slowly as she looked up at him.

"Come with me." He walked her to the bedroom, where a white box tied with a large ribbon lay on the bed.

She smiled. "What is this?"

"Open it."

Regan took a deep breath and slid the bow from the box. "Zach..." She laughed as she pulled a long white satin negligee from the box and held it against her body. There was a smoldering in her eyes, and he knew at that moment, inside of her burned a flame as hot as the one heating him up.

"I couldn't resist. Though I'm not sure you'll have it on long." He couldn't help but think about what seeing her in it was going to do to him. If she didn't hurry and try it on, he wasn't sure she'd have a chance. Never in his life had he been so aroused.

"Let me go slip it on, then." She walked across the room toward the bathroom, keeping her eyes locked on his.

"I'll wait here."

Zach laid down on the bed, propping himself up on his elbow, and waited for her to make her appearance.

When Regan returned, she'd slipped into the negligee and pulled her hair up, away from her slender neck. She'd glossed her lips, and the twitching in his pants was probably as obvious to her as it was to him.

Regan sauntered toward the bed, running her hand over the fabric that clung to her curves. He sat up. "You look wonderful." He stood and slid his hands around her waist, feeling the warmth of her skin through the thin material.

She lifted her lips to his ear. Her breath was hot. "Kiss me." She closed her eyes, and he watched her for just a moment before lowering his lips to hers. Pliant under his, her mouth easily opened to him, and her body molded to his. Her breasts pressed against his chest, her thighs against his thighs. The negligee was so thin he could feel the heat of her against his already aroused body.

He slid his hands up the sides of her body, enjoying every curve she offered under the satin. Wanting to taste her, need burning through him, he moved his kisses from her lips to her neck. Regan's pulse quickened under his tongue, and he felt the tightening of her hands on his arms.

Zach turned her toward the bed and gently lowered her beneath him. He moved his kisses from her neck to her silk-covered breasts. Her nipples peaked beneath the white cloth. Gently he teased them with his thumbs as she arched against him.

His hands moved from her breasts and he began to gather up the silky fabric at her waist. He was happy to find the negligee was all she wore. Time was theirs, and he meant to enjoy every moment thoroughly, kissing her stomach and down her legs, taking time to nibble at her knees and ankles and back up again.

Regan squirmed with delight as Zach savored her body inch by inch. She tangled her fingers in his hair as she moved against him. He cupped her, and a gasp escaped her throat. When he slid his fingers inside her, she pulled him closer to her as he licked, teased, and drove her to the peak of climax, then again.

Zach watched her as he pleased her. It drove him mad to see the smoky change in her eyes as she gasped in pleasure.

Regan sucked in breaths, and her eyes softened in color. Then she reached for his shirt, releasing buttons as quickly as her fingers would allow while he slid his pants to the floor. She opened up to him, pulling him inside of her, urging him deeper.

"Tell me you love me," he said softly as he rocked against her,

Her eyes fluttered up to look into his. "I love you."

"I want to always please you, Regan. I love you." He continued to push them both to where their bodies blended into one.

He felt the piercing of her fingernails in his back and her legs wrapping around him, pulling him tighter to her. He moved his mouth over hers, searching for the warmth of her tongue. She was moving with a rhythm that mimicked his. He felt his body tighten as she pulled him deeper.

He buried his face against her neck as he released, and she shuddered beneath him. He wanted to take that moment and save it. He wanted to push away all plans, give her the ring he'd bought her, and convince her to marry him.

Instead, he lay there above her, catching his breath.

"I don't ever want to move," he said once he could speak.

"You'll have to sooner or later." She laughed huskily. "But for now, hold me tight."

CHAPTER 52

Zach slept for the first time in weeks. When he woke and the sun peeked through the curtains, he sighed. Regan lay beside him. Her white negligee lay discarded on the floor. Her hair fanned over her pillow, and her chest moved with the slow rhythm of her dream.

He touched her shoulder and ran his fingers slowly down her arm as he kissed the back of her neck. She stirred, rolling slowly toward him. He pushed back her hair and gazed at her.

"God, you're beautiful in the morning," he said.

"You look like you finally slept." She looked up at him, her eyes still hazy.

"Finally." Zach kissed her gently. "I'm going to take a shower and then order us up some breakfast." When she lazily closed her eyes and nodded, he added, "I'd enjoy someone washing my back if you're up for it."

"I think that's something I could manage."

When Regan emerged from the bedroom dressed in a new black suit and black sling-back pumps, she was ready for the meeting. She took in the view of the room and laughed aloud.

She wasn't sure what Zach had been thinking when he ordered breakfast.

There were plates of eggs and pastries. There were bowls of fruit and cereal. A pot of coffee and two different juices sat in the middle of the table.

Zach looked up from a piece of toast that he was picking apart. "I'm nervous." He wore a custom-made dress shirt with his initials embroidered on the cuff in a deep blue, which made him look even more sophisticated.

Regan kissed him gently on the lips and brushed a crumb from his tie. "Zachary Benson, how many times have you gone to the table and signed contracts?" She tried to keep her calm for him, but inside her stomach fluttered like a jar full of butterflies fighting for their freedom.

"I know. It's this investor. He's…well, he's a piece of work. I just don't like the way he conducts business and the conde-scending way he treats his trophy wife." He picked up his coffee and sipped. "If you don't walk out of the room and quit today, I'll be surprised."

"Why would I do that?"

He set down his mug and pushed it back and forth across the table in front of him. "Because if you stay on as my assistant, you'll have to become very involved with this man and his associates."

"I'll be fine and so will you."

"When this meeting is over, you and I are taking a long walk on the beach."

"Now that sounds like a great idea." Regan helped herself to a few bites of food from each plate. She too wasn't very hungry. Seeing Zach's reaction to meeting with the man made her nervous too. But she knew he'd be fine. He always was. Though he was worried, Zachary Benson was an exceptional busi-nessman with an eye for detail and the skill to close any deal.

Besides, she and John would be by his side. Nothing could go wrong.

The clock had ticked toward nine o'clock when there was a knock at the door. Regan rose from the table and answered it. John stood before her, smiling broadly. "Let's make this happen!" He'd dressed casually for Tyler's funeral; a dress shirt and a tie. But today he wore a suit with a jacket and a full Windsor knot in his tie. It was painfully obvious it wasn't his preferred choice of clothing. She smiled as she watched him adjust his tie.

Regan grabbed her purse and bag full of notebooks and contracts. John started for the elevator, and Zach held the door until she had walked through. There were nervous smiles between them.

When the elevator door opened, Regan took one step inside, then she realized what she'd forgotten and her stomach dropped.

"I forgot the portfolio with the contracts." She slipped her hand into the closing gap of the door. "I'll get them and meet you downstairs in the business office." She stepped out and smiled encouragingly at Zach as the door shut, closing her off from him.

Regan ran back to the room, gathered the portfolio, and had one more sip of coffee before racing out the door. She pressed the button for the elevator and stepped in when it arrived.

She hoisted up her bag and the portfolio as the door opened. As she walked from the elevator and into the corridor, a man and a woman exited the other elevator. With her arms full and her bag slipping from her shoulder, Regan's balance shifted, and she bumped into the couple, dropping the bag and portfolio, scattering papers everywhere. Carlos's joke of walking through the door and falling on her face ran through her head. Silently she cursed him as she began picking up papers.

"I'm sorry," Regan said as the woman scurried to help her.

The man only stood looking down at them. "You're clumsy. Come on, Charity, we're late," he scolded as the woman rose.

Regan kept her head low. The voice. She knew that voice.

The butterflies that filled her stomach finally broke free from the jar, and now she could feel the shards of glass as they stabbed her from deep inside her. She cautiously looked up to see Michael Hamilton and his trophy bride stride away. Her heart began to pound uncomfortably in her chest as she sat back on her heels. Instantly her palms grew damp and tears stung her eyes. Every fear she'd ever had surfaced, and her breath caught when she tried to form a plan that would get her out of the hotel. The scenario her brother had warned her about had arrived. Michael and Zach's worlds had just collided.

Regan gathered the papers and ran toward the office. She burst through the door, causing John and Zach to jump from their chairs. She dropped the papers onto the table. Her breath was short and sweat beaded on the back of her neck.

Zach reached for her. "Sweetheart, what's wrong?"

Regan's entire body shook, and her heart was pounding so hard in her chest it was painful. Zach's eyes scanned her but she couldn't answer. She tried to suck in a breath and calm herself. She just had to get out of the room as calmly as she could, and it would all be okay. Michael Hamilton didn't have control over her —not anymore.

"Is this your assistant?" Michael asked from across the room, tapping his pen on the table. "She's a wreck. I don't think we can..." When Regan lifted her head, he stopped. "Oh, God, Regan?"

Regan didn't move and made sure to keep her eyes from looking right at him. She couldn't. Every muscle in her body had frozen.

"Regan?" Michael's voice softened malevolently as he walked toward her.

She shifted her eyes to Zach, and he met her stare with confusion. She couldn't do this. "Zach, I have to go." Regan dropped her bags and the portfolio and swung her purse over her shoulder as she ran for the door.

CHAPTER 53

Zach let the papers and the portfolio Regan had dropped fall to the floor. His investor had scared the hell out of her and was chasing Regan out the door, and Zack intended to put an end to whatever had frightened the woman he loved.

By the time Zach made it into the hallway, Hamilton had grabbed her by the arm. "Regan, don't run from me."

"Michael, leave me alone." Her words were short and sharp, but muffled under a blanket of fear that Zach didn't understand.

"You're alive." He yanked her toward him. "Dammit, you're alive."

"Yes, I'm alive. No thanks to you!" Regan's face had flushed red with anger.

Zach sprinted toward them with a need to pull her from the grasp of the lunatic that was holding her so tightly she couldn't move. "Regan, what's going on?"

Michael Hamilton didn't release his stare or his hand from Regan. "Mr. Benson, this has nothing to do with you. Please dismiss yourself."

"Like hell it doesn't." Zach took another step, but Regan pulled herself up straight and glared at Hamilton.

She pulled against him. "Let me go. You have no right to hold me like this."

"Where do you get off being alive?" he growled. "Your brother told me you died. You and that damn baby!" His words were bitter and hateful.

She wrenched her arm, unable to free herself from his cruel grasp. "Go to hell!"

"Regan, what is he talking about?" Zach inched closer. He wanted to grab the man and throw him against the wall and kill him for causing her pain, but the negotiator in him cautioned him to keep her safe. He noticed John behind him, and was silently thankful for the support. "Is this the man Curtis said put you in the hospital?"

"Zach, go in the office. Please…" She was sobbing now, and Michael's eyes grew angrier.

Zach had to keep calm. Had to know what was going on so he could make the right decisions. "Sweetheart, tell me…"

"Sweetheart?" Michael shifted his eyes to Regan. "Stupid slut. Are you sleeping with your new boss?"

"This has nothing to do with you." She sobbed harder, and he yanked her closer to him. Zach moved in, but John pulled him back.

Michael's jaw jutted up toward Zach. "Mr. Benson, this woman is nothing but trouble. You'd do yourself a favor by firing her right now." Michael's voice didn't sound the same, Zach realized. The man was almost inhuman with his commands.

"I don't understand." Zach eased from John's restraining grip. "Regan, tell me what's going on."

"Let me." Michael had both her arms pinned by his hands. His stare focused on her. "I've been under the impression for a year now that this bitch died. Her brother looked me in the eye and told me she and our baby died."

"Baby, what baby?" Zach pleaded for her to talk to him. His stomach tightened, as did his throat. He didn't know what was going on, but he knew Regan was suffering.

"Oh, God, Zach, go away." She sucked in a breath. "Michael, please…"

"Stupid bitch!" When his hand came up to strike her, Zach moved in. He was at the man, pushing him away from the woman he loved. His fists whaled on him, bloodying his lip and bruising his face as they fell to the floor, fists swinging. Too soon, John pulled Zach from Michael. He saw Regan run down the hallway for the stairs.

"You son of a bitch!" Michael managed to clamber to his knees while John held tight to Zach.

Charity Hamilton stood at the door, dainty mouth open, and watched her husband struggle to stand.

"I will press charges," he growled.

"And I'll have her counter them," Zach threatened.

Michael smiled as he wiped the blood from his lip. "She won't. She's afraid of me, and now she'll be afraid of you." He pulled his wife's arm until she followed him. "I thought she was dead, Mr. Benson. Now that I know she's not, I intend to find out where my bastard child is." He started down the hall, and when Zach lunged toward him, John held tight to his arms. Hamilton turned back. "Oh, and Mr. Benson, I'm sure you can assume that our agreements and business arrangements are over."

"I wouldn't want to do business with you," he said as Michael stepped into the elevator.

John released his grip after the doors had closed.

Zach bent over and rested his hands on his knees, his pulse pounding in his head like a jackhammer. He forced himself back upright.

"Regan," he shouted as he ran for the stairs with John following him.

He charged up to their floor and pushed open the door to the suite, but she wasn't there. Her suitcases hadn't been touched. She'd simply fled.

He ran back down to the lobby while John called her cell phone.

Zach searched the lobby, but there was no sign of her. John arrived a few seconds later, reporting that she hadn't answered her phone. Asking around finally produced someone who said she took a cab to the airport.

Zach plowed through the lobby doors and took the next cab to the airport in hopes of finding her.

REGAN SHIVERED in the California heat in the backseat of the cab that rushed her away from the hotel. Never had she considered that her new path would cross with Michaels, except when her brother mentioned that they ran in the same circles, but now it had. For the second time, the man had ruined everything she'd ever worked for or wanted.

She'd taken the first cab across town and then changed cabs. This one took her to John Wayne Airport; she was certain Zach would look for her at LAX.

Two hours later, she was flying toward Alabama. She'd rent a car and drive to Nashville.

She needed the time away. She knew Zach and John would be looking for her, but she feared that Michael Hamilton would be looking for her as well.

Regan sat back in her seat. Her secrets were out. Zach would know she was unworthy of his love now. She'd borne the child of Michael Hamilton under horrible circumstances. She'd convinced Curtis to lie to him and tell him she'd died, rather than risk another beating like the one that had almost killed her. Michael had believed him and moved on. She'd been stupid to believe she was safe.

She wiped madly at the streams of tears that rolled down her cheeks. In one year, she'd lost everything only to regain a bit of her dignity and pride back. How was it possible that in a moment's time she'd lost it all again? There was no way Zach would look at her the same way now.

She closed her eyes tight and held back her tears. She very quickly realized she'd done what Mary Ellen had warned her not to do. She couldn't care less about her employment status at the moment, but not only had she lost Zach, she'd lost him the contract on his biggest build ever.

As the flight landed in Alabama, Regan took a deep breath. It was time to start over. Again. Arianna would be in New York for a while. She could move up there and hide in the anonymity of Manhattan.

CHAPTER 54

Zach paced outside Regan's house. She should have beaten him back to Nashville by several hours. Where could she be?

Fear had cost him any rest on the airplane. What if Michael Hamilton found her? John had stayed in the hotel, in their room, in case she returned there. Zach had to protect her from the madman who—he didn't even want to think about what that man had done to her.

It was edging toward seven, and the sky blazed orange. Finally, Carlos and his children pulled up in front of the house.

Zach watched Carlos' eyes scan him. She'd talked to her brother, that much he could tell. The man's dark eyes burned with fury, and he couldn't blame him for wanting to come at him. But he could see Carlos holding his calm.

"You three go in the house. I'll be up in a little bit," he ordered his children as he walked toward Zach. They each said hello as they passed.

Zach knew from the kids' laughter as they jostled each other on their way into the house that Carlos had kept Regan's troubles from them.

"Please tell me you've talked to her," Zach pleaded, grabbing Carlos's shoulder as soon as the children walked through the door.

Zach dropped his hand, sensing Carlos's tension. Then an tense stare from Carlos followed. Carlos didn't quite trusting him.

Regan's brother tucked his hands into his pockets and rocked back on his heels. "I've talked to her."

"Is she all right?" His voice wasn't steady. He saw no point in trying to keep calm.

"That depends on your thought of all right," Carlos said evenly and then let out a breath. "I'm going inside to get us a couple of beers. I don't want my kids to hear us. Have a seat on the step." Carlos walked into the house, and Zach climbed the steps heavily and took a seat.

Carlos returned with two beers. He handed one to Zach and sat next to him with the other. They sat in silence for a moment, sipping the beers and waiting for the other to talk.

"She's scared," Carlos finally said, looking out over the street where children played. "He tried to kill her. He tried to kill them both to wash his hands of them." He dangled the beer bottle by its neck. "Worst part is, he loved her and she loved him." Carlos shook his head. "He was too caught up in the money and social aspects of his life. He honestly did love her, but in the end I truly think he lost his mind."

Zach was sure of that. He'd seen the man's eyes. He'd heard his voice. No well-mannered man treated his wife the way that Michael Hamilton had treated his.

"What did he do?" he asked, though he wasn't sure he could handle hearing the specifics of Hamilton's attack on Regan. But he needed to know. Zach loved her. He needed all the details.

Carlos turned his head and gave Zach a long, thoughtful look. "He almost beat her to death."

Nausea clenched his stomach as awful images played out in

his mind. He made himself listen to the rest of what Carlos was saying.

"He'd married that other woman, and quite frankly he had to dispose of Regan and the baby or he'd lose the wealth and privilege he'd just married into." His jaw tightened and his voice carried the disgust he obviously felt over the situation.

"She came back home then? Back to Nashville?"

"The moment she found out he'd married that other woman. She was hurt and angry, but she figured she still had her baby and she could go on, just the two of them."

Zach took a deep breath and thought of the scar on her stomach. A lump formed in his throat. He'd never even considered that it was a cesarean scar. "Tell me about the baby."

Carlos shook his head and sipped his beer. "She was Regan's life. It gave her pride and purpose that she'd be someone's mother." He smiled. "I never saw her. None of us did except Curtis. He was the only one with Regan when she gave birth."

Zach swallowed the lump lodged in his throat. "The baby died?"

Carlos shook his head and he latched his look onto Zach's. "No. Because of Regan's injuries, the baby was born six weeks early. She spent weeks in intensive care. Regan fought for her life, and the baby fought for hers. She signed papers for adoption. She gave her to a family who could love her and raise her the way Regan couldn't. It was the best choice she could make for both of them."

"But she wanted the baby." And she had a family who would support her through anything—emotionally, financially, whatever she needed. He'd seen the way they came together for him and his mother after his dad died. "Why didn't she keep her?"

"She was afraid he'd find them and take her daughter away from her, or finish what he started. She did what was best for the baby." Carlos shook his head again. "She ordered her to be taken out of the room. Curtis said she screamed at them to take her. She closed her eyes so she'd never see her."

Zach scrubbed his hands over his face. It was no wonder she'd shied away from him when he confessed his love and spoke of marriage and babies. There was such pain there. And the nightmare she'd had, she was yelling for someone to take her away. It all made sense now.

Carlos set his beer down on the step and turned to fully face Zach. "When Hamilton came looking for her, Curtis told Hamilton that they had both died. Regan didn't have any other choice. If she pressed charges, it would just keep him in their lives. If he thought she was dead, he'd leave her alone. They never would run in the same circles. He dashed off to Italy for a few months to avoid any heat, and he never showed up at her door again. As far as we were concerned, he was gone." He picked back up his beer and drank down the last bit in the bottle. "The baby turned a year old last Tuesday."

"That's why she called in sick to work? I was worried about her. She wasn't any kind of sick I'd ever seen."

"Her heart was broken." He began to pull the label from the bottle.

"I love her." Zach caught Carlos' stare. "I want to marry her. I want a life with her. None of this matters. Not one damn bit."

"If I didn't think you were sincere, I'd kick your ass," Carlos said with a hint of humor.

"I know." Zach stood and Carlos followed. "Where is she?"

Carlos shook his head. "I can't tell you. Give her some time."

He'd felt as though he'd been socked in the stomach, but he couldn't blame them for protecting her. "Please put in a good word for me. All of this is the past. It doesn't change how I feel for her."

"You'll tell her soon enough." Carlos offered his hand, and Zach shook it before walking away.

CHAPTER 55

When Regan pulled up in front of her parents' house, it was midnight. Her eyes stung from the hours she'd shed tears. She'd stopped multiple times along the drive, trying to decide what to do. Go home or go straight to Arianna's in New York? She'd chosen her mother's arms and her comfort for the night. Zach would surely look for her here, but her family would keep him at bay. And if Michael came looking for her—they'd take care of him in any way necessary.

Her mother was waiting for her at the door and enveloped her the moment she reached her, holding her to her bosom as Regan sobbed. Carlos had called her as Regan had asked him to do; she just couldn't make the call herself and hear her mother's voice while she drove away from the man who had hurt her so badly, again. Her mother held her as she walked with her to her bedroom. The bed had been turned down, and the lamp on the nightstand gave a soft, comforting glow to the room.

Regan fell onto the bed and lay back. Her mother pulled her shoes from her feet. "You are going to rest. Eventually this was bound to happen, but I won't let it destroy you, and neither will your family. Michael Hamilton is a bastard. Zachary Benson isn't."

"Mama, it can't work now." She wiped her eyes.

"Someone gave you and your sister to me so I could love you. People don't look at you different because of that, do they?" Regan shook her head. "So imagine what a wonderful thing you did giving up your angel to someone. Don't you think he'll see how special that was?"

"But, Mama, I lost him the biggest contract of his career. And I wasn't honest with him about the baby. How can he still love me?"

"Regan, you are a wise woman. You know that he will see past all this." Her mother kissed her and left the room.

Regan rolled to her side. It didn't matter. She couldn't see him again. She was too hurt and too humiliated. It was over.

∽

ZACHARY PACED his office for two days. Any business he tried to attend to only ended with him thinking about Regan.

Mary Ellen had come to his rescue, bringing the baby with her. She sat on his couch, nursing her daughter. "You're being an ass. Just go to her."

"I can't. She won't see me." He pulled his fingers through his hair as he paced again by the window. "I've been by her house. Carlos tells me she's not there. I've gone to the hospital, and Curtis says to give her time. Her mother smiles at me, kisses me on the cheeks, and says that her daughter loves me." He leaned against the wall. "If she loves me why won't she see me?"

"Zach, until you have a child, you can't imagine the pain of giving one away. Imagine making that decision thinking you were going to die," Mary Ellen said in a calm adoring manner. "Do you love her?"

"Yes, I do love her." His heart ached when he said it.

"Are you angry with her?" She lifted her daughter over her shoulder and patted her back.

"No. How could I be?"

"She thinks she's done you wrong."

"But she's done nothing." He moved to her and sat down next to her on the couch to ease the wobbling in his knees.

"Be patient, then."

He wasn't sure how he was supposed to be as patient as everyone had said. He was dying inside. It hurt.

"I've done a few things that I know she'd like. If I can just get her to be with me for a few minutes, I can show her that I still want forever. I'm not going anywhere, and I don't want her to either. I want forever, and that's what I've planned for." He offered to take the baby from Mary Ellen and held her carefully in his arms. The baby adjusted and Zach settled. "Will you help me get some time with her?"

Mary Ellen buttoned up her shirt and smiled at Zach. "Of course I'll help you. I picked her for you, after all. I knew she'd be the one to take care of you forever."

CHAPTER 56

*R*egan had sent in her official letter of resignation to Benson, Benson, and Hart. She'd packed up her belongings at the house and had decided the best thing to do would be to head to New York without a word to anyone. When she was settled in with Arianna, she would call and let her family know.

Carlos stood at her bedroom door as she zipped her suitcase. She'd hoped to be gone already, but nothing ever got past her family.

"The office called." His voice was placid. "They got your letter."

She pulled the suitcase from the bed and dropped it to the floor. "Good, then they know I'm not coming back."

"Oh, I think he figured that out by the way you ran." The calm in his tone was replaced by the snippy undertone that set her blood to boiling.

"Carlos, butt out. This has nothing to do with you." Anger and humiliation bubbled in her stomach. "You have no idea what I've gone through." She wished she hadn't said it. He knew so many other things about pain. He knew the pain of moving to a new place and having his parents die right in front of him. He overcame having a new family thrust upon him that wasn't his own. He'd suffered the pain of losing his marriage and watching the woman he loved marry his best friend. He knew pain.

"I'm not butting out. You're being a jerk. You should hear him out," he argued.

"I have nothing to say to him."

"Fine." He turned from the door. "They're expecting you to pick up your things. They said he'll be out of the office after two."

"Great. I'll go on my way out."

He didn't react other than to walk away.

REGAN FELT sweat drip down her back as she walked through the lobby of Benson, Benson and Hart. She hadn't anticipated returning to the building. She'd wanted to leave it all behind her.

There was no one at her desk, and the door to Zach's office was closed. She tried to convince herself that she was relieved he wasn't there, but a little bit of her wanted to see him one more time.

She noticed a box on the floor with her personal belongings in it. Quickly, she picked up the box and started out of the office.

Mary Ellen stopped her in the doorway, a wide and welcoming smile on her lips. "Regan, it's wonderful to see you."

Seeing her there put finality to her resignation; she hadn't expected to feel let down. "Mary Ellen, you're back?"

"Yes, he called immediately and begged me back. The man can't do anything on his own." She looked her over as she held her daughter in her arms. "How are you?"

"I'll be fine." Regan glanced around the office and then at the baby, wanting desperately to reach for her and touch her. "I guess I'll go."

Mary Ellen handed her a piece of paper with an address and

driving instructions on it. "You need to go here to get your check."

"Can't they send it to me?"

"No. You have to sign for it," she said. "I know he added a severance package with it. He feels bad that you had to deal with Mr. Hamilton."

Regan nodded. She didn't want charity, but it certainly would help her start her new life wherever she landed.

"Thank you." She tucked the paper into her purse.

"Regan, take care." Mary Ellen smiled.

Regan wished she could smile back, but like her brother had done to her earlier, she simply turned and left the office.

REGAN BEGAN her drive out of Nashville. She followed the directions Mary Ellen had given her. She was sure she'd taken a wrong turn. The city began to disappear, and acres of land sprawled around her.

Soon she saw the name of the road she was to turn down. It was unpaved and lined with oak trees. Regan's mouth fell open when she came to the end of the road. In the clearing stood a house, the most beautiful house she'd ever seen. It was white with decorative shutters and a porch that wrapped around it. On the front porch sat two white rockers gently rocking in the breeze.

She looked down at the piece of paper Mary Ellen had given her. The address matched. Surely there had been some mistake.

Regan parked the car in front of the house and looked around. Flowers bloomed in pots on the stairs. A carpet lay at the door welcoming visitors. The front door was open, and she tapped on the screen door.

There was no answer, but someone must be home.

"Hello. Hello, is there anyone here?" She yelled into the house.

"You can go in and look around if you'd like," a man said behind her.

After a moment's panic, she recognized Zach's voice. She turned to see him leaning against her car.

Her breath caught in her lungs. He looked wonderful standing there so casually. The sunlight shone on his sandy hair, giving him a golden aura. A smile settled on his perfect mouth. Oh, how she'd missed his mouth.

"Mary Ellen said I needed to come and get my check. I had to sign for it. I thought I was in the wrong place." They started toward the steps at the same time.

"She was right." He pulled the envelope from his pocket and handed it to her, his fingers lingering on hers.

"I'm sorry I lost you the contract." She averted her gaze to the ground.

"I guess it's good that you quit before I could fire you, then." His words made her eyes shift to his, but he was still smiling.

"She said you had a severance package for me, but really that wasn't necessary."

He shrugged. "You may change your mind when you see it." He nodded to the paper. "You still have to sign for it."

"Oh, right." She opened the envelope. It didn't contain a check. She held up the piece of paper. "What is this?"

"Read it."

"Zach…"

"It's not a check, but it does require a signature," he said, climbing the next step closer to her, but she fought the urge to touch him.

The paper shook in her fingers. It was the ultimate contract, and its sentiment squeezed at her heart until she thought it would burst. "It's a marriage license."

"You're right." He tucked his hand in his pocket and pulled out a blue velvet ring box. The ache in her chest moved to her throat and stole her air. "I've been carrying this with me since L.A."

He opened the box. An enormous solitaire ring caught the sunlight, winking at her, and Regan gasped.

"Zach, I don't understand." She lifted her gaze from the glimmering ring and looked into his calm green eyes that smiled lovingly back at her.

"What's not to understand?" He took the ring and slid it onto her finger. "Regan, will you marry me?"

She refrained from jerking her hand back. It didn't make sense. She was soiled. She was damaged goods. There was nothing for him to still want from her, yet he looked at her with those loving eyes. Her knees went weak. "Why would you want to marry me?"

"Do you want a list?"

"But I wasn't honest with you. I've had a baby with another man." Cold sweat broke on her brow, and she brushed her hand across her forehead. "I lost you the biggest contract of your career. How could you want to marry me?"

"Because I love you. Those things are part of you." He moved his hand to her cheek. "You gave a family a child they couldn't have. What a wonderful gift. You gambled at love and lost. Everyone does."

"But Zach…"

"If you want your daughter back, we can contact my lawyer. It's only been a year. Isn't there some kind of clause?" She shook her head adamantly. Oh God, what was he offering? Regan looked away from him for a moment and gave into the contemplation. Her daughter. Her little girl. She could hold her, see her, love her as she had since she'd felt her first flutter of life in her belly. Then the reality of it forced its way back into her delusion. Her baby was better off without her. Her daughter had a family, and to strip them of that relationship would be a horrible burden to live with. It would be better to live without love again than to hurt a child.

Zach's thumb rubbed against her cheek, and she looked back

at him. He smiled down at her. "You are very special to me, and I'm not going to let you run away from me."

He pulled her in a quick move to the end of the step so they were eye to eye. Just as quickly he wrapped his arm around her waist and pressed their bodies together. The speed of his movement made her gasp, but then the warmth of his lips was on hers and no matter how much she wanted to be sensible and break free, she couldn't. His lips were as intoxicating as his green eyes, his scent, his voice, and his touch. If she'd walked away, she'd regret it forever. It would kill her little by little to say goodbye to him forever.

When Zach pulled away, she opened her eyes and watched him. His lips parted into a grin that sent a river of warmth through her. He brushed her lips with his thumb. "You're going to marry me and live in this house I bought for you."

"Excuse me?" A bubble of excitement rose into her chest. She turned her attention back to the house behind her.

"You heard me. You said you wanted Tennessee sprawling land and two rockers on the porch."

"Zach..." She looked around her through moist eyes. There were two rocking chairs on the porch, which wrapped around the house. The trees that lined the road rustled in the wind. It was just as she'd described to him. This was just what she'd wanted.

"Regan, if you turn me down again, I'll tie you to the spindle," he teased with humor in his voice.

She settled her gaze over him. She did love him. Running away wasn't going to change that.

"So I'm fired?" She finally smiled.

"As my assistant." His hand was in her hair, and she moved in even closer to him, wanting to feel him near. "But I need a partner, in life and in business.

"And you want me to be that partner?" She rested her forehead against his. "If you'll accept the position." He slid his other hand to her waist, and her body relaxed against his as she gave into her need for him.

"I guess we'll have to go inside for negotiations. I'll have some executive decisions to make." She ran her hands up his chest. "So I can walk, or you can carry me inside."

He laughed and hoisted her to his waist. She wrapped her legs around him and circled her arms around his neck.

"You'll be signing that contract," he urged as he carried her past the rockers and through the front door of the house built on sprawling Tennessee land. His arms held her tightly and his hands caressed her back.

She kissed him, and warmth filled every part of her. "We simply can't do business without the contract. Partner."

EPILOGUE

The caterers prepared in the kitchen, and the florist placed arrangements on each table under the large tent in the yard. Audrey found immense pleasure in organizing the people who came in and out of the house, Zach knew. He hadn't seen her smile that much since before his father had died.

Zach's wedding to Regan had brought her purpose and happiness back to her life.

Regan's mother, sister, and Simone had all scurried up the stairs to the spare bedroom to help Regan get ready. They'd soon been followed by women carrying cases of makeup and hair tools.

He wondered what kind of talk was going on behind that closed door.

The men had been banished to the downstairs, and as the wedding drew closer, to the mother-in-law suite to get ready.

Zach had closed billion dollar business deals, but waiting for the moment when Regan actually said *I do*, mad him more nervous than he'd ever been. In the back of his mind, he knew she was a flight risk until the moment they said their vows and exchanged rings.

He chuckled to himself. She wasn't going anywhere. He knew every secret she'd ever kept, and vice versa. Simone had made sure that if there was any part of Zach's life he hadn't told Regan about, Simone had filled in the blanks. Yes, he might not have had a sister born to him, but Simone came in close enough.

"You boys all need to get changed. I'll send everyone back," his mother said as she blew a kiss his direction.

Zach watched as Carlos' ex-wife and his daughter hurried up the stairs to the room where Regan got ready, and Carlos walked toward him with his sons.

"You look nervous as hell," Carlos teased as they boys followed their uncle into the room at the end of the hall.

"I am nervous. Were you this nervous when you got married?"

Carlos shook his head. "We were too young and stupid to know better," he said on a laugh. "We nearly eloped. We couldn't wait."

Zach saw the flash of regret in Carlos' eyes, but the smile was genuine. If he didn't know any better, he'd think that Carlos was still in love with Madeline, even though she was someone else's wife.

"I'll be fine when it's over," Zach admitted as he and Carlos joined the others in the *Groom's Suite*, as the sign on the door announced.

◞◟

REGAN'S MOTHER tied the bow on the back of her dress and sniffed as she did so.

"Mama, don't cry," Regan said watching her in the mirror.

"Hush. My daughter is getting married, and I'm moved."

Adrianna retrieved the veil off the bed and carried it to the mirror where Regan stood. Regan watched as her sister lifted the veil and placed it on her head.

Regan helped set it into place among the curls that were

sprayed into place.

Once the veil was clipped on, Regan, her mother, and her sister looked at their reflections in the mirror.

"Mama, I hope I'm as happy as you and Daddy are."

Her mother wiped the tear from her eye with the handkerchief Regan had given her as a gift. "You will be. Zach is a good man, just like your father."

Regan took one more look in the mirror, and smiled. Yes, he was a good man.

ZACH STOOD in his mother's rose garden, Simone by his side, and Regan's brothers next to her. He watched his mother wipe tears from her cheeks as Mary Ellen did the same a few rows back.

Everyone who meant something to them was gathered in his mother's garden to share their special moment together.

The moment Zach saw Clara walk through the door with her mother, his heart raced faster. It would only be a few moments until Regan was his forever.

Madeline stepped to the side and let Clara walk down the aisle, waving at her father, dropping rose petals on the ground. She was followed by her brothers, who each carried a pillow with a ring on it.

Adrianna followed the boys, and Zach noticed John's eyes were fixed on her as she walked down the aisle. Then, he saw her.

Regan was accompanied by both of her parents, one on each arm, as they walked her toward him. For a moment he thought his knees might give out.

"She is *magnifique!*" Simone whispered in his ear.

Yes, she was he thought.

When Regan and her parents reached him, they stopped. Her mother kissed her cheek, and then her father did the same.

"Take care of one another," he said, directing the statement to both of them before his wife moved to kiss Zach on the cheek.

As her parents took their seat, Zach gathered Regan's hands in his. "You do look, *magnifique*," he said, repeating Simone's sentiment. "I'm so glad you're going to marry me."

"I've never wanted anything as much as I want to be your wife."

"Then let's make this official."

The minister began the ceremony, and Zach was sure every word was important, but he hadn't heard any of them. The only words he heard were Regan saying, "I do."

AFTER THE CEREMONY, they dined, toasted with champagne, and cut into the beautiful cake Regan had chosen. As the night grew later, everyone moved to the dance floor, and Zach wrapped his arms around his beautiful bride.

"This is exactly how I dreamed this night would be," she said as she watched Clara and Eduardo holding hands and dancing as she and her brothers had many years ago.

"Your brother looks happy," Zach nodded in Carlos' direction.

Regan turned to see him dancing with Madeline, and each of them smiling as if it were happy to be with one another in that moment. When Christian tapped his father on the shoulder to cut in and dance with his mother, Regan batted away a tear.

"I think I'll make our sons take dance lessons," Zach said as he took Regan's hand and twirled her away and back to him.

"Why would you do that?"

"So that at weddings they can spin you around the dance floor."

"I think that's a wonderful idea. We'll name our first one after your father."

Now she watched as her new husband batted away tears.

"I think he'd appreciate your executive decision."

A SECOND CHANCE

We hope you enjoyed Bernadette Marie's
The Executive's Decision.
Continue the family saga with an excerpt from book two,
A Second Chance.

A SECOND CHANCE

CHAPTER ONE

*A*t the end of the long, tree-lined drive stood the house, welcoming her just as the owner would. It wasn't the first time Madeline Carson had made the trip out to Regan and Zach Benson's house, but she couldn't help but wonder if it would be the last.

She batted back the tears that stung her eyes. No, she wasn't going to cry for herself. She was there to celebrate the birth of Regan's baby boy. Tyler Alan Benson. A child welcomed into the world by two people who were so very much in love.

Oh, she was adult enough to admit she was jealous. Who wouldn't be? Zach doted on his wife of three years. A baby would only enhance the perfect relationship that her ex-sister-in-law had with her husband.

There had been a time when she'd felt that optimism about a man, love, and her family.

The first tear fell.

It had been five years since she and Carlos Keller, Regan's brother, had divorced. Five years, and she still mourned it every day.

After her marriage to Carlos ended, there was his best friend,

Matt. He'd been there to console her in her time of need. That need had led to a relationship, and they'd married only six months after her divorce had been finalized.

The marriage had ended the twenty-year friendship between Matt and Carlos, but who could blame them?

Neither Carlos nor Madeline could really pinpoint what went wrong to end their marriage. It simply had fallen apart. There were money issues, of course. Then the kids came along, and the money was even tighter as Carlos finished graduate school and she worked two jobs. The very things that were to have made their family stronger had actually pulled it apart.

Matt hadn't meant any harm when he had come to console her. He was playing the part of a friend to each of them. Things simply had changed between him and Madeline, and they'd fallen in love. Or so she'd thought at the time.

Madeline pulled to the side of the driveway and wiped at her eyes.

No, it hadn't been love. It had been comfort. Matt needed to take care of someone, and she was willing to let him take care of her. He'd let her stay home and raise her children. She couldn't have asked for more.

Now even that had fallen apart.

Madeline glanced at the messenger bag on the passenger seat. Inside it were the divorce papers that Matt had served her with three days ago. So far, she hadn't had the courage to sign them. She hadn't even had the courage to discuss it with her children. They would get to that. As soon as Carlos brought them back to her after his week with them, they'd realize Matt had moved out. She'd like to think they'd be a little upset that he was gone, but she knew they wouldn't.

Oh, it would hurt for the moment. It would hurt more because they'd know it hurt her, but they were too in love with their father to want another man in their lives, or hers.

Sure, Matt had been a good role model and a loving man to

them all. He simply wasn't their father. For the first time in days, she smiled through her tears. Her children loved their father and he loved them.

She took a few cleansing breaths. Matt's leaving couldn't have come at a worse time. Having your husband walk out on you never happened at a convenient time, but she had a bigger battle to face now.

Madeline put her hand to her chest and looked down at the swells of her breasts against her shirt.

She had cancer and she hadn't told a soul.

Sadness filled her body with a heavy fullness, and anger riddled her mind. Madeline had never imagined this would happen to her.

"Well, now isn't the time to sob over your sad life," she said to herself as she pulled down the visor and looked in the mirror. She wiped off the smudged mascara and fixed her hair. "This is Regan's moment. It's time to celebrate life."

Once she successfully pulled herself together, she started toward the house.

The chairs on the porch rocked in the breeze. The November air had chilled, but the ground was still dry. That would be changing soon, she thought as she parked the car.

Madeline looked at the house. It had been Zach's engagement present to Regan. Or, as Regan referred to it, her bribe to marry him, which had worked in his favor. Over the past three years, Regan had added her touches. In the spring, the flowers would all bloom around the porch and lay out a colorful spread of welcome. As it was, the drive was paved with leaves that had finally given up their homes on the branches of the trees that lined the road.

She climbed from the car and opened the trunk. The large box she'd brought for Regan and Zach sat wrapped in bright yellow paper, reminding her that a new life was just beyond those doors. A cousin to her children, a nephew to her ex-husband, and a blessing to Regan and Zach.

She lifted the box from the trunk and moved it to her hip. Then she shut the trunk, walked up the front steps, and pushed the doorbell. When she heard it chime, she realized that she'd probably woken the baby.

Regan pulled open the door and smiled. "Madeline. I'm so glad you were able to come by. Please, come in." She stood back to let her through.

"You look wonderful," she said, but she saw the signs of motherhood streaked across poor Regan's face. Her eyes were hollow and dark from lack of sleep. The elegant attire worn by the wife of one of Tennessee's most prominent businessmen had been swapped for a pair of comfy sweat pants and an oversized T-shirt to encompass her swollen breasts. "This is for you and Tyler." She handed the box to Regan.

"You didn't have to do this."

"It's a box of necessities. Diapers. Diaper-rash cream. Nipple cream for the mama."

"Thank you," Regan said on a sigh.

"Just a few other things I think you can use up. I didn't buy him any clothes. I figured Zach's mother would want to do most of that."

"You're right. Audrey will make sure he's the best-dressed child at the playground. I think she cleaned out the Baby Gap." She shook her head. "Zach tells her to quit buying him things, he's only a week old, but she insists."

"I'd have to agree. Grandmothers get special rights."

"Would you like to see him?" Regan offered.

"Of course."

Regan laced her arm through Madeline's and escorted her to the living room. Madeline smiled when she saw the bassinet near the sofa with the sleeping baby. Her heart ached a bit with the memory of all of her own children sleeping in it. "Your mother gave you the bassinet?"

"Yes, she wants everyone to have a chance to sleep in it. Carlos and Arianna were the only two of her own children that didn't get to."

The Keller family was an eclectic mix, Madeline thought. Regan and Arianna had been adopted by the Kellers, but had been with them since Regan was an infant and Arianna was two years old. Their little brother, Curtis, was the Kellers' only natural-born child, and he was a year younger than Regan. Carlos had been adopted by Emily and Alan Keller when he was seven, after a car accident had killed his parents.

When Madeline had given birth to Eduardo, Emily gave her and Carlos the bassinet for their children. Now it was Tyler's turn. "I guess Clara was the last one to sleep in it," Madeline reminisced.

"I can't believe she's eleven."

"Tell me about it. The boys are both teenagers." She looked at Regan. "I'm not that old, am I?"

Regan touched her arm. "Heavens, no."

They laughed, but when Tyler stirred, they both stopped and watched.

"I fed him only fifteen minutes ago. He should be pretty happy for now. Would you like to hold him?"

"Oh, Regan, he's sleeping. Don't bother him."

"Give me a break. You drove forty-five minutes out here to see him. I know you, Madeline. You came to hold the baby." Regan reached for her son. "He'll sleep just as fine in your arms as he will in that bassinet."

She adjusted the blanket around him as she handed him to Madeline.

A SECOND CHANCE

CHAPTER TWO

*M*adeline sat down on the couch with the baby, who cooed against her. "He's so perfect."

"He is, isn't he?" Regan adjusted into the corner of the couch and relaxed.

"Eduardo had hair like this." She smoothed her hand over Tyler's thick, dark hair. "Christian and Clara were both bald. Remember?" Regan nodded her answer with a yawn. "Time flies."

Madeline let Tyler wrap his tiny hand around her finger, and she felt the tug in her heart. It seemed so long ago when Carlos had sat by her side in the hospital and they admired their first baby. "I wonder if his hair will stay dark like yours or if he'll get his daddy's light hair."

"Hmmm," was all Regan said. Her head had rested to the back of the couch, and her eyes had closed.

Madeline simply smiled and sat quietly. She'd been there too. It would never cease to amaze her how mothers did it. They could go and go with no sleep and provide the essentials that their babies needed. But when exhaustion took over, it was like running right into a wall.

The struggles of motherhood were just like the cancer that

was taking over her body. In order to survive it, she would have to love herself as she loved her children. She would need to have hope, just as she had when her children became their own people and began to experience new things. And she'd need to remember to take care of herself as she'd neglected to do for the past fifteen years while she doted on her own babies. It would be easier if Carlos were there with her.

"Well, little man, you've been born into one of the most wonderful families in the world. You'll be well taken care of," she whispered, kissing him atop the head and wondering if she'd see him grow up.

"You look natural doing that," Carlos said from the doorway, watching her.

His voice startled her, and she froze, trying not to wake the baby as her heart pounded in her chest. "Dear God, you scared me to death." She tried to ease back into the couch without stirring Tyler. She looked up at the man who had once captured her heart and somehow continued to do so. His long, lean body and handfuls of wavy black hair played with her imagination too often. "How long have you been standing there?"

"A few minutes. Did you knock her out?" He nodded toward his sister.

Madeline let out a sigh. "She's so tired. I was surprised Audrey or your mother weren't here to help her."

"Yeah, right. You know Regan. She wanted to do it alone. Besides, Audrey had a hair appointment."

"Where are the kids?"

"They're putting their things in your car. I told them to stay outside so they didn't bother the baby. Clara is pouting, but the boys are fine with it."

Madeline looked back down at the sleeping baby in her arms. "Well, sweetheart, I guess I'd better go. I'm glad I got to meet you."

"You don't have to put him down. Stay as long as you'd like."

"Oh, I should get them home and settled." She rose and put Tyler back in the bassinet. She laid a kiss on her fingers and gently pressed it to his cheek. "Good-bye."

She stood from the bassinet and felt the room begin to spin around her.

"Whoa." Carlos was at her side steadying her. "Are you all right?"

"Yeah." She tried to regain her balance. "I'm fine."

"You don't look so well. Why don't you sit down?" He held tight to her arms.

"I really should be going."

"Madeline, there's no need for you to run. You're still part of this family."

She smiled and nodded. The entire Keller family had always made her feel right at home, even after she and Carlos had divorced.

Madeline took a deep breath and soaked in the feeling of Carlos's hands on her. She missed him, and that, on top of everything that was happening to her, wasn't helping her steady her emotions. Instead, his nearness and the heat of his body were stirring up feelings she had no right to have, not anymore.

"I'm okay now." She reached her hand toward his chest, but he didn't let her go.

Carlos eyes scanned over her slowly. "You're sick. You should let me call Curtis and have him come look at you."

"No." She shook her head. "You're not calling your brother to come and check up on me. I'm fine. I'm just coming down with something. All the better reason for me to go home before I get this little man sick." She looked back down at the baby sleeping in the family bassinet. The sadness inside her stirred again. What she wouldn't give to hold her children and watch them sleep with Carlos by her side once more.

Carlos steadied his eyes on hers and then stepped back. "If you need me, you call."

"I will."

"Let Matt know what happened."

Madeline nodded. Once she had turned to Matt for comfort—whom was she going to turn to now that he was gone? "Thanks for meeting me out here with the kids."

"Sure. Oh, by the way, Mom says there's still room for two more at the table on Thanksgiving. You and Matt are welcome to come."

"Thank her for me, will you? I think I'll just have a quiet Thanksgiving at home. I'll bring the kids by on Thursday morning after we watch the parade."

"The parade. Still your most favorite thing on TV?"

"And it always will be," she said, smiling, thinking about the time Carlos had maxed out every credit card they had to make sure she witnessed it live on the streets of New York. That was a lifetime ago, she reminded herself. Too bad she'd fought him over it instead of realizing the sentiment behind it.

She touched his arm as she walked past him, and then hurried out to her car where her children waited for her. Their smiles took away the pain she'd been feeling. Even when everything around her seemed to be shattering, she still had her children.

Panic suddenly filled her, and she fought back the emotions that were clawing at her. She wondered how long she had left to be their mother.

PLEASE REVIEW

We hope you enjoyed *The Executive's Decision*
by Bernadette Marie.
If you did, we would ask that you please rate and review this title.
Every review helps our authors.

Rate and Review: The Executive's Decision

ABOUT THE AUTHOR

Bestselling Author Bernadette Marie is known for building families readers want to be part of. Her series The Keller Family has graced bestseller charts since its release in 2011. Since then she has authored and published over fifty books. The married mother of five sons promises romances with a Happily Ever After always...and says she can write it because she lives it.

Obsessed with the art of writing and the business of publishing, chronic entrepreneur Bernadette Marie established her own publishing house, 5 Prince Publishing, in 2011 to bring her own work to market as well as offer an opportunity for fresh voices in fiction to find a home as well.

When not immersed in the writing/publishing world, Bernadette Marie can be found spending time with her family, traveling (mostly to Disney parks), and running multiple businesses. An avid martial artist, Bernadette Marie is a second degree black belt in Tang Soo Do, and loves Tai Chi. She is a retired hockey mom, a lover of a good stout craft beer, and might have an unhealthy addiction to chocolate.